MURDER

ON THE

SPANISH SEAS

MURDER

ON THE

SPANISH SEAS

Wendy Church

The following is a work of fiction. Names, characters, places, events and incidents are either the product of the author's imagination or used in an entirely fictitious manner. Any resemblance to actual persons, living or dead, is entirely coincidental.

ISBN: 978-1-951709-85-3
eISBN: 978-1-951709-97-6

Library of Congress Control Number:
available upon request

First hardcover edition May 2022
by Polis Books, LLC
44 Brookview Lane
Aberdeen, NJ 07747
www.PolisBooks.com

POLIS BOOKS

For my mom

PROLOGUE

Fortunately for me, it was July in Spain, and the water was a comfortable seventy degrees. What wasn't fortunate was landing in it from the foredeck of the cruise ship on which I had, until very recently, been a passenger. Hitting the ocean from seventy feet up was like smacking into concrete. I felt the bones in my right foot crack as I entered the water. *Damn it.*

My foot was useless but I kicked painfully up to the surface, sucking in mouthfuls of air as I broke through. I lay floating on my back, catching my breath, and feeling lucky I'd landed in the water and not on the dock on the other side of the ship.

As my head started to clear, I realized I was clutching something in my hand that had survived the fall. It was a small black box.

I was looking at the box and piecing together what happened when I heard splashing. Another body burst through the water close by, and then a powerful male hand grabbed my non-broken foot and pulled. I got a mouthful of water as he dragged me toward him. When I was close enough, he reached for my arm and then my hand, his strong fingers prying mine from the box.

I held on as we thrashed in the water. After a few moments, he stopped trying to pull my fingers away and instead crushed them around the box. I felt my hand collapse under the pressure and we both sank again below the surface.

DAY 1

CHAPTER 1

On the list of the places I never expected to be, this had to rank in the top five. Or maybe it's the bottom five. I'm not sure how that works.

Not that Barcelona isn't nice. It's an interesting city, and its Palacruceros Terminal isn't bad, as far as port terminals go. But taking an ultra-luxury cruise had never been part of my plans.

I'd been on board the *Gold Sea Explorer* for about an hour and was on the deck, leaning against the railing. Things had been calm, but I was now looking down at a disturbance in the terminal that was rapidly turning into something more serious.

A group of twenty or so men at the security checkpoint on the quay were forcing themselves into the boarding area. They pushed and shouted as security staff ran toward them from all directions of the pier. Passengers scattered as staff wielding batons and talking into radios tried to form a circle around the mob. Just when they seemed to be gaining control of things, two of the men broke through the ring and then the flimsy security gate. As they ran through the roped-off area toward the gangway, embarking passengers dropped their hand luggage and fled. On the gangway, the cruise ship staff who had been welcoming passengers backed off, leaving the men a free route to board. It wasn't clear where the men were going, and I was wondering if it was time to relocate myself.

I'd been reluctant to go on this trip. It was a gift from my best friend, Sam, and while the idea of being stuck on a ship for ten days with hundreds of people was closer to my own version of hell than a vacation, the fact that I was recently unemployed made accepting a gift of the world's most expensive luxury cruise a fairly easy decision.

As I watched the two men run up to the gangway, I was questioning that decision. I looked behind me to see if I had a clear path to the rear of the ship.

"*Gelditu!*" a deep male voice boomed from the top of the gangway.

Both men stopped in their tracks and looked up at a uniformed man blocking the entrance to the ship.

The pause gave the pursuing security staff a chance to catch up and they tackled the men to the ground. As they were handcuffed and led away, the man who had yelled a command at them turned and headed back inside. As quickly as it had started, things settled back down.

I looked out over the boarding area, scanning the recovering mob of people for Sam. It didn't take long to spot her. She'd made it through the security gate and was cutting a path through the crowd with a team of porters struggling under her baggage. Her brightly colored bikini top, wraparound skirt, sunglasses, and one of those hats with the very wide brims that you imagine movie stars wearing all looked perfectly natural on her. I saw her start up the gangway and waved and smiled.

My smile faded fast when I saw what she was carrying. Her two-year-old Chinese Crested dog, Chaz, sat in her arms. Chaz was seven pounds of pure ugly, and it was always a shock to see the two of them together. Imagine Elizabeth Hurley cuddling with Jabba the Hut and you get the idea. Sam was tall and stunning, with long brown hair, high cheekbones, and olive skin that reflected her ancestry. Chaz looked like the canine version of end-stage Regan in *The Exorcist*. Gray and hairless save for a Dr. Seuss tuft of hair on his head, he had an unnaturally long tongue that had taken up permanent residence outside his mouth, which was bursting with crooked and gapped teeth. His look was capped off with demonic eyes that bulged out of his face like damp, gangrenous growths.

Sam looked up to me and waved. The railing was crowded with

passengers, but this was definitely a "one of these things is not like the other" situation, and when she made it to my deck, it was easy for her to pick me out. At thirty I was younger than most of the other passengers, and as far as I could tell, none of the other women were wearing jeans and a T-shirt. And unlike many on this trip, I was decidedly not Mediterranean-looking. In addition to my love of whiskey, my Irish roots had provided me with straight dark hair, pale skin, and blue eyes. I guess I look OK. Not like Sam, but passable, in a Debra Winger sort of way.

Sam gave me a warm but careful don't-crush-the-dog hug as Chaz growled a warning. I did everything I could to avoid those potentially dangerous teeth, although it's unlikely he could bite through anything, given that the upper and lower sets didn't look like they would ever actually meet each other. I honestly don't know how he managed to eat.

She saw the look on my face. "I had to bring him. The other dogs pick on him when I'm gone."

"That's because they know he represents an existential threat to their gene pool."

Sam has six dogs and numerous cats, all rescues, and I was on great terms with all of them except for Tiny Torquemada, who hated me with a fiery passion.

"I thought they didn't let pets on board."

"He has his own quarters and a full-time attendant."

Of course he did.

We made our way to the elevator that would take us to our suite. The cruise line catered to the wealthy, and this particular ship to the fabulously wealthy. Sam and I were staying in the Neptune suite, of which there was only one, and it took up almost all of deck fourteen at the very top of the ship. I'd gotten a quick look at it when I boarded earlier. It included three bedrooms and two bathrooms on an upstairs floor, connected to the lower floor by an open spiral staircase running through the center. The living area on the main floor featured Bugatti couches and various other designer furniture arranged around a coffee table, a fully stocked kitchen and teak-trimmed wet bar, a $250,000 Steinway piano, and a 1,000-square-foot balcony that wrapped around the suite, providing a view of most of the ship and a near 360-degree view around it.

The suite was also equipped with a steward call system. Every room had a $3,500 Ming call unit that looked like a squat salt shaker, if that salt shaker was gold-trimmed, leather-covered titanium with "Gold Sea Explorer" embossed across the top. When pushed, it summoned our own private concierge, Benat, who'd escorted me to our suite earlier. To his credit, and the credit of the English butler school from which he'd no doubt matriculated, the "Holy mother of fuck" I'd uttered when seeing the suite hadn't fazed him in the least.

Sam had thought I needed to get away, and she'd been right. I'd been working the last few years as an investigator and expert witness in corporate malfeasance cases, which is normally about as action-packed as it sounds. But my most recent trial had simultaneously turned me into a household name and left me jobless. Jesse O'Hara, Financial Investigations, was now Jesse O'Hara, Unemployed. Again.

The case involved Capitalon, a global finance and investment corporation whose stock value had skyrocketed in the last couple of years, primarily based on a combination of their charismatic celebrity CEO Joshua Bistek and what turned out to be massive corporate fraud. Bistek's involvement alone had made the case high-profile, must-watch TV, and I was the prosecution's star witness.

My expertise is in forensic accounting and finance. I'm something of a whiz with numbers and can cruise through financial reports and spot irregularities that tell me a story very quickly. I'm also good on a witness stand, and had been in growing demand by prosecutors. I fit the bill as an expert witness with PhD credentials and the ability to accurately recall details while impressing juries with unemotional testimony. But I'd had trouble maintaining the requisite stoic demeanor in this case. Jason Bistek was a self-absorbed, incompetent assbag, and as the walking stereotype of the out-of-control *nouveau riche*, he'd had little time to actually run the company, leaving it in the hands of his ethically-challenged CFO who'd been manipulating the books to show profits that didn't exist on investments that never happened. They'd squandered millions, and caused thousands of people to lose their jobs.

The last two days of the trial had been a slog of tedious cross examination by the defense team, all ten of them, and I was starting to lose my shit. Bistek had zero business skills, and in response to the hundredth question from the defense about whether or not he was really *that* incompetent, I'd blurted out to the court and the world, "He's a complete fucking idiot. Asking Joshua Bistek to run a multibillion-dollar global organization is like asking a baby to build a space shuttle."

The crowded courtroom had broken into laughter and social media went nuts, leading to an explosion of memes featuring babies and space shuttles. But as soon as the words came out of my mouth, I knew I'd blown it. As an expert witness it doesn't pay to be hyperbolic, and in the wake of the trial my business had completely dried up.

It was too bad, because I was really good at this, described by people in the industry as being a "tough and unflappable witness" (true) that "didn't pull any punches" (also true) with a "photographic memory" (kind of true). I do have an unnaturally good eye for details and near-perfect recall, which pairs nicely with an unrelenting inquisitive streak. I also have something of a sixth sense when it comes to knowing when people are lying or hiding things, an artifact of my natural distrust of humans in general.

In shocking and unrelated news, I'm currently single.

We made it to our suite and Sam was checking out the rooms. She looked pleased, which meant something as she'd been taking cruises since she was a kid. "I'm a little surprised you made it," she called over her shoulder as she opened the door to the balcony. Sam knew my opinion of cruises (large-scale E. coli delivery systems) and up to now my sole experience with them had been numerous viewings of *The Poseidon Adventure* and *Titanic*.

"The only reason I agreed to this was because you told me Ryan

Reynolds was going to be here. And you said the magic words."

She turned to me and raised an eyebrow.

"Seven bars."

She laughed. "Dinner in an hour, after the muster drill?"

"Sure. What's a muster drill?"

"It's a safety drill. We're required to go through it before the ship leaves port. They'll let us know when it starts. It should be soon." She stepped out onto the balcony.

Chaz followed her, taking a moment to turn and growl a warning at me in case I was thinking about joining them. He was putting me on notice that us being on vacation did not mean he was taking a vacation from hating me.

CHAPTER 2

We'd been in our room a short while when the announcement that the muster drill would be starting came over the ship's PA system. A few minutes later there was a series of loud bells. Benat came to our door and escorted us down to our designated muster station next to the railing on the pool deck. Directly above us were a set of lifeboats I hoped we wouldn't be using.

We were joined by passengers from decks thirteen, twelve, and eleven, and we all listened to instructions delivered over the PA system while the crew member who would be responsible for getting us into the lifeboats demonstrated the procedure.

I was leaning against the railing, looking out at the terminal that was now almost empty. "This is fine, but what's the rush for the drill? We've barely had time to check out our rooms."

Sam was watching the demonstration. Without turning around, she said, "It used to be that they were required to hold the drills within twenty-four hours of departure. But since the *Costa Concordia* incident, they now do them before the ship leaves the dock."

"The *Concordia*?"

"Yes, a cruise ship in Italy. It sank shortly after leaving port, so none of the passengers knew where to go or what to do. A number of people died."

OK then. I turned away from the railing and paid a little more attention to the spiel, which turned out not to be that bad. I was surprised when they said it was over. The whole thing had taken less than ten minutes.

"That was relatively painless," I said as we walked back to the elevator.

"Good thing. We'll be going through that twice a day for the duration of the cruise."

"What?"

She pushed the button to our floor. "Yes, at seven am and ten pm. Passengers are required to be reasonably sober for those drills, so you'll need to be careful."

"*What?!*" We hadn't left port yet, and there was still time for me to get off the ship. I'd get my bags later.

Sam saw the expression on my face and started to laugh.

"You're kidding, right? Please tell me you're kidding."

She nodded, laughing too hard to answer.

We parted ways at the suite, her to unpack and get ready for dinner, and me to wander around the ship. This particular cruise line was especially known for its very high-end food and alcohol, which I decided was time to confirm via my own market research. My heart was still pounding from the scare of twice-daily sober muster drills, and an aperitif or two would be just what the doctor ordered.

Elevators linked the passenger decks, but I took the stairwell down to deck eight, which on the ship's plan posted in our room looked to be the center of things. Opening the door to the deck, I found myself in the center vestibule of rich people's Wonderland. The sweeping atrium spanned ten levels, and an ornate staircase wound up through the middle of it, rising through the levels, upon which were a variety of shops, restaurants, and bars. Passengers glided by the full-length windows, examining tchotchkes and menus posted on the glass, everything surrounded by glittering soft lights and gold trim. It made the *Poseidon's* grand ball room look like a high school gym on prom night, although a giant Christmas tree could still do a lot of damage in this place.

I wandered up the gently sloped staircase, looking in on a few of the ship's bars. They were already filling up with boisterous plutocrats. Everyone looked happy, expectant, and eager to mingle with each other, so I moved on.

The passengers were what you would expect on a luxury cruise. Everywhere I looked it was Versace this, and Gucci that, and the women and most of the men were wearing jewelry that represented more money than I would make in a lifetime. From the snatches of conversations I picked up, it was a diverse crowd of blue bloods, including Spanish, French, and English, both British and American versions. I know this as I've traveled a lot and am pretty good at recognizing languages. Not that I'm fluent in any of them, but I'm comfortable ordering beer and cursing in at least eight. As far as I could tell, no one was cursing or ordering beer at the moment.

The international flavor of the passengers was a benefit, as I like being around people from different countries, largely because if I can't speak their language, I'm under no obligation to talk to them. And while I really appreciated Sam's gesture behind gifting me the cruise, it represented more of her preference than mine. Sam's the world's biggest extrovert. She loves meeting people, finds something to like in most of them, and expects that everyone will like her back, which is not a bad assumption, as just about everybody does. My people world is limited to a small number of close family and friends, a few who like me and the rest who are obligated to.

The upper decks seemed to be filling up fast, so I migrated downward. I found what I was looking for on the lowest level of the atrium. Deck four included a theater and an ice skating rink, but no restaurants or clubs, and only one small pub. Between the theater and the rink was one unadorned hallway, down which I could see a few doors that looked like offices. Unlike the other bars and restaurants, there was no floor-length window in front of the pub, just a small pane of frosted glass.

I entered to a dimly lit space with dark walls surrounding a leather-lined bar, behind which was a selection of high-end labels. More importantly, it was completely empty except for the bartender. I took one of the eight seats and ordered a Jameson.

"Jameson Rarest Vintage Reserve?" The bartender's name was Enzo, evident by the large name tag he and every other crew member were wearing.

"Yes, thanks. Make it a double."

No way the Vintage Reserve was part of their regular stock. Sam thinks of everything. I absentmindedly touched the four-inch scar on my forehead, mostly hidden by my hair, that marked the starting point of my friendship with her.

Enzo poured a healthy shot and set it in front of me. Good bartenders know when you just want to be left alone and he didn't bother me with small talk, thereby guaranteeing us a close, ten-day relationship.

I sat there thinking about the trouble at the boarding area. The ship had left port since then, so whoever had caused the problem was a safe distance away at this point, probably locked up and maybe facing jail time. Likely a local disturbance, but it would be something to look into. I was already wondering what I was going to do on the ship for ten days, and it might help relieve the boredom to have something interesting to occupy my mind.

My thoughts were interrupted by a man and a woman entering the bar. I'd seen the woman board earlier. She was in her sixties or so, and like everyone else on this cruise, except for me, clearly from a lot of money. Maybe it was because I was on a cruise ship, but she reminded me of Shelly Winters—a little overweight but sturdy, her hair artfully styled and a blonde-orange color that most likely came from a hairdresser. Her makeup was classic and understated, with a modest amount of color framing her ice blue eyes. She was wearing an expensive-looking light green skirt, blouse, and jacket set, accessorized by what looked like a 500-carat wedding ring on a fleshy white finger that bulged around it. I'd seen her board the ship with the man she was with now, along with a young woman I assumed was her granddaughter.

The man was middle-aged, and they seemed familiar. A son, maybe? He had dark brown hair in a buzz cut, thick eyebrows, very dark brown eyes, and a large nose that looked like it had been broken a few times. Possibly at the same time he acquired the prominent scar that ran from just outside his left eye down to his chin. He was plainly dressed in a dun pullover, dark cargo pants, and functional-looking boots. Even under his loose clothes I could see he was powerfully built. He carried a small black backpack over his shoulder that he set on the floor when they took their seats at the bar. His expression was intense, and they seemed to be arguing in what sounded like Russian.

The woman ordered and the bartender put two shot glasses in front of them, along with a fairly spectacular glass bottle in the shape of a skull. Very cool, if a little creepy looking. The bartender poured two shots and they both drank.

They talked in low tones for several minutes, the discussion gradually growing more heated, and his voice increased in volume until he was nearly shouting at her. To her credit, the woman didn't back down. She calmly responded without raising her voice.

At one point, the man leaned into the woman's face, practically spitting at her. Out of nowhere, her hand came up and slapped him hard on the cheek. The crack echoed in the small space.

Whoa. This trip might be more interesting than I thought.

The man stopped, stunned. I wondered what kind of medical services were on this ship, because if this guy punched her back she'd end up at least unconscious.

The old girl had a pretty good right hand, and his face was already starting to show her handprint. He looked like he was going to explode, and I waited for his retaliation, but to my surprise he leaned back and just glared at her. He checked his watch, then smacked his hand hard on the bar and left the pub.

The woman was red-faced but composed. She nodded at Enzo, who poured her another shot. She drank it immediately and got up to leave, heading straight for the door and not acknowledging that there was anyone else in the room.

I looked at Enzo, who shrugged. Maybe this was standard behavior on cruise ships.

I finished my drink and debated having another. Like a lot of high-end luxury cruises, this one was all-inclusive. We could eat and drink whatever we wanted to with impunity. But I had ten days to get my money's worth, so I decided to head back to our suite.

On the way out, I saw the Russian man leaning against the wall. His eyes were closed and he was breathing deeply. After a few breaths, his face adopted a bland expression, and he opened his eyes. I expected him to go to the elevator, or the central stairs, but instead he went down the little unadorned hallway and stopped near one of the doors. In a short while it opened and a crew member came out. They seemed to know each other, at least well enough to have a conversation. They shook hands.

No, not shaking hands. It looked like he handed the crew member something. From where I was standing it looked like an envelope. Then he took the backpack off of his shoulder and handed that over as well. The crew member took the backpack and went back through the door. The Russian watched it close behind him, and then turned and walked to the elevators.

What was that about?

He hadn't looked at all like he had in the pub with the woman. Instead of angry, he was more...businesslike. But what kind of business could he have with a crew member four hours into the trip?

It didn't take much to ignite my healthy, some would say pathological, curiosity. And once that happened, it demanded to be satisfied. Sam said I was a slave to it. Maybe, but it made me a good investigator. Well, a good former investigator.

Who was this guy, and what had he said to get smacked in the face? And why was he giving things to a crew member? I wanted to follow the crew member to see if I could get a look in the backpack, but there was a key pad next to the door he'd gone through, and I didn't have the code. I decided to tail the Russian for a few minutes to see what else he was up to.

I watched him get in the elevator and waited to see where it stopped. Twelfth deck. One of the pool levels, and the highest outside deck on the ship. I quickly walked up the atrium stairs to level ten and took the stairwell the rest of the way.

This pool deck was set up in two half levels. The pool itself was on deck twelve, but a shallow set of stairs led up to an additional sunning platform toward the rear of the ship. The platform was full of lounge chairs that were in the process of emptying out as everyone headed in for dinner. Behind the lounge chairs was the ship's funnel, a typically iconic feature on cruise ships. This one was no different. While our vessel was relatively small, carrying only two hundred very wealthy, versus a more standard two thousand not-so-wealthy passengers, they hadn't skimped on the funnel. It was the ship's dominant feature, rising from the deck to well above the top of the ship like a giant blue-green winged bird, if that bird were a Transformer.

I got to the deck just in time to see the Russian disappear behind it. I followed up the short set of stairs to the lounge chair area, and walked carefully to the side of the funnel on which he'd disappeared, and peeked around.

He was facing the rear of the ship, looking down. He had his phone out and was taking pictures. Every now and then he would take one of the water or the rear of the ship, but it looked like his primary interest was whatever was directly below the funnel. He took pictures for about a minute.

I waited until he finished and left, then walked to where he'd been standing. From here I could see down to deck ten, the fitness level that included another smaller pool. Directly below me was a crew-only restricted area, surrounded by a low barrier that contained some machinery and a deep well that went down numerous levels. Rising up from the well were a couple of long vertical cylinders that looked like storage tanks. Probably some kind of fuel.

I waited behind the funnel until I thought he'd walked away, then came from around it. He'd left the lounge area, and I just caught him walking back through the door to the stairwell. I went quickly back down the little stairs to the door and opened it slowly. He wasn't in the immediate hallway, so I stepped in. I heard steps, and then a door open and close below me, so I started down the stairs. I was about to open the door to deck eight and the atrium when I felt a hand on my shoulder.

I jumped, startled.

A low voice growled softly, "Why are you following me?"

I turned around and came face to face with the Russian.

"I, um, I'm not following you…" I reached for the door handle to the atrium.

He grabbed my wrist in a viselike grip and pulled me away from the door, then put both hands on my upper arms and moved me to the wall. I couldn't believe how strong his hands were. He leaned in close to my face, his dark eyes boring into mine.

Normally, when someone gets this close, you can smell something… their breath, their body, soap, cologne…something. But with him there was nothing. Just a suffocating force that pinned me to the wall.

His fingers tightened painfully on my arms, digging into my skin and holding me immobile. I wondered how he'd been able to come up behind me without making a sound. Silently, like a cat. Not the kind that gets up on your counters and plays with plastic bag ties and Q-tips, but one of the big ones in the jungle. The kind that moves through bushes and over leaves without leaving a trace or a sound, secure in the knowledge that he's the apex predator, and every single thing in the jungle is his for the taking.

"Do not follow me. Understand?"

I looked at him, unable to speak. I guess there was a first time for everything.

His hands squeezed tighter. Both of my hands were starting to go numb.

"Nod if you understand."

I nodded.

He stared at me a moment longer before loosening his grip, then walked through the door of the stairwell and out into the atrium, glancing behind at me one last time before the door closed.

I stood there for several minutes while the blood returned to my lower arms. Eventually, I got myself together and moved away from the wall. My arms hurt where he'd grabbed them.

He was really strong. And really mad. Why? What was he doing that was so secret?

I looked at my watch. *Shit.* Sam would be waiting. I hurried up the stairs to our suite.

CHAPTER 3

Sam was sitting on our couch when I got back. I rushed past her with a mumbled, "Sorry," and went up to put on clean clothes and run a brush through my hair. As I was changing my shirt, I could see finger-shaped bruises starting to form on my upper arms.

I'd decided not to share the interaction in the stairwell with Sam. I'd gotten myself into trouble before with what she referred to as my "excessive nosiness," and I wasn't in the mood for a lecture from her right now.

We left the suite and headed for the restaurant, sans-Chaz, who was undoubtedly being hand-fed free-range, organic, endangered species steak by his personal attendant. Sam had picked a restaurant on deck nine, Playa, one that featured regional cuisine ("Iberian-inspired food"). It was one of the larger venues on the ship, with high ceilings and an entire wall of glass that let in the ambient light from the atrium. All of the seating was at group tables, and we were placed at a round table with several couples and one man by himself.

I did my best to avoid talking while Sam charmed the group. She has this rare combination of beauty that captivates men but doesn't threaten other women, and a warm, sincere interest in people that draws them to her like a magnet. It didn't hurt that she was in a sheer black cocktail dress and a pair of four-inch heels she had no trouble walking in. I was wearing what Sam referred to as "Jesse casual," which was slim-fit black jeans, a black Michael Kors three-quarter sleeved jacket over a black T-shirt, black jump boots, and a necklace with a locket I'd gotten from my mom, my only jewelry except for a watch I still found useful even in the era of cell phones.

As an expert witness, dressing the part was key, so my courtroom attire had been unerringly professional. I had two Brooks Brothers suits purchased solely for that purpose. But everywhere else I was firmly committed to comfort over style. I'd learned long ago that trying to pull off the perfectly accessorized lady look wasn't part of my skill set, and once I accepted that, the act of dressing myself became much less stressful.

The meal was served in courses. During the first one we went around the table and introduced ourselves. The two couples were from Barcelona and traveling together, they did this a lot. The men were wearing Rolexes and the women looked like they were keeping the diamond mines in business all on their own.

Sitting next to me was a single man who introduced himself as Ander Ibarra. He looked a little out of place in his off-the shelf business suit, a tie, and a watch that was not a Rolex. He was polite and answered questions, but didn't offer any more information about himself. This made him immediately more interesting to me, as I've found that the less someone talks, the more they have to say. Ander looked to be around thirty, with straight black hair that went to just above his shoulders. He had a large nose and warm, intelligent brown eyes. He was trim and handsome in a rugged kind of way. I made an effort not to stare at him.

The marketing about the cruise's superior food wasn't kidding. We started with beef filet carpaccio, langoustine bisque, and fresh bread. The main course was Iberian ribs cooked with honey and parsnip foam, followed by Crema Catalana, a kind of crème brûlée. All of this was washed down with unlimited ice-cold cava that was in a constant state of refresh by the wait staff. Apparently, they'd been instructed to never let a glass get more than half empty, which was fine with me.

The conversation flowed with the cava, and over the course of the meal I learned all kinds of things I didn't really need to know about the fabulously rich, like where they go online to buy rich people things (JamesEdition.com), where they vacation during the winter (Gstaad or Aspen), and what brand of private jet was the best (Bombardier). At one point, someone asked Ander where he was from.

He took a small sip of cava. "San Sebastian."

Smirks crossed the faces of the Spaniards as one of the women made a comment in Spanish to her husband.

My Spanish wasn't great, but I caught the word *lenador*, which I thought meant lumberjack. San Sebastian is in Basque Country, and I knew enough about the region to know that many Spanish view the Basque as backcountry hicks.

Ander smiled graciously, ignoring the jibe. "I am a teacher."

The woman said, "Where is your beret?"

The Spaniards giggled.

"It is at home," he said patiently.

They returned to their giggling and discussion amongst themselves in Spanish, which continued until dinner ended. I thought it was pretty rude, but Ander didn't seem to mind. As usual, Sam was surrounded after the meal by several people from our table who wanted to spend more time with her. I was accustomed to this, and put on my "I'm waiting for my friend, and I'm not interested in talking" face. It got a lot of use when I was with her.

After twenty minutes she said her goodbyes and turned to me. "I'm going to check in on Chaz. Want to come?"

I couldn't think of many things I would like less. "No, thanks. I'm going to wander around."

She knew what that meant. "You know we have a full bar in our suite."

"I know. I'll see you in a while." I started to walk away, but paused and turned back to her. "Hey, can you do something for me?"

"What's that?"

"Do you remember those three people who boarded together, the older woman, the man who looked like her son, and the younger woman?"

"No…I don't think so."

"They were Russian. I think they might be the only Russians on the ship. Can you get his name?"

"I'll try. Why? Did you see someone you're interested in?" She gave a sly smile. Sam was always trying to hook me up.

"He's having some kind of argument with the woman he boarded with. She hauled off and smacked him in the pub. I'm curious about him."

Her eyes sparkled. Sam is really good at getting information out of people because they can't help but tell her things. It's one of her superpowers and she loves using it.

"It might be nothing. Just seemed strange. Mostly, I need something to do."

"OK. I'll have it by the end of the night."

I knew she'd have it within the hour. "Great, thanks."

We parted ways, and I headed back down the stairs to deck four, where I made a beeline for my pub.

There was one person at the bar. I was surprised and not disappointed to see it was Ander from our table at dinner. He saw me and nodded, looking at the seat next to him. I sat down, and Enzo poured me a shot. He put it down next to Ander's dark reddish-brown drink.

"What are you having?"

"Kalimotxo." He looked at my blank expression. "Red wine with Coca Cola. Very popular where I come from."

To each his own. But, yikes. "Sorry about the assholes at our table tonight."

He smiled, revealing strong white teeth. "I do not care what a few *diruz josias* think. Many Spanish believe everyone from the Basque Country is either a lumberjack or a terrorist."

"Which are you?" I asked, surprising myself by smiling back.

"Neither. I teach economics and law in the International Business Management Program at Deusto University."

Smart *and* good looking. Nice. I put away my drink in one sip and nodded to Enzo, who refilled my glass.

"Your English is good."

"It has to be. The program is taught in English." He turned a little in his seat, facing me. "And there are no terrorists at this point. The separatist movement is over. Rightly or wrongly, the treaty has been signed and the ETA is virtually done."

Rightly or wrongly? I filed that one away for later. I knew the ETA was the military arm of the Basque separatist movement. ETA stands for Euskadi Ta Askatasuna, which roughly translates to Basque Homeland and Liberty. Back in the nineties the ETA had been responsible for some of Spain's most deadly terrorist events.

"Virtually?"

"Like most nationalist movements, there are always holdouts..." He looked down at his drink.

I thought about the protestors at the quay and the two men who had tried to force their way onto the ship. But he didn't look like he wanted to talk about it, so I changed the subject. "Do you cruise often?"

He chuckled. "No, it was a gift of sorts from my university. And I clearly do not belong with this group of people." He gestured down at his attire. "You?"

"No. It's my first and probably last one. It's not really my thing. It was Sam's idea."

"The woman at the table...Sam. Are you two together?"

"Yes," I said, and then realized what he meant. "I mean, we're friends. This trip was a gift to me."

"That is a very nice gift. Why isn't it your thing?"

I explained to him that I wasn't really into crowds, or small talk, or intestinal parasites. "But so far it's been interesting."

He raised an eyebrow, encouraging me to go on.

"There was some kind of disturbance at the quay when we boarded. A few guys tried to storm the ship."

He nodded. "Yes, some demonstrators."

"Do you know what it was about?"

He hesitated and took a sip of his drink. "No."

"And it also looks like we might have a domestic conflict on board already." I described what I'd seen earlier with the Russian couple in the bar.

He leaned forward, encouraging me to continue. I liked that he had a curious streak.

"What do you think was going on?" He'd set his drink on the bar and was looking at me intently.

"No idea. It was all in Russian."

"I saw them earlier. There was a young woman with them."

"Yeah, I think they all might be related. Maybe it's her granddaughter. She didn't look any happier than he did to be here."

He paused, thinking. Then, "Russians…unhappy is their happy place." We both laughed.

I wasn't used to smiling this much, and my face felt funny. It reminded me of how I felt after going to the various professional conferences I'd been forced to attend over the years, where the muscles in my face responsible for smiling and pretending to care became fatigued from overuse.

Ander took another sip of his Coke-wine drink. "What are you drinking?"

"Irish whiskey."

"They have a good selection here."

"Yeah, no kidding. Four top shelf tequilas, six bourbons, five single malt scotches, eight vodkas, and four gins. Not bad for a little pub."

Ander looked at the shelves of bottles on the wall, his lips moving as he counted.

I mentally smacked myself for doing what Sam called my "memory thing" right off the bat. People generally didn't respond well to my ability to perfectly recall everything around me, although it didn't seem to bother him.

"What do you do for a living?" he asked.

"At the moment, nothing."

He waited for me to keep going and I didn't. My employment record was not one of my strong points. The last three years as an expert witness represented the longest uninterrupted stretch of my working life. One of my physicist friends, part of my small circle of brainy social outcasts that I'd met in graduate school, described my career as "a series of high-speed random walks into brick walls."

As an academic rockstar I'd graduated at the top of my class, and landed an enviable position right out of college with one of the big five accounting firms. In retrospect, it's hard to imagine a worse fit for a foul mouthed, too-smart young woman with a bad wardrobe, deep-seated anger issues, and no social skills than a prestigious Midwestern accounting firm. I was let go after six weeks, learning in my brief exit interview that dropping F bombs in front of senior partners was not appropriate.

This was followed by a position with a boutique financial services company. My supervisor really liked me and was sorry to have to fire me, taking time to explain things in a way he hoped would help me going forward. He knew I was into food, so had used a restaurant analogy.

"Imagine you're in a kitchen in the best restaurant in the world, cooking superior cuisine that people come from all over the world to eat. Then imagine that food being brought to customers by angry servers who throw the plates on the tables and walk away. That's kind of what it's like working with you. You're a five-star meal served by meth addicts in withdrawal."

Rinse and repeat, I went through five more companies in four years, my productivity inevitably overshadowed by some fatal breach of decorum that resulted in immediate dismissal.

My essential challenge was summed up succinctly by my last

manager as "a million-dollar brain and a ten-cent personality." This was fairly accurate, although I thought on that scale my personality rated at least a quarter. But in any case, that was when I decided I needed to work for myself, and started the financial investigations and expert witness business.

I thought it was a little too soon to share my work history with Ander. He was smart, nice looking, and apparently single, so if there was a chance we might connect on the cruise, I didn't want to blow it the first night by letting him know too much about me.

Exercise was always a safe topic. "Are you into sports?" He looked fit and must have done something to keep in shape.

"I ride to work. Cycling is popular where I come from. You know Miguel Indurain is from Navarre."

I nodded noncommittedly. Between my aversion to spandex and sanctimony, I wasn't much of a cycling fan, but even I knew who Indurain was. He'd won the Tour de France multiple times.

Ander went on. It was odd how quiet his body was. I spent a lot of time in bars, and people almost always fidgeted while they talked. They'd turn their drinks in their hands, peel beer bottle labels, swing around in their chairs, something. He was comfortably still. "I used to play rugby, but that is a young man's sport. And I do some climbing. Mountaineering is very popular as well. Have you heard of Alberto Iñurrategi Iriarte? He is from the Basque Country, and is one of eight people in the world to climb all fourteen of the eight-thousand-meter peaks in the world, each Alpine style." In response to my puzzled look, he said, "That means without oxygen or Sherpas, and few camps."

I supposed that was notable, and tried to look impressed.

"And Josune Bereziartu, she is from Lazkao, and is the first female to have climbed the grade difficulty 9a5 14d."

I had no idea what that meant, but assumed it was also incredible and nodded.

"And you?"

"No organized sports anymore, but I work out regularly. And I like to watch professional sports, especially football."

"You mean American football, yes?"

"Yeah. I'm not much of a soccer fan."

Football, for me, was more than a sport. It was inextricably entwined with the few happy memories I had of my childhood. Sunday morning game time was special because I could usually count on my dad sticking around for that. The more he started to drift away from us, the more important that time watching games together became to me. Eventually it was the only time I saw him. In the end that had gone away too. But the safe, warm feeling that football evoked in me remained. It was a little ridiculous, but I would still get excited every fall for the season to start, turning the TV on to whatever game was playing, even if I didn't care about the teams.

We'd lived in Chicago most of my life, but Mom and Dad were from Cleveland and were huge Browns fans, so I was too. I still am, despite it being a lifelong exercise in futility.

"But you know what you call soccer is the original football, yes?" He smiled.

We got into the inevitable "soccer is the real football" discussion, about the "beautiful game," and the purity of soccer compared to American football. I'd had that argument many times before with soccer fans and at this point found it tedious, but it didn't bother me with Ander. He was having fun with it, and unlike other people didn't take it as a personal affront that I wasn't a soccer fan. We argued good-naturedly for a few minutes and then moved on to other subjects. He was an avid reader, and well versed in history and politics. It was refreshing to be with someone who didn't find my own varied interests overwhelming.

I'd known ahead of time there wouldn't be many singles on this cruise, which was fine with me. Something about being stuck on a ship with a bunch of strangers sucked the urge to connect right out of me. But I could feel it coming back.

We finished our drinks, the first of many that lasted late into the evening.

DAY 2

CHAPTER 4

I woke up late the next morning with a slight hangover, something I'd probably need to get used to on this trip. I put on jeans and a T-shirt and went to meet Sam on the pool deck where I knew she'd be sunning.

She was surrounded by a group of admirers that would no doubt grow daily. I sat down in the deck chair next to her.

She looked me over. "You were out late. I'm hoping it's because you got lucky last night?"

"If by lucky you mean I managed to avoid groups of people and drank good whiskey, then yes, very."

She sighed. "You know, if you give it a chance, you might actually meet some interesting people on this trip. You'll live longer if you have more friends." Which was probably true for most people.

The deck was slowly filling up with what looked like uninteresting people. Mostly couples who were sunning, sleeping, or drinking. The Olympic-sized pool was already in use by several people swimming laps. I recognized one of the swimmers as the young woman I'd seen board with the Russians.

I leaned back in my chair, taking a sip of the coffee that had magically appeared from one of the stewards. "I have you. You're like having ten friends." More like a hundred.

The ship was smoothly cutting through the water, although I could barely tell by the movement of the deck. Sam looked up at the sky, closing her eyes. "I found out your Russian man's name. It's Boris

Alekseev."

"What did you have to do to get the name?"

"I'm having drinks with Palben, the chief purser." Her eyes were still closed but I could see the start of a smile forming on her lips.

"Isn't crew fraternization with passengers frowned upon?"

"Normally, yes. But he's an executive level officer, so he gets more leeway."

"Thanks. I owe you."

"No, you don't. He's cute. And he can get me a behind the scenes tour of the Guggenheim when we get to Bilbao."

"Is 'behind the scenes at the Guggenheim' a euphemism for hooking up?"

"No, you're invited too."

"Great. Thanks for doing that."

Crew members were moving unobtrusively among guests with trays of drinks, bottles of cava, and ice buckets. The crew member to passenger ratio on this cruise was very high, almost one to one, but the crew, for the most part, was either out of sight most of the time or managed to blend in to the surroundings. I could see from their name tags that they represented a variety of countries. There were a lot of Spanish-sounding names, which made sense given that most of this cruise took place around Spain.

On the far side of the pool, I spotted Ander leaning up against the railing, looking around. He saw me and waved. I waved back.

"Well, I did meet someone. Remember the guy from our dinner table? The one from San Sebastian? I had drinks with him." I pointed to Ander.

She looked across the deck and brightened. "There you go!" She looked him over. "He's nice looking in a rustic kind of way." She looked back at me. "Is he smart enough?"

Sam knew my dating history. My longest relationship in the last year had been a three-day weekend with a guy I'd met at the gym. He was gorgeous and a great guy, and it was a vigorous, sweaty affair, but, as usual, I got bored and ended it. That was par for the course. Inevitably, within a few dates, the guys I met would turn out to be either not smart enough, or boring, or both, and I'd cut them loose. Sam called me a cerebrosexual, and I supposed that was true. Occasionally, I'd hook up with someone after consuming mass quantities of alcohol, which always made other people seem more interesting. At least until it wore off.

"It seems like it."

We watched Ander from across the deck. He found who he'd been looking for, and walked toward the railing at the bow where he met up with a crew member. An officer by the look of his uniform.

I leaned over to Sam. "Who's he talking to? Is that the captain?"

"No, it's the first officer, he's the second in command on the ship. I think his name is Inigo."

"They seem chummy."

Whatever they were discussing was private. Two passengers walked to the railing next to them, looking out over the water. While they were within earshot Ander and Inigo stopped talking. A few moments later, the couple left, and the men resumed their conversation, their heads bowed together. While they were talking, another crew member walked up to Inigo and handed him a note. He said something to Ander, then turned and walked away toward the bridge. Ander left after him and we saw him go into the stairwell.

"I wonder what that was about," Sam said.

I wondered too. I continued to scan the deck. On the other side of the pool, standing off to the side, was a crew member by himself. He was the only one not waiting on passengers. His head moved slightly as he gazed around the deck through mirrored sunglasses.

"What do you think he does?"

Sam looked him over. "I'm guessing he's the ship's security officer. They're required to have one."

The security officer was short and skinny, with thinning black hair that was cut short. He was standing unnaturally straight, possibly to

36

make every one of his five feet and six inches count. He held his hands behind his back in what looked like a military parade position. Kind of a ridiculous posture on the deck of a luxury cruise ship.

"Not likely he's going to sneak up on anyone." The guy wasn't exactly subtle, his face fixed with an exaggerated look of suspicion.

"He's part of a team, and there are probably some who are undercover as well. Security on cruise ships is serious business."

"Why? What are they worried about?" It hadn't occurred to me that criminal activity would be a thing on a cruise ship.

"Terrorism, and there's a lot of drug smuggling that goes on. It's big business." She took a sip of cava. "There was a bust on one of the Caribbean cruises I took a few years ago. A couple of crew members had picked up some cocaine in Jamaica and tried to bring it into the US. Because of this there are usually security cameras everywhere on cruise ships."

"I haven't seen many cameras." Actually, not a single one.

"Yes, that kind of surveillance doesn't fly with this clientele. People with this kind of money tend to avoid cameras. Instead, they do extensive pre-trip checking on everyone. It's not practical on a cruise with two thousand people to do in-depth vetting, but with fewer passengers it makes sense."

I recalled the forms she'd had me fill out prior to the cruise, the administrative version of a complete colonoscopy. At this point, there wasn't much they didn't know about me. I thought it was to make sure our cruise didn't have any undesirables on board. Now that I thought about it, it was a little surprising that they'd let me on.

Sam continued. "In lieu of cameras, every floor with passenger suites has a concierge."

"You mean like Benat? I thought he was here to help us."

"He is. But each floor's concierge is also responsible for keeping an eye on the passenger suites. Theft is a common problem on cruise ships. This is in addition to a lot of other security measures. We all went through a metal detector when we boarded, and we're going to do that every time we re-board after port calls. Remember how they took your luggage when you got on?"

I nodded.

"Everyone's bags were taken when we get on the ship. They were turned over to handlers, and we didn't get them back until they'd been processed. They use dogs to sniff out drugs and explosives. Those are the things I know about, but for obvious reasons, they don't make a point to share all of their security procedures with the passengers."

Hearing all of this, I wasn't sure if I felt more or less safe, but realized I was hungry. "Are you up for an early lunch?"

"Sure."

We picked up her things and walked to the elevator. One of Sam's goals was to try all of the restaurants on the ship, so we went to the top level of the atrium and into the first open lunch venue we saw.

Bistro Entrecôte ("Alternative French") was a small, intimate restaurant. Pendant lights hung above tables set with black and white tablecloths, and vintage photographs hung on brick veneer walls. The tables included a mix of small two-tops and larger settings.

Sam liked being with groups for meals, and we joined a table that included a mix of international big shots from various countries and their spouses, one young trust fund couple from France, and a Dr. and Mrs. Ken Beverly.

After surviving a round of introductions, I put my head down and focused on my salad. Sam was her usual scintillating self, drawing people out and making each one feel like they were the most important person on the planet.

"So, Dr. Beverly, what kind of doctor are you?"

"I'm a proctologist."

My head popped up, and under the table, Sam put her hand on my leg. As he described his practice, I could feel her hand tightening on my thigh, silently begging me for restraint.

"That must be interesting—" Sam started, and I quickly interrupted her.

"Are you into astronomy?"

He smiled at me. "Why, yes, how did you know?" He started to regale us with details of his high-end home telescope and nightly findings, while I waited for an opening to ask him what his favorite planet was.

Sam saw where this was going and didn't give me a chance, deftly steering the conversation to subjects less dangerous but not nearly as funny.

She kept it up until lunch ended. We went back to our suite, me sulking at the lost opportunity for ass doctor-related comedy, and Sam relieved that we'd gotten out of there without major embarrassment.

Once we got back, she started packing her small deck bag. "I'm going back to the pool. Want to come?"

"Sure. Give me an hour. I'm going to check out the ship." I waited for her and we left the suite together, her heading for the elevator and me for the stairwell.

I'd heard it takes people days to figure out how to navigate large cruise ships, so I'd done my homework prior to the trip. Our ship had fourteen decks with passenger suites located on eight of the levels. A notable feature was that it had *only* suites—no plebian cabins or staterooms. This meant that if we hit an iceberg and started sinking, there would be no steerage class to lock below deck while the aristocrats bogarted the lifeboats. But, as with all other cruise ships, the higher up you went, the more expensive the accommodations. Sam had paid an obscene amount of money for the privilege of our top-deck suite. The least expensive suites were on level seven, twenty of them, for the least fabulously wealthy.

The shops, restaurants, bars, and clubs were sprinkled throughout the levels. We'd spent the morning on the main pool deck, one of two. The other one was on the sports level, which included a fitness center, jogging path, putting green, bocce court, paddle tennis, and a climbing wall that I suspected would get little use. Deck five was the casino, and on the lowest passenger-accessible deck was the theater, ice skating rink, and my little pub. Three full-service spas were sprinkled among the decks, and a tepidarium, whatever that was. I'd also learned there was a library and a "surfing simulator".

The bridge was located on the highest level of the ship, the same as our suite. The crew's quarters and all of the ship's other operations were on the lowest levels. Things like materials storage, engineering, utilities, waste management, and medical facilities made up decks one, two, and three. Those levels and the bridge were off-limits to passengers except during tours. Sam and I would have a chance to see those decks, as unbeknownst to her I'd signed us up for an engine room tour.

I took my time and walked each deck. With only two hundred passengers on board, I was already able to recognize most of them, my near-photographic memory not restricted to numbers and documents. I eventually found myself on the lowest accessible level. Resisting the urge to go to my little pub, I went back to the stairwell and headed up to the pool to join Sam.

***

I'd fallen asleep on the lounge chair next to Sam and woke to a soft throat clearing. I opened my eyes to see our concierge Benat standing at the foot of our lounge chairs.

"Dr. O'Hara, Miss Hernandez, I am sorry to disturb you.

It was still weird to be called "Doctor," but they had done their homework and knew I had a PhD. And they'd probably figured out that with this particular clientele, it was better to err on the side of excess formality and titles. Benat didn't know yet that I wasn't really a member of this clientele.

"If you are amenable, the captain has requested you join him at his table tonight for dinner. He will be in the restaurant Casa Roca on deck seven at six o'clock."

I looked at Sam, who nodded her head eagerly. "Sure, thanks, Benat."

"Please call me Ben." All of the crew, with the exception of the captain, went by first names, part of the "family" atmosphere the cruise line promoted. They didn't resemble my family in the slightest, but I was happy to add him to the short list of Bens I knew, currently including Ben Franklin, Ben Stiller, Ben Hur, and Ben Gay.

He smiled, gave a little bow, and left. I thought he was pleased that his charges had rated an invitation from the captain so soon, which I suspected was because of Sam's fast-growing reputation as a dazzling conversationalist, and me because we came as a set.

Sam clapped her hands happily, hurriedly packed up her things, and left for our suite. Beauty takes time, and she would use the full hour before dinner to look fabulous.

I followed her in a half hour, dressed in five minutes, and spent the rest of the time waiting for her on our balcony, looking out at the water.

CHAPTER 5

Since it was the captain's table, Sam went all out with her most impressive evening wear, a custom Reem Acra silk gown that looked like it was glued on. It was off-white with teal highlights and a low back, and she completed the look with her favorite family heirloom earrings and necklace set given to her by her grandmother. Sam thought it was a waste to spend money on jewelry, which was a source of dismay to her grandmother, who'd gifted her a number of priceless pieces probably originating from medieval Spanish royalty.

I was in "upscale Jesse Casual," the primary difference between that and normal Jesse Casual the Christian Louboutin boots that replaced my jump boots. Sam had long ago given up trying to get me to invest in a more elaborate wardrobe.

I'd heard that cruise ships were basically short periods of killing time between meals, and it was already starting to feel that way. But at least we were eating in style. Casa Roca was one of the fancier spots on the ship, with a menu designed by the three Roca brothers of El Cellar de Can Roca in Girona. The captain (Xose de Maria de something de something) personally greeted each diner as we joined the table. I recognized him as the guy who'd been at the top of the gangway during the boarding process when the two protestors had tried to get on. He was about sixty, and his most distinguishing feature was a goatee/mustache combo reminiscent of Colonel Sanders.

Joining us at the captain's table were the Russian woman I'd seen the first night in the bar and the younger woman she'd boarded with. I was surprised and a little disappointed that Boris wasn't with them. By now the shock of the confrontation with him in the stairwell had worn off, and I was more interested than ever in finding out what was going on with him. The younger woman was quiet and looked uncomfortable, which, to be fair, could also have been said about me.

The meal started again with introductions, a ritual I suspected we were doomed to repeat at every damn meal on the trip. In addition to us and the Russians were two couples: the Hendersons, and a woman and man from Madrid who introduced themselves as Alejandro and Valeria. The Madrid couple was like Sam in that they pegged the high end of the attractiveness scale. Alejandro was tall and dark haired, with flawless chiseled features and dimples that deepened when he smiled, which he did often, no doubt to display his perfect teeth. Valeria could have been a supermodel, other than she looked like she'd eaten a meal in the last week. She was also tall, with long dark hair and Everest-like cheekbones setting up a face that needed no make up to look flawless.

My thoughts were interrupted by the too-loud introductions being given by the Hendersons, John and Trish. They were from the US and into real estate, and each other.

Trish had big blonde hair and a large, red lipstick-lined mouth set in a wide, genuine, and, I was to learn, permanent smile. She was wearing a low-cut top that was about two sizes too small. John's assets were less obvious, but he seemed nice enough.

"We're John and Trish Henderson! We just got married!" they shouted as they leaned in together to show how much in love they were.

I tried not to throw up in my mouth.

"Guess how we met?" Trish asked, somehow managing to sound both breathless and deafening at the same time.

"Band camp?" I offered.

Sam kneed me under the table.

"Noooo…on a cruise!" She giggled and leaned into John, who gave

43

her a kiss.

As I worked on getting my appetite back, I wondered how Trish and John had warranted an invitation to the captain's table, which all of a sudden seemed much less exclusive. As it turned out, the Hendersons' cruise package included one meal with a high-ranking crew member, and the captain had apparently drawn the short straw. He smiled politely as they fawned over each other.

The introductions continued. We learned that the Hendersons were from Chicago, which surprised me. We must have really run in different circles, as if they'd been anywhere close to mine, I would have heard them.

The Russian woman introduced herself as Svetlana Peshkova, and the young woman as her granddaughter Tatiana. Tatiana stared into her lap during the introductions. She was about twenty or so, and looked like she wanted to be anywhere but on this ship, which wasn't surprising. What twenty-year-old wanted to go on a vacation with their grandmother? Well, me, I guess, but I'm pretty sure I'm an outlier.

I introduced myself quickly, but not quickly enough. Trish Henderson was a fan of Court TV.

"Wait…you're Jesse O'Hara? *The* Jesse O'Hara? The 'baby and the space shuttle' Jesse O'Hara?"

"Yep."

"*Holy cow!* What's it like to be in a real courtroom?"

"Well, there's usually a judge, and a jury, and lawyers."

Trish and John nodded solemnly at my unique insight while Sam kneed me again under the table.

The rest of the meal was like that. Between courses of langoustine en croute, ceviche, and Bullit de Peix, there was small talk, shouting from the Hendersons, and the occasional question about my work. Sam effortlessly guided the conversation around the table, and, as usual, kept everyone enthralled. Everyone except Svetlana, who said little. I caught her staring at me a few times.

After three hundred hours, dinner started winding down. As the dessert and coffee were being served, the captain stood up and lightly touched his fork to his glass to get our attention. Speaking in accented but clear English, he said, "Thank you all for joining me this evening. I hope you have enjoyed the trip so far, and be assured, the best is yet to come. Tomorrow, we port in Cadiz, which, for many of you, will be the start of an excursion inland to Sevilla. Some of the crew are also from this region of Spain, so if you have any questions, please feel free to ask them."

He smiled and raised his glass for a toast, which we all joined. This signaled the end of the meal, and I got up to leave as soon as it was polite. Unfortunately, not soon enough, as I found myself cornered by the Hendersons.

"We'd love to have breakfast with you tomorrow!" Trish shouted.

I nodded in what I hoped was a noncommittal manner and extricated myself, looking around for Sam. She was talking to Alejandro and Valeria. The three of them were smiling and standing very close to each other, and Sam was lightly touching Alejandro's arm. I knew what that meant. She'd likely be hooking up at least one night on this trip.

After saying her goodbyes to Alejandro and Valeria, Sam joined me. Like everyone else within five hundred feet, she'd heard the invitation from the Hendersons.

"They could be fun."

"Yeah, I'd love to, but I'm already scheduled to be poking my eyes out with a fork then."

"Why do happy people make you so angry?"

"Happy people don't make me angry." This was probably a complete lie. "But I left my earplugs at home."

We walked out of the dining room into the atrium and Sam headed back to the special pet quarters to visit the tiny Toxic Avenger, who was probably getting a full body massage from a team of specially trained Swedish massage yogis. I was feeling adventurous and decided to try out one of the other bars on the ship. I walked a few shops down to where I'd noticed a sports-themed bar earlier.

Joe's Place was based on the cruise line's perception of an American sports bar, containing a number of TVs, a couple of nice pool tables, and a long bar. There were a few people sitting at tables and only one man at the bar, so I deemed it safe and sat down and ordered a beer.

I recognized the guy at the bar from the pool earlier where he'd been with his young wife and infant son. He'd since changed out of his pool clothes and was now wearing a collared shirt open several buttons down, highlighting a large gold medallion resting on a furry black chest. His hair was oiled and slicked back in the very latest in combover technology.

He raised his glass to me in a remote "cheers" but didn't seem interested in talking, which worked for me.

Above the mirrored backdrop was a large TV showing a live baseball game. I was surprised they had it on, as in my experience, Europeans were completed baffled by Americans' fascination with baseball. It was a bonus for me though, as in addition to Sunday football games, my favorite memories as a kid with my dad were when he would take me to Cubs games. He loved baseball and would patiently explain the intricacies of pitch counts, hitting approaches, and the game's peculiar physics. When I was old enough, he started playing catch with me every night after work.

This was prior to his deciding that blackout drinking with his friends was more fun than spending time with his family. But I ended up with great hand-eye coordination and a pretty good arm.

As luck would have it, the game was the Cubs versus the Mets, and it had just started. After years of futility the Cubs were in the playoff mix, and the game actually meant something.

It was pleasant sitting at the bar, watching the game, and I got into it. *This trip might not totally suck after all.*

I was on my second beer when the TV went silent, followed by the crackling introduction of the PA system.

"This is the captain speaking. All passengers, please return to your suites. Crew members, be advised that Charlie is on board." This message was repeated in Spanish and French, then again in English: "All passengers, please return to your suites immediately."

CHAPTER 6

The bartender removed our drinks and the wait staff politely urged people to get up and out of the restaurant. They were trying to be courteous, but I could see looks of concern on their faces.

Passengers streamed into the atrium from other restaurants, bars, and shops, some looking worried and some annoyed. Ship staff directed everyone to the elevators and stairwell. The look of calm affability that had been on nearly every crew member's face since we'd boarded had disappeared. They were now serious and focused on getting all of us back to our rooms as efficiently as possible. Passengers demanding to know what was going on were gently but firmly guided along.

Sam was already in our suite when I got back. She was sitting on the couch reading a magazine, looking a lot less worried than I felt. Ben was at the door and looked relieved to see me. Once I was inside, he turned and left, closing the door softly behind him.

I walked over to the kitchen and opened the refrigerator for a beer. Ben had gotten the memo and it was stocked with Guinness. If we were going down, I was going to do it with a drink in my hand. "What the hell is going on? Do you think it's a fire?" I'd heard this was one of the primary risks on cruise ships.

"I don't think so. They called a Charlie code."

"Who's Charlie?"

"Charlie means some kind of security threat. It's one of the codes they use to alert the crew without alarming passengers." She didn't seem worried, which calmed me down considerably.

"A security threat? What does that mean? Someone used a salad fork for their steak?" I couldn't imagine any of the passengers I'd seen as a threat.

"It could be one of a number of things. The most common security issues on a cruise ship are theft and sexual assault. But it could also mean an unauthorized passenger or, in rare cases, piracy."

I walked out to the balcony and looked around. It was dark now, although the sky was clear and an almost full moon laid a carpet of light over the calm water. There were no other ships in the area, so it was unlikely we were under attack by Captain Jack Sparrow. Below us on the two pool decks, I could see small groups of crew members walking around, peering into containers and under equipment.

"Sam, look." She joined me, and I pointed to where we'd gathered for our muster drill the first day. They were lowering the lifeboats.

Were we sinking? I hadn't felt us hit anything, and as far as I could tell, the ship was still moving through the water as smoothly as before. On the other hand, this was how it had started with the Titanic. A small bump that eventually led to Leonardo de Caprio and Kate Winslet saying tearful goodbyes in the ice cold Atlantic.

Her eyes got wide. "Chaz…" She pushed the Ming button on the balcony to call Ben.

I doubted we were sinking, but if so, one benefit would be that there would probably not be room in the lifeboats for dogs. Yes, it would be a horrible tragedy if Chaz were lost at sea and marooned on an island. But maybe he would end up in a Swiss Family Robinson-type of situation, living out the rest of his days in a small, primitive community, chewing up someone else's stuff. Sam would eventually get over it, and replace him with a real dog that didn't hate me.

We watched as they lowered the lifeboats down to the deck one by one. I was relieved to see that it didn't look like they were readying them for usage. They were looking for something.

As we were the only passengers on deck fourteen, Ben was at our door quickly. "Yes, Miss Hernandez?"

"Ben, what's going on? Is Chaz still in his room? Can I get him?"

"I do not know. And I am sorry, but I must ask you to stay in your suite until the captain gives the all clear signal. I am sure Chaz is fine." He bowed and left.

There was nothing to do, so we waited, watching from our balcony until the sun went down. Eventually, the crew members left the decks. It didn't look like they'd found anything.

With nothing more to see, we went back into the suite. Sam grabbed a bottle of prosecco from the kitchen and we settled in on the couch in comfortable silence. I looked at her, curled up in the cushions, calmly reading her magazine. One of the things I really loved about her was her utter lack of drama. She just didn't expend any energy worrying about things she had no control over. As someone who was constantly assessing everything and everyone, all of the time, I found her profoundly calming.

We were probably going to be fine, but just in case, I said, "Sam, if anything happens, I just want you to know...you've been an awesome friend."

She looked at me affectionately. "You too."

"Really?"

"Of course. You're devastatingly loyal, and the most honest person I've ever met. It's refreshing. You're also brilliant. Things would be much less interesting without you." She winked at me while she sipped her prosecco. "But nothing's going to happen. Someone probably misplaced her diamond necklace."

All right then. She went back to her magazine and I sunk into the soft couch and closed my eyes.

***

Three hours later the PA system came alive again.

"Hello, everyone. This is the captain speaking. I am sorry for the inconvenience. You are all welcome to resume your activities."

"So that's it? What the hell was that about?"

Sam had jumped off the couch. "I don't know," she said, grabbing her bag and walking out the door, "but I'm going to check on Chaz." Little Lord Voldedog was probably just fine, but she wouldn't be able to focus on anything else until she made sure.

Maybe the ultra-rich were accustomed to leaving problems to be solved by underlings, but I was used to knowing what was going on around me. I headed out to the pool deck to take a look for myself.

It was close to midnight, and the railing, the pool, and all of the fixtures and furniture were lit up with small lights, giving the deck a festive look. After doing a complete circuit around the perimeter, I walked over to the area behind the funnel where I'd seen Boris taking pictures the night before. I looked at the machinery and then leaned over the security gate, peering down at the storage tanks. I couldn't see much past the top of the tanks, just shapes, no details, and wished I had a flashlight. I peered into the well, squinting against the darkness. Two decks down, I could see something that hadn't been there the night before. A small dark form was resting against one of the tanks, swaying a little bit, like it was hanging from something. I was sure I hadn't seen it when I'd followed Boris out there the night before.

Maybe this was what the crew had been looking for. If so, ship security needed to know about it.

I headed down to deck four, where I'd seen the security office in the same unadorned hallway as the door to the crew's quarters and the lower decks. It was closed, but I saw a light on inside and knocked.

The security officer opened the door. Now I could see his nametag, Balasy. Close to ballsy. I wondered if he was. I peered around him and saw two other crew members in the room.

"Yes?" Unlike the rest of the crew, he didn't appear to have the same mandate to be excessively polite to the clientele. His mirrored sunglasses were off and I could see his eyes. They were not at all friendly.

"Excuse me, I think there's something on deck ten that you might want to take a look at."

"What?"

"You were looking for something, right? During the security alert?"

He stared at me, narrowing his already small eyes into tiny, albeit bulging, dots. They were set off perfectly by his pointy nose, complete lack of a chin, and a wispy failure of a mustache.

"It's next to one of the big storage tanks behind the funnel."

He continued to stare at me.

Jesus, don't rush into anything.

Finally, he said, "And you know this how?"

"I saw it."

"When?"

"Just now."

He dramatically sighed, rolling his eyes and exhaling through his thin lips. "It is dark out. I'm sure you didn't see anything. Please, we are very busy here." He started to close the door.

I put my foot in to keep it from shutting. "Look, I'm just trying to help. "See something say something", right? And you were clearly looking for something. That's why we had the security alert, isn't it? I'm telling you, it wasn't there yesterday."

He looked down at my foot and said haughtily, "I am the ship security officer, miss, and you are now interfering with my work. Please leave." He obviously did not think a mere passenger could be of any use to his important work.

I removed my foot and he semi-slammed the door in my face. I heard it lock. *Officious ratface asshole.*

Now what? If what I'd seen in the well was some kind of bomb, we were in danger. If so, it would serve him right for ignoring me. But the satisfaction I would get about being right would be quickly overshadowed by the ship sinking and our collective drowning deaths. On the other hand, it seemed unlikely that if they'd been looking for something dangerous, they'd give the all clear before finding it. They'd probably found what they'd been looking for, and what I saw was unrelated to the security alert.

But I was uneasy. My gut instinct was rarely wrong when I noticed things. Whatever was in the storage tank well hadn't been there the night before. And after meeting him, I wasn't exactly filled with confidence in the security officer's capabilities. I would go back tomorrow and take a look when it was light and I could see better.

I went back up to deck ten to take one more look around. We were close to pulling into our next port and the ship was slowing down. Almost no one was left on deck, just one couple on the far side. I couldn't see them very well, but he looked very drunk, sagging down against the railing. The woman was holding him up, like he was probably getting ready to puke over the side. I didn't want to be anywhere near that, so I turned back inside and went up to our suite.

Sam wasn't back yet. I grabbed a beer from the kitchen and stepped out onto to our balcony. The moon was almost full and I could see land. We'd left the Mediterranean, passing through the Straits of Gibraltar and into the Atlantic Ocean. We were putting in at Cadiz, our first port of call, one of four stops on the Iberian Peninsula. I was glad we'd be in port tomorrow; I was more than ready to get off the ship for a little while. It was already starting to feel too small.

I thought about what I'd seen in the well behind the funnel, and about Boris's little photography excursion. It was a strange place to take pictures, and his reaction to me following him had been extreme. I rubbed the bruises on my upper arms. He was up to something. I could feel it, literally. Fortunately I had ten full days stuck on the ship to figure it out. It probably wouldn't take me that long.

I heard Sam come back into the room. "I hope you don't mind. I asked Ben if he could spend the night with me." She was holding Chaz tightly in her arms.

"No problem, I'm going to bed." I headed up the staircase, taking a quick look around to make sure all of my stuff was picked up, as he'd busy himself with chewing up anything of mine he could get his dirty little paws on. He looked misshapen and crippled, but I knew from previous experience that he could move like a fucking ninja when he had the opportunity to get into my shit. I'd lost a fair number of shirts to his gnawing teeth. But Sam loved him, and I didn't object to him staying with us. Like they say, you can choose your friends, but you're stuck with the family you're born with, and with the pets of your best friends, even if they are demon spawn from hell. Or something like that.

Like the interaction with Boris in the stairwell, I didn't share with Sam what I'd seen near the funnel, or my exchange with the security officer. She wasn't all that spooked from the Charlie code, other than being separated from Chaz, but I didn't want to make her uneasy.

I fell asleep quickly. At one point during the night I was woken up by the ship's PA system calling for someone named Oscar. I didn't know who Oscar was, and wondered why they had to alert the whole damn ship to find him, but drifted back to sleep before I could think more about it.

DAY 3

CHAPTER 7

I got up early to hit the gym for a workout, in part to make up for the five thousand calories of food and wine I knew I was going to consume on shore. Like Sam I was slim, but unlike her, it didn't come easy. My lineage dates back to corpulent Irish potato eaters, and it took daily workouts to not end up like my ancestors, which in one surviving grainy black-and-white photo shows my great-great grandmother and friends wearing size XXXL shirt dresses, smiling broadly and exemplifying the changing norms for beauty since the early 1900s. The twelve-person elevator limit was clearly not established with my family in mind.

Normally I attended a local gym at least five days a week, and my workouts involved intense self-defense sparring and a fitness regimen. I wasn't a particularly disciplined person, but this was one area of my life that I took seriously.

In my early twenties I'd taken up Krav Maga, a fighting scheme designed by the Israelis. Unlike many martial arts, Krav Maga is less an art from and more a ruthless and efficient way to stay alive if threatened. It's basically a no-holds barred system to protect yourself, and is particularly great for women, as many of the moves rely on leverage rather than strength. The Krav Maga classes I'd taken were primarily geared for self-defense, but the instructor made sure we understood that even using it in defense, we would be dealing out damage. If I were being honest with myself, I'd have to admit that part appealed to me.

The fitness area of the ship was on deck ten, the same deck as the pool. It was, not surprisingly, empty, and also, not surprisingly, very well equipped. The room was packed with modern treadmills, stairmasters, free weights, and a set of Cybex weight machines.

I stepped on the treadmill and started running. The treadmill was in front of a mirror, and I fixed my gaze on the scar on my forehead that brought me back to the day I met Sam.

***

I was at Northwestern University on the Evanston campus working late on my dissertation. I'd been at it for three years and was almost done. I often picked random buildings in which to work, and this time I'd chosen Kresge Hall, the art building on the south side of campus. I'd spent little time there in classes, but it was a nice place to get some reading done as it was open late and relatively quiet.

It was almost 11 p.m. and I needed to wrap up and head home. All of the coffee I'd consumed was catching up with me, and given that I was in for a long walk and a trip on the L, I decided it would be prudent to hit the bathroom before leaving.

It was almost time for the building to close, and as I neared the women's bathroom on the main floor I was surprised to hear voices. I walked in and saw a young woman lying on the tile floor with four men standing around her. Two of them were holding her down. All but one had beers in their hands. The other was unzipping his fly.

The men were large and muscular. I thought I recognized one of them as formerly on the football team. He'd been highly recruited, but then had been kicked off his freshman year for reasons that were never made public. I'd seen the woman before around campus. She stood out as she was tall and, for Evanston, glamorous looking. Her name was Salbatora, but everyone called her Sam.

It sounds funny, but no matter how much you're exposed to things like this on TV, it doesn't really prepare you for seeing it happen in front of you. Maybe because there's no ominous music playing to signal that something bad is happening. In any case it took me a minute to comprehend what was going on.

Sam saw me and we locked eyes. Her makeup was smeared on her tear-streaked face, her dress was torn, and one of her shoes had come off and was hanging around her ankle by a strap. Her very large, dark brown eyes were wide, and she looked terrified.

While I'd learned from a brief stint in counseling that I had deep seated anger issues, I was not inclined toward physical expressions of it. My rage leaked out, according to the therapist, in sporadic bouts of depression, sarcastic and often juvenile dark humor, and verbal assaults, rather than physical aggression. In retrospect, I thought that had I said something to these guys, it's likely they would have run out, not wanting to deal with the repercussions of a witness to what they were doing. But it was late, I was tired, and something about what I was seeing triggered my rage for the first time in a physical form. Catching them, and me, by surprise, I went completely berserk.

"You fucking motherfuckers!" I grabbed the trashcan near the door and threw it, yelling at the top of my lungs, then ran toward the one who'd been unzipping his fly, throwing punches and kicking.

I had no idea what I was doing. I'd never struck anyone in anger in my life, and was beyond inept in this situation. But it didn't matter. I went at them with a fury, flailing wildly and calling them every name I could think of, which was a lot, as my list of insults is world-class and legendary among my friends and family.

This was the part where you'd like to think that the heroic young woman, fueled by righteous anger, got the best of the bad guys who had been taken by surprise. But the notion of a slightly raised red mark caused by the plastic trashcan I'd thrown scared no one. The man I threw it at batted it away with a sneer, and all four of them turned their attention away from Sam and to me.

They walked toward me, balling up their fists. They didn't even bother ducking my weak punches and wild kicks, but instead just focused their efforts on getting me under control. Once two of them had a hold of my arms it was over, and they proceeded to methodically beat the holy crap out of me.

Big, heavy punches to my stomach, face, and back. I heard a snap as one of my ribs broke, and I felt my nose give way from another shot to the face, followed by sticky blood pouring out. As I sagged to my knees, one of them raised his beer bottle and I watched it come toward my head. I heard or maybe felt a loud crack, and that was the last thing I remembered. As I was losing consciousness, I thought about how movie fights always took way longer than this one.

I found out later that with their attention on me, Sam was able to get up and run out to yell for help, which in a near-empty university building on a campus at night is a pretty useless endeavor. But she'd pulled a fire alarm, and I figured that's when they stopped beating me and ran out. Their testosterone was up, and I'd interfered with their fun. I was fairly certain if she hadn't done that, they would have raped me and killed me, and then possibly raped me again.

I woke up in a hospital room. I knew what it was right away as I'd spent a lot of time in them as a kid, usually the result of injuries sustained from losing some kind of self-imposed gravity challenge.

My mom was sitting on the bed close to me. She touched my face gently. Her eyes were red, and I could see she'd been crying. "Jessica Maureen O'Hara. What did you get yourself into this time?"

Mom never used my full name unless she was really angry or really scared. She'd named me after Maureen O'Hara, her favorite actress, and her idea of a "nice Irish girl." That was before she'd learned I was anything but.

I started to talk but my throat was too dry and my voice didn't work. I gestured toward the pitcher of water next to the bed. She reached for it, and poured me a glass and handed it to me. I tried to drink it, but for some reason it wouldn't go down.

It felt like we hadn't talked in a long time, and I had so much to tell her. She looked beautiful. I wanted to ask her what skin regimen she was using. It looked like she hadn't aged in the last ten years.

"Jesse. Jesse, can you open your eyes?"

I woke up in a hospital bed surrounded by beeping machines. Mom wasn't there, of course. A nurse was standing by the bed, holding my wrist.

I did a quick inventory of bodily damage. There was a dull ache in my left side, and I lifted a hand to my face and touched my very tender nose. I'd be sporting some really nice black eyes for a few days. There was a sizable bandage on my forehead and I had a massive headache.

"The doctors say you don't have any internal bleeding. Two of your ribs and your nose are broken, and they think you have a concussion. It took twenty-four stitches to close the cut on your forehead. They want to keep you here for a couple of days." She looked me over and said, "Are you up for seeing someone? Visiting hours are almost over, but there's someone here for you."

I looked to the doorway and saw Sam, and nodded.

The nurse left the room, and Sam came in and walked toward the bed. "How are you feeling?" she said.

"You should see the other guys." I was pretty sure the other guys didn't have a mark on them, unless they were allergic to plastic.

Sam sat on the bed. "I'm Salbatora. Most people call me Sam." She took my hand and leaned forward, looking me in the eyes. "Thank you."

"Are you OK?" I asked.

"Yes, I'm fine. In much better shape than you are."

"What happened?" I asked. "Do you know those guys?"

"No, I don't know them. I was in the art studio late, and they followed me into the bathroom. If you hadn't come in…" She looked down at the bed.

I wasn't all that surprised. Sam was well known on campus. She was beautiful, outgoing, and popular. Even I knew who she was, and I wasn't exactly running in the cool kid circles. The men had probably had their eyes on her for a while.

60

"I don't remember much after going in. What happened?" Mostly I was wondering why I was still alive and un-raped.

"I pulled the fire alarm."

Smart girl. Yell "rape" and nothing happens, but no one wants to get burned to death.

She squeezed my hand gently. "Why on earth did you take them on? They could have killed you."

I wasn't sure how to explain the physical debut of my deep-seated anger issues. "I really hate bullies."

She tilted her head and waited for me to continue. I stayed silent, and she didn't push it. After a few moments she said, "I've never been rescued before. I'm not sure what to do." She looked around the room. "Do you need a fruit basket?"

We both laughed, which for me resulted in significant pain in my midsection. Broken ribs and humor were not a great combination.

The nurse came back in to let us know that visiting time was over.

Sam got up to leave. "Is it OK if I come back tomorrow?"

"Sure." I realized I was looking forward to it.

I was in the hospital for two days. Sam visited me both of them, and then weekly after I moved back home to recover. We spent hours together. It was strange, as talking about my life and feelings wasn't usually my thing. But our shared experience in Kresge Hall broke down my formidable wall of distrust, and I found myself telling her things I'd never shared with anyone. I had the feeling it was the same for her.

Her full name was Salbatora Hernandez de María de los Remedios Cipriano de la Santísima Álvarez-Cuevas, and her stunning features were the result of her mixed Spanish and Jamaican heritage. Her grandparents on the Spanish side were aristocrats, and grew their fortune during the Franco years, primarily via black market alcohol and cigarettes. They'd been living the dream until the atmosphere in Spain got too dangerous even for them. The entire family left for the US, settling in Inverness, one of the wealthiest Chicago suburbs.

Her mom grew up in Inverness, and like a lot of kids of very wealthy parents, spent her early adulthood traveling the world. After two years, her travels came to an abrupt end when she'd gotten pregnant with Sam, and returned home married to a poor Jamaican man, Sam's father. The family wasn't thrilled with the match, but they accepted it. The couple were producing the family's first grandchild.

Sam grew up a member of the uber-privileged class, but somehow managed to not turn into a complete asshole. She was an artist and a philanthropist, and spent a fair portion of her time rescuing animals and sometimes people. She'd bought her own house in Chicago's Edgebrook neighborhood, eschewing the tonier suburbs for something closer to the city and its vibrant art scene. When I was well enough to move around she invited me over.

Her house was less a house than a compound. It sat on the edge of ten acres, the main structure covering 6,000 square feet, not including several separate smaller buildings. Sam lived in one half of the main house, and rented out the other half, as well as all but one of the unattached buildings, for next to nothing to young artists in need of studio space.

Behind the house were fruit trees and several herb and vegetable gardens, surrounded on three sides by undeveloped low forest in which her rescue dogs and cats roamed freely. Walking around the grounds, I saw none of the precious landscaping I was used to seeing with typical Midwest mansions. Native plants surrounded the house, which itself was lightly ornamented and seemed to blend into the surroundings.

On my first visit I met her personal menagerie, which at the time included her five rescue dogs and an unclear number of cats. This was pre-Chaz, as Sam had apparently not yet discovered the Satan's Spawn pet rescue organization. The dogs generally stayed in a group and were a funny-looking pack. They included a 160-pound Landseer Newfoundland that she'd gotten from the closure of an illegal puppy mill, a Bernese mountain dog/lab mix, a beagle from a New Orleans shelter that had been almost dead when they found him, and that she'd nurtured back to health and eventually to obesity, a permanently happy golden retriever, and a mixed breed that defied categorization. The only thing they had in common was their utter devotion to Sam.

Like the outside of the house, the inside was functional but not opulent, filled with lots of wood furniture, warm-toned floors and walls that gave it a homey, rustic look. The one area she splurged on was the kitchen. It was large and outfitted with numerous pantries, a large central island, and an eight-burner Viking gas stove, above which was an industrial grade hood that she'd had custom designed.

Sam loved to cook and designated Fridays as group dinner night. She would do all the cooking, and it wasn't unusual for fifty or more people to show up, who typically included most of the artists who used her studio space, her friends from nonprofit organizations, and occasionally a few family members. In the summer she would set up long tables in the backyard, and in the winter she would open up the very large dining room in the main house.

Between the studios and her frequent fundraising events for various arts and animal causes, Sam's community of friends was large, though I realized over time that she had few people with whom she completely confided. She had many acquaintances and scores of people who loved her, but hardly anyone she trusted completely. But the shared experience in Kresge Hall's bathroom created something between us that couldn't be duplicated through normal channels. So even though she was a well-adjusted adult from a fully functional family, and I was the poster child for ACOA, we became close friends.

It turned out that there were no legal consequences for the men who had attacked her. As their attorneys pointed out, they didn't actually rape anyone, and technically it was me who had attacked them. But the incident did have several significant impacts on my life, the most important of which was my friendship with Sam. It also was the impetus for me to learn how to defend myself.

I came across a listing for "Krav Maga for Self Defense" at a nearby Jewish Community Center. The price was right (it was free) and the center was walking distance from my apartment. The class was taught by a short, paunchy Israeli in his fifties, Mort Lowenstein, who I absolutely believed could kill me with a paper clip and not break a sweat. It was co-ed, and I was surprised at how some of the moves were not only simple, but could be used to neutralize larger, stronger attackers. When the first class ended, I signed up for more, eventually getting good enough that I worked with the instructor to help him teach the beginner classes. The focused training helped me recover physically and emotionally from the attack in a way that therapy never did.

I also started carrying a boot knife. I found a used, fixed blade three-inch Worden DATU that fit snugly and discretely on the outside of my jump boot. I wasn't completely certain I'd be able to use it if the time came, but it made me feel better wearing it.

I tried to get Sam to join me in Krav Maga but physical confrontation wasn't really her thing. She did decide to take up shooting, and had a range built in her yard. She worked closely with a private instructor for several months, after which she practiced almost daily. I got the sense that she was a bit embarrassed by it and didn't do it in front of others, but occasionally she would let me watch.

Her weapon of choice was a small caliber Beretta that fit in her purse. After a few years of regular practice she got very good at it. She never showed any outward signs of trauma after the attack, but like me with my boot knife, she rarely left home without her pistol.

The thirty-minute timer went off on the treadmill and I moved to the weights. I worked out for another hour in the empty gym, then headed back to our suite.

On the way back I stopped by deck ten to get another look inside the storage tank well, this time during daylight. Stepping through the doorway to the deck I could see a group of crew members standing at the well. Yellow barrier tape had been put up around the opening. Ballsy was there, as was the captain. They were talking, or rather the captain was talking. He did not look happy. Ballsy was looking down, contrition replacing his previously haughty demeanor. He was being scolded.

I walked toward them, getting within a few feet before one of the crew members put his hand out and gestured me back. I was close enough to see that one of the crew members standing next to the captain was holding a black backpack. It looked a whole lot like the one I'd seen Boris hand over to the crew member the first night.

It was unzipped and empty.

CHAPTER 8

After a quick breakfast Sam and I left the ship. On our way out we passed an official-looking group of people in uniforms at the bottom of the gangway, talking with Ballsy and the captain. Ballsy handed the empty backpack over to one of them. Also with the group was a dog, a yellow lab, wearing a harness. It was going nuts, whining and making little barks. I turned around as we walked by and watched the group head up the gangway.

"I wonder what that was about," Sam said.

She waited for me to weigh in, but I stayed silent, which might as well have been a colossal "I know something I don't want to share" red flag.

She raised an eyebrow. "You know something. Spill it."

"I saw the captain and Ballsy with that backpack this morning. I think they pulled it out of the storage tank well behind the funnel."

"*And*?" Sam always knew when I was holding something back. It was irritating and comforting at the same time.

"Last night after the Charlie code, I went out to the deck. I saw something in the well that hadn't been there before and reported it to the security officer. He didn't appreciate my help but must have gone back to check. I think it was the backpack."

"Do you think that's what they were looking for during the alert?" Her eyes got wide as she thought through the implications. "And does that mean they gave us an all clear announcement before it was really all clear?"

"I'm not sure. The captain was chewing Ballsy out when I got up there this morning. Maybe because Ballsy told him everything was fine, but then they found something that wasn't supposed to be there next to the tanks. If it's what they were looking for, the all clear was premature."

"Could you see what was in the backpack?"

"No. It looked like it was empty. But they might have taken out whatever was in it before I got there."

"I wonder what it was."

"They were bringing a dog on board…and they only use dogs for two things, right? Drugs or bombs." And cadavers, but I didn't want to say that.

"Yes. But either way, I'm glad we're off the ship. This is your vacation. We're supposed to be relaxing, not worrying about things like this."

I nodded, even though I wasn't glad. I wanted to know what was going on. Sam was right, I was in many ways a slave to my curiosity. But I needed to do my best to put it away for now. She'd gone to a lot of trouble to put this trip together for me, and I didn't want to seem ungrateful.

One of the perks of this cruise was having our own driver at each port of call who would be at our disposal for the day. We went toward the terminal and past the group of passengers on the quay, most of whom were looking around to get their bearings. We found our driver, Tano, in the taxi area of the terminal, holding up a sign with Sam's name on it.

He introduced himself in English. "You are going to Sevilla?"

"Yes," Sam said.

He opened the car door and we got in, and as he pulled out of the taxi area I got a good look around. The port of Cadiz was near the historic section of the town, which looked within walking distance from the cruise terminal. I hadn't been in many ports, as most of my travels had been via planes, trains, and automobiles, but this one was nice, with clean, spacious walkways that looked like they would take you to the center of town. It would be an interesting destination in its own right, but we were heading inland to Seville. A lot of the other passengers from our ship were getting into cars, and I guessed they were doing the same thing. Among them were Svetlana, Tatiana, and Boris. He was looking around, and his gaze eventually came to rest on me. He stared for a long moment before getting into the driver's seat.

My upper arms were still sore from where he'd grabbed them. I was glad I was wearing a three-quarter sleeved T-shirt as the bruises were in full bloom, currently a colorful set of purple and red lines.

My thoughts about Boris were interrupted by Tano. "Have you been to Sevilla before?"

"No," Sam said. "Can you tell us a little bit about it?"

He smiled. "Yes, I am from there. Sevilla is over two thousand years old and one of Spain's oldest cities. The name comes from Hisbaal, a reference to the ancient god Baal of the earliest known inhabitants, the Tartessians. It was taken over by the Romans in 200 BC, who ruled until the eighth century when the Muslims conquered a large part of the region. They lasted until the thirteenth century, when they were defeated by the Castilian Christians. There are many interesting historical landmarks that reflect these various cultures. A lot of cruises that port in Cadiz stay for several days to accommodate multi-day trips to give people a chance to see them."

This was interesting and well beyond my existing knowledge of Seville, which amounted to one Bugs Bunny cartoon about the Barber of Seville that was based on an actual opera. I never saw that opera (or, well, any opera), but that episode was one of my all-time favorites.

While we were driving out of the terminal, Tano slowed down and then stopped, muttering something under his breath that might have been a curse. In front of us was a group of people in the middle of the street, blocking the exit. Many were holding signs in a language I didn't recognize. Traffic in and out of the port was stopped.

I turned to Sam. "Do you know what the signs say? What are they protesting?" Unlike me, she was actually fluent in a number of languages, the result of a multinational family and years of European boarding schools, which was also the source of the slight English lilt to her accent.

"It's Euskara, the Basque language from the northern region of Spain. It looks like they're demonstrating something about a prison." She said a few things to Tano in rapid Spanish.

He seemed disdainful and explained in English, "One of Spain's maximum security centers is here, the Puerto de Santa Maria prison. It holds political prisoners, including terrorists. Some groups claim the prisoners are mistreated." He honked his horn. "One of the Basque prisoners died last week. The prison is saying it was suicide, but some say the circumstances are suspicious."

"Isn't the Basque Country a long ways from here?"

"Yes, over a thousand miles." He leaned out of his window, yelling at the protestors and honking his horn again.

We waited about five minutes until port security was able to manage the crowd back onto the sidewalks. Tano drove out the terminal exit and a short way on city streets, and then onto a long bridge that linked Cadiz to the mainland. The bridge put us directly onto the highway that would take us to Seville.

The ninety-minute drive took us through the Andalusian region of Spain, of which Seville was the capital. The landscape was unremarkable, primarily lowlands, a mixture of green and brown. Mostly brown at this point.

"Sam, did you hear the intercom go off last night?"

She was looking out the window. "No, I must have slept through it."

"They were looking for Oscar."

She turned to me. "Oscar is the code they use on cruises to designate to the crew there is a man overboard."

"Oscar?"

"Yes, it's like Charlie in that it activates their emergency procedures without alarming the passengers. I heard it on a cruise once before. One of the passengers got very drunk and fell overboard."

Or went over on purpose, I thought. If there weren't seven open bars, I might have already thrown myself off.

"Apparently it's not all that uncommon. Fortunately for the drunk man, it was warm and calm, and they were able to find him and get him out before hypothermia set in."

"I wonder who it was." The one thing I did know was that if it were Trish Henderson who fell overboard, they'd have no trouble locating her in the water. "It seems like a coincidence that it happened right after we were confined to our rooms, doesn't it?"

"Yes…maybe that was the reason for the alert? We saw the crew looking for something. But maybe they were looking for some*one*. Maybe that's why the dog is on board, to look for whoever is missing."

That made sense. And if so, the security threat had nothing to do with the backpack. But it still didn't explain what was going on with Boris and the crew member he'd given it to, and what the backpack had been doing in the well. Now that we were off the ship and away from the fray, I decided to completely level with her.

"There's something else. That first night, I saw Boris meeting with one of the crew. He handed him something that looked like the backpack they found in the well. I also saw him taking pictures around the funnel."

"What were you doing on the deck looking at the funnel? Is that why you were late for dinner?"

"Yeah, I, uh, followed him. He wasn't too happy about it. He got a little aggressive with me."

"Aggressive? Aggressive *how*?" Sam wasn't generally reactive when I got into trouble, as it was a semi-regular occurrence. But she was a little more vocal when she thought it put my physical safety at risk.

"It was nothing, he just made it clear he didn't want me to follow him." I didn't tell her about the bruising on my arms. "I also saw him give the crew member an envelope."

She thought for a moment. "It might be nothing. Crew members often interact with passengers, and sometimes they exchange things. They might be running a little operation on the side to offload some things from Russia."

"But these are really wealthy people. How could it possibly be worth his time to sell stuff on the side to a crew member?"

She looked out the window without answering.

I pressed her. "What do you think we should do?"

"Do? Why do we need to do anything?"

I was getting a little exasperated. "Sam, we had a security alert and then someone went overboard. They found a backpack in the storage well, and it looked a whole hell of lot like the one I saw Boris give to a crew member. We just saw them take the backpack off the ship, and now they're bringing a group of officials and a dog on board."

"You're right, Jesse, yes, I'm sorry. I just want this trip to be nice for you." She dipped her head, something she often did when she was working things out in her head. "It seems like the first thing would be to talk to the security officer."

"Yeah, I tried that. He wasn't interested. And now that he's been chewed out by the captain, I can't imagine he'll be more receptive to my help."

"What about Ben? He's supposed to be our liaison to everything on this ship."

"Good idea." *Why didn't I think of that?*

This wasn't a first for Sam. When I'd get stuck on something I was trying to work out, she'd listen to me talk about it, saying nothing, then ask the one salient question, or make the one key observation that moved things forward. Not surprisingly, it was often something people-related. Humans were her sweet spot and my blind one.

When we got back to the ship I'd talk to Ben and see about getting a message to the security officer. It might be better received coming from a crew member than from me.

Now that I had a next step, I could put away the mystery and focus on our day in Seville.

Sam and I had previously negotiated our shore excursions. She was into art, and I was into history, so we agreed that while in Seville we'd do more history, and focus on art in a later port of call. Our plan for Seville was to start with a tour of some of the most interesting historical monuments and buildings. Sam had mapped out a three-hour walk that would take us by the major landmarks. It would be self-guided, as I wasn't into tour groups. The idea of walking around in a group at someone else's pace filled me with dread.

It was going to get hot, so we planned to be done and inside eating lunch by one or so, and then spend the rest of the day in the air-conditioned Museo Arqueológico de Sevilla, Seville's renowned archeological museum.

As we entered the city, I pulled out my phone to check the starting address of our tour.

Sam put her hand on my arm. "I hope you don't mind; I made some other plans for us. We're not going to do it self-guided."

Dammit. "For fuck's sake, Sam, you know how much I hate tour groups. We agreed to do this on our own."

She smiled. "I'm sure you're going to want to do this one."

I was sure I wasn't. I scowled and looked away from her out the window.

"Look, just give it a chance. If you don't like it after five minutes, we can go off on our own. Deal?"

"Deal." I was certain it wouldn't take me five minutes to decide to bail.

Sam gave Tano the address to our starting point, and he dropped us off at the street corner of Calles Gerona and Alhondiga. The streets were narrow, made up of large square cobblestones and surrounded on all sides by three-story buildings that looked like apartments built above a variety of small businesses. There were no historical landmarks in sight.

Sam got out of the car and told Tano we'd call him when we were ready to go back to the ship. He drove away with a wave.

She looked around and made eye contact with a young man standing alone on the sidewalk. "Itzal?"

"Yes, Miss Hernandez?" He walked over and shook hands with her.

"You must be Dr. O'Hara. I'm Itzal. I'll be your tour guide today."

Not for long you won't, I thought as I shook his hand. I checked my watch so I would know exactly when five minutes had passed.

"Shall we get started?"

"Yes!" said Sam.

Itzal turned and walked through a doorway on the corner of the street.

I turned to Sam with a puzzled expression on my face.

She said, "Oh, yes, I forgot to mention. Itzal is the guide for one of Seville's Tapas, Taverns, and History tours. It's normally offered to groups in the evenings, but he agreed to do it privately for the two of us during the day."

I couldn't help the sheepish smile that was taking over my face. A personalized tapas pub crawl. Sam had nailed it and she knew it.

"I honestly I don't understand why you don't trust me at this point," she said, walking through the doorway.

I wondered too as I followed her. She'd never let me down. The folks in the ACOA support group I'd attended exactly once might have a lot to say about my trust issues. Maybe it was something to explore later. Later in life, that is, when I would have nothing better to do.

We followed Itzal into a tavern, where he grabbed a table. Even though it was only eleven o'clock it was already filling up.

"Our tour starts here, at El Rinconcillo, the oldest tapas bar in Sevilla. It dates back to 1670." He handed us some menus.

The place was homey and rustic, with hams hanging from the ceiling and several of the walls filled to the top with very old shelves completely loaded with bottles of various alcohols.

"Tapas are the specialty here and are not ordered from the menu.

If we want tapas, we will need to order at the bar. What is your preference?"

I was interested in an authentic tapas experience and put down my menu. "Why don't you order for us? What would people who live here eat? And, uh, drink?"

He smiled and got up to go to the bar. He spoke to the man working behind it for a few minutes, and then came back with a bottle and three glasses. "Food is coming." He poured healthy amounts of wine into each of our glasses. "We will start with this Ocnos, it is a regional chardonnay from the north of Sevilla. Good for lunch."

I liked that they had a special designation for an appropriate lunch wine. He finished filling our glasses and we toasted.

"Sevilla is the tapas capital of Spain. What we are going to do today even has a specific name here, *tapear*, which means 'tapas bar hopping.'"

We had a term for it in English too. Day drinking.

Itzal was a wealth of information, and it didn't take long for me to appreciate having a guide. "The word *tapas* means lid, or cover. Originally, tapas were thin slices of bread or meat, usually pork. Tavern goers would use them to cover their glasses to prevent fruit flies from getting into their wine or sherry, which historically was very sweet.

"One story is that tapas started during the reign of King Alfonso the tenth. He was ill, and had to take small bites of food with wine between meals. Once he recovered, he decreed that no wine was to be served in any of the inns in his land unless it was accompanied by something to eat. Some historians also believe that the emergence of tapas across the region was the result of the Spanish Inquisition, who used them as a test to identify Jews who would not eat pork."

Our food arrived and he stopped talking while the servers put a number of dishes on the table. The plates held thin slices of ham, fried fish, some cheeses, and a few things I didn't recognize.

"What's this?" I asked, pointing to a casserole-type dish that looked green with flecks of red in it.

"That is espinacas con garbanzos, it is a specialty of this region. Garbanzo beans and spinach with paprika."

We dug in. I put some espinacas con garbanzos on my plate and tried it. It was smoky and hearty, and while I wasn't a huge spinach fan, it was a struggle to stop eating it and try the other things.

Between bites, Itzal said, "When we leave here, we will wind our way through the city and eventually end up at La Giralda, the bell tower of the Sevilla Cathedral and the most iconic landmark in the city. On the way we will stop at two more tapas bars I think you will like."

We left before we got too stuffed, and over the course of the next few hours, Itzal took us on a circuitous path that wound through and around town and by the major landmarks. We did tours of the Real Alcázar de Sevilla, one of the oldest and largest palaces in Spain, and still the home of the Spanish royal family. Next was the Torre del Oro, the Golden Tower, originally erected as a watchtower to prevent invasions from the nearby Guadalquivir River, and then used as a prison during the Middle Ages. We walked by La Casa del Flamenco with its Auditorio Alcántara. The Casa was an artifact of the region's history of flamenco dancing, dating back to the fifteenth century, and still a big part of the music scene in Seville. While we walked, Itzal regaled us with stories about the famous people and events that had played a role in the city's rich history, including Julius Caesar, Christopher Columbus, and the Spanish Inquisition.

In between historical sites we stopped at two more tapas bars. At Casa de la Viuda we sampled the simple but delicious *papas sevillanas*, Sevillian dressing potatoes, that used only olive oil, parsley, and vinegar to elevate potatoes to something greater than the sum of its parts. Our last restaurant stop was Bar Alfalfa, which specialized in handmade brusquetta, where we tried a number of vegetarian and meat-based bruschetta. They didn't resemble the American hors d'oeuvre of the same name in the slightest.

We left it up to Itzal to order the appropriate drinks along the way. This ended up including a variety of local wines, beer, and in one case sherry, which normally I wasn't a big fan of, but matched up well with some of the tapas.

As promised, the last stop on the tour was the fifteenth century Seville Cathedral and its famous bell tower La Giralda. We stood outside on the sidewalk looking up while Itzal shared the building's history. Built originally in the twelfth century as a mosque minaret, it had been converted to a cathedral when the city was taken over by the Christians in the thirteenth century. At almost 350 feet high it was still one of the largest churches in the world. It was the dominant and most recognized structure in Seville, and made a fitting end to a terrific tour of the city.

We were saying our thank yous and goodbyes when Itzal looked up the street and said, "There is a very good tapas place just around the corner. Are you up for one more?"

Sam looked at me with an expression that said this was my day, so it was up to me.

I nodded enthusiastically. "Definitely."

We followed him a short distance and then into a small place, Bodequita Romero, at the triangular corner of three cobblestone streets. Like the others, there were hams hanging from the ceiling, but this place had a more modern feel, being relatively new at only seventy years old. We tried two more of the region's iconic tapas: montadito de pringa, a stewed pork sandwich seasoned with paprika, and fresh grilled cod, both accompanied with ice cold Cruzcampo beer.

We took our time, enjoying the atmosphere and Itzal's company. He was originally from Bilbao, and we were surprised to learn that prior to becoming a tour guide, he'd worked for the Basque Nationalist Party.

"That's a big change. What made you decide to go into tapas tours?"

He shifted in his seat, his omnipresent smile fading. "The nationalist movement is over. My family worked for generations to bring autonomy to the Basque people, and we were unsuccessful." He looked unbelievably sad.

I was sorry I brought it up, but he quickly regained his cheer and we continued to talk and drink. At one point, Sam looked at the antique clock on the wall. "It's getting kind of late. We should probably head over to the archeological museum." I looked at my watch and was shocked to see that five hours had gone by. We said goodbye to Itzal and went out to the curb where Sam pulled out her phone to call Tano to pick us up.

It would be nice to spend some extended time in AC for a little while. My only concession to the heat had been the selection of a white instead of black T-shirt, and I was starting to regret not bringing anything but jeans on this trip.

We planned to spend the afternoon at the museum and then head back. Because Seville was a popular destination for cruise passengers, they'd set the required boarding time back from five to eight p.m. Even on a luxury cruise, they'd been clear that the ship's schedule would wait for no one, and we didn't want to be left behind. At least, Sam didn't want to be left behind. We'd planned to be back to the ship by 7:30 so as not to cut it too close. It was almost four now, which gave us a good two hours at the museum.

Sam was frowning at her phone. "They're calling everyone back to the ship."

"What?"

"It's leaving earlier than planned. They want us to reboard and are going to leave as soon as everyone is back on."

"Do you know why?"

"No." She called Tano, and he arrived within a few minutes to take us back to Cadiz.

Seville had been clear and very hot. As we drove closer to the coast, it cooled, and by the time we got to the terminal, it was overcast and significantly colder. A lot of people were getting back to the ship at the same time, and we joined the line that had formed to go through the metal detector at the top of the gangway. Some of the passengers were loaded down with shopping bags that had to be scanned and, in some cases, investigated, which irritated a number of them who were already annoyed that their excursions had been curtailed. The very wealthy were not used to having their plans fucked with, much less having to wait in line.

As we were standing there, I saw Svetlana and Tatiana get out of a car. The car drove off after they stepped out and I didn't see the driver. Boris had been with them this morning when they'd left, but now it was just the two of them. I wondered if he was already on board, and if not, if the ship really would leave him behind in Cadiz. Part of me was hoping that was the case. He seemed like trouble. But part of me hoped not. I wanted to find out what he was up to.

The two women were arguing loudly. I had no idea what it was about, but imagined it could be something like this:

"You are ungrateful. I bring you on this very expensive cruise and all you do is pout. There are many children in poor countries who would love to be here."

"Yes, thanks very much for bringing me on the Cocoon Cruise, where the requirement for admission is age-related senility. The only people within fifty years of my age are children, and the biggest entertainment is waiting to see who will keel over first from clogged arteries or gout."

"Watch your mouth or I will slap you. You know how much I like slapping."

James Bond films notwithstanding, I didn't believe Russians were any less virtuous than other people. But these three were a real piece of work.

Their argument stopped abruptly as they got into line, both staring straight ahead.

We were almost to the front of the line when the people ahead of us stepped aside to make way for a group of men carrying something down the gangway.

As they passed by us, I could see it was a stretcher, covered in a sheet. Underneath it was the outline of a body.

CHAPTER 9

It was almost eight o'clock by the time we got back to our suite. I sank gratefully into the couch and Sam called Ben, who was at our door within a minute.

"Yes, Miss Hernandez?"

"Ben, what's going on? Who were they taking off the ship?"

Ben looked uncomfortable, looking away and holding his hands tightly together. "We lost someone overboard last night. They found him today in the water."

"Do you know who it was?"

"I do not know. They are not releasing the name until his next of kin are notified."

"Is that why our stay in Seville was cut short?"

"No, there is a storm coming, and the captain wants us to be away from here before it comes in."

I started humming the tune of *The Wreck of the Edmund Fitzgerald*.

Sam didn't bother looking me, asking Ben "Are we in any danger?"

He smiled calmingly. "No, this is an excess of caution. The captain wants your trip to be as smooth as possible, and leaving early will insure that happens."

He turned to leave, but I stopped him by asking, "Ben, what happened the other night? What was the security alert about?"

The smile left his face, and he hesitated. Without looking at either of us, he said, "It is nothing to worry about."

I usually knew when people were hiding things from me, and he was doing it now, but I didn't call him out on it. I got up from the couch and walked to the doorway. "Ben, can you do something for me?"

He brightened. He didn't like talking about unpleasant things. Changing schedules, security alerts, and people going overboard weren't on the agenda to make our trip as wonderful as possible. Fielding requests for guests was back in his wheelhouse. He raised his eyebrows expectantly.

"I know they pulled a backpack out of the storage tank well. I saw one of the passengers give something that looked like it to a crew member the first night. Can you speak to the security officer and tell that to him? And that I would like to discuss it with him?"

Ben struggled not to frown. This wasn't the kind of request he wanted to accommodate. And I guessed Ballsy wasn't someone anybody wanted to talk to. But he nodded, then gave one of his little bows and left.

The door closed, and I turned to Sam. "Who do you think went overboard?"

"Very drunk passengers occasionally fall over the side on cruises. If a crew member went overboard, he probably did it on purpose. It's rare, but not unheard of for them to commit suicide. The hours, the pay…some people just aren't cut out for it."

"There seem to be a lot of 'rare' occurrences on this ship."

"Yes, well, I don't think we have to worry. If something was really wrong or we were in danger, they'd get us off of it right away. On the other hand, if you hear a 'kilo' call over the PA, that's a different story." She turned and headed for the kitchen. "Do you want something to drink?"

"No. Wait, what's 'kilo'?"

"It's a code for the crew to go to emergency stations."

Jesus. Good to know. I looked out the sliding glass door to the balcony, and up at the gathering clouds. "I hope the storm doesn't interfere with our plans tomorrow."

"What plans?" She was pulling a bottle of something out of the fridge.

"I signed us up for the ropes course."

She turned toward me, a look of minor horror on her face. "*Ropes course?*"

"Yeah. They're known for having the best one in the industry. Didn't you notice all of the scaffolding on the back part of the ship? Tomorrow is a scheduled cruising day, no ports of call, and I didn't want us to get bored. We're slotted for the eleven o'clock session." I smiled at her and went up the stairs to take a shower.

DAY 4

CHAPTER 10

"You look relaxed," Sam said. "Maybe you should cruise more often."

We were drinking coffee on our balcony. We'd slept in late, the five hours of walking in the heat the day before had taken it out of us. She was right, I was relaxed. And it was strange…it usually required a fair amount of alcohol to get me to this state. Maybe there was something to this cruise thing.

There was a knock at our door. I went to open it and saw Ben. He looked the same way he had the last time he visited us, which was to say, uncomfortable. He avoided making eye contact with me.

"Good morning, Dr. O'Hara."

"Hi, Ben." I waited for the bad news.

"There has been a bit of a change to our itinerary. We will be missing…several ports of call. Our next stop will be Bilbao. We will cruise for the rest of the day and through the evening, and plan to arrive there tomorrow morning."

"Why?"

He looked past me and out the window. "The large storm that is coming through, it is moving toward the coast and north. In order to avoid it, we must go directly to the Bay of Biscay."

"OK, thanks, Ben. Hey, did you have a chance to talk to Ballsy yet?"

"*Balasy*, yes. He, uh, told me that he would talk to you when it was appropriate."

I knew what that meant. Ballsy would rather go down with a sinking ship than accept help from anyone, particularly a passenger, and maybe especially a female one. Whatever. I'd made an effort to help him. Now I would just have to find out what was happening on my own.

"OK, thanks Ben."

He looked relieved I didn't ask him anything else and left.

We'd be heading to the northern coast and turn into the bay, bypassing Lisbon, Porto, and La Caruna, none of which was all that interesting to me. I was glad we'd been able to see Seville but didn't care all that much about the others.

I walked back to the balcony and sat down. I hadn't noticed it before, but the sky toward the south of us was definitely darkening. The wind had picked up too; looking down I could see whitecaps. "The storm is bigger than they thought, and we're going to be skipping the next three stops. We're going straight to Bilbao."

Sam looked surprised. "That's very unusual. It must be a large storm. But it makes sense that they would want to get away from the ocean side of the peninsula, and into the bay as soon as possible.

"Have you ever been on a cruise ship during a storm?" I was kind of looking forward to it. The calm water was getting monotonous.

She thought for a few moments. "No, some rain, but nothing major. People don't buy these cruises to sit in their cabins, so the ships take care to avoid bad weather. The routes they take are generally not ones that have risk of storms or even rain." She took a sip of coffee. "I do remember a few years back one came through this area. I think it was Hurricane Vince, the same year as Katrina and Rita. There were a lot of hurricanes that year, so many that they started running out of names for them. It was considered rare at the time for this region. But I wouldn't worry about it. These captains are very tuned in to the weather, and I'm sure we'll be giving any storms a wide berth."

I was no stranger to sea disasters, having watched *The Perfect Storm*, *Poseidon Adventure*, *Adrift*, and *Castaway* multiple times. And I wasn't all that worried about it. I like storms, and big weather in general. It feels like nature reminding us there's something bigger than us. In any case, I'd come prepared with a month's supply of Dramamine.

"Did Ben talk to the security officer?"

"Yeah. Ballsy's not interested in my help."

She raised an eyebrow. "You're going to do your own investigation, aren't you?"

I didn't answer. I didn't need to. Sam knew I couldn't help myself.

***

Sam and I were the first people to arrive at the ropes course. The course was laid out on the fitness deck at the rear of the ship, and was made up of extensive metal scaffolding with a series of poles and platforms, in between which were various configurations of ropes, logs, cables, and netting. It looked like a giant tinker toy set.

I'd done a ropes course once before as a team-building exercise at one of the companies I'd worked at, when I was still part of a team. The layout of the course on the cruise ship was similar, albeit with a few key differences. We were on a ship and not in the woods, and several of the elements—ropes course sections are called "elements"—were set up out over the water, including some planks and a couple of fairly long zip lines. Ropes courses are designed to have participants move from station to station via the different elements, each presenting a unique challenge in crossing the space. I counted forty elements on this course.

Since breakfast the sky had gotten darker. Clouds were starting to gather overhead, and it looked like it might rain. I could feel the breeze picking up, although it was hardly noticeable from the ship's movement.

Our course leader was checking some equipment when we arrived. He looked up and smiled. "Hi, I'm Harry. We're just waiting for a few more people."

A few moments later, a middle-aged couple in matching blue athletic outfits walked over. They looked like they were in their sixties, although they could have been older. They were both tan and seemed to be in good shape.

I was surprised to see Tatiana join us. She was alone, no Svetlana and no Boris, who I'd not seen since the three of them took off in their car in Cadiz. I wasn't even sure he was still on the ship. At least I wouldn't have to listen to them all arguing with each other. Her face displayed the same bored look she'd worn since the first day.

Sam wasn't very excited about doing a ropes course and was doing her version of pouting, which was, admittedly, undetectable to anyone who didn't know her well.

Looking over her shoulder, I said, "You can cheer up now. Your buddies are here."

She turned around and saw Alejandro and Valeria. Based on how they'd flirted at dinner the other night, I thought that would brighten her mood, and it did. They all hugged and did the two-cheek kissing thing. Anyone watching them greet each other would think they were long-time friends.

This wasn't bad, I thought. Seven people, should be fun.

Harry looked over our group and said, "We're all here, so let's get started! I'm Harry. I'll be leading you through the ropes course. Everyone will wear one of these harnesses." He held one up to show. "Some of the elements are very high out over the water, but don't worry, you are strapped in and there's no way you can fall off the course. Please, everyone, take one of the harnesses and put it on."

He handed each of us a harness, and as we were putting them on he went around and made adjustments to make sure they were secure. While he did this, we did a small round of introductions. We learned that the middle-aged couple were the Marchands, Juliette and Jean Pierre from Lyon. Tatiana mumbled her first name, looking down at the deck and avoiding any eye contact.

Harry continued, "This course is the largest one in the world on a cruise ship. It has forty different elements, involves two hundred and fifty feet of track, rises to one hundred feet over the water, and—"

"Hey!"

Harry was interrupted by loud voices coming from two couples coming toward us. They looked very happy, probably related to the fact that they were drunk off their asses. Not bad for eleven in the morning. Such is cruise life, or maybe their lives every day. Hard to say.

"We want to do some fuckin' ropes too!"

Australian by the accent. That brought us up to eleven people. Shit. It would take forever to get through the course, as it would move as fast as the slowest person in the group. And the Aussies were too drunk to be anything but slow.

The two couples were going through the rack of harnesses, and struggling to figure out how to get them on. One of the men put it on his head and the others guffawed.

Harry walked over to them and said politely, "I'm sorry, but we're full up for this session."

I wasn't sure if that was true, but I guessed they didn't want really drunk people on the ropes course. It could end badly. I imagined one of them vomiting from one hundred feet up. Might be spectacular, in a gross kind of way, and I wondered how the fabulously wealthy would respond to getting puked on. That was almost worth keeping the Aussies in the group to find out.

"Wuh?" The one with the harness on his head turned to the group.

"He's telling us to rack off, mate. S'OK, we're not devo." I heard a mumbled *"bugger"* and *"fuck me dead,"* but they didn't seem too put out. They turned and walked away, all equally unsteady, and weaving together in a group, like a drunk amoeba.

Harry continued with his introduction. "There are two versions of the course, a basic one and a more advanced one. Everyone will start with the basic course. Those who are feeling adventurous can continue with the more advanced section. The first element is here." He pointed to a set of stairs. "We go up these stairs to the starting platform. We want to have only one person on each element at a time, and no more than two people on a platform at a time, so once the first person is halfway across an element, the next person in line can climb the stairs to the platform." He started up the stairs, calling down, "Who wants to go first?"

Sam was first in line and climbed up the stairs. I stepped aside to let Alejandro and Valeria go next so they could continue flirting. After them came me, then Tatiana, and last the Marchands.

The first element was a simple rope bridge, made up of two thick ropes tied together and one line above to be used as a handhold to help with balance. Harry hooked Sam's harness into the metal track, gave it a yank to make sure it was secure, and stepped back to give her a free path to go out onto the ropes. Sam stepped gingerly onto the thick ropes and, realizing they were secure, walked calmly if not confidently across the space to the next platform.

No one had any trouble with the first element. I crossed it in a few seconds, barely needing to hold the line above to keep myself steady. The subsequent elements were similar, none posing much of a challenge, and the group moved capably in a line from platform to platform. Alejandro, Valeria, me, and Tatiana handled the elements with ease. The Marchands were slow but steady, as was Sam.

The basic course was simple, so to keep it interesting I tried to see how fast I could get across each space. I noticed Tatiana going through them quickly as well, about as fast as me.

"It's not a race," Harry said when we'd gone through several elements, noticing how rapidly the two of us were moving.

Bullshit it's not a race. I could feel my competitive juices kicking in, and I sped up.

The course included two eight-foot beams that hung well off the ship and out high above the water. Each of us took our turn "walking the plank." I wasn't sure why they thought it was a good idea to recreate a nineteenth century execution practice on a cruise ship, although standing on the edge of the plank looking down at the water was very cool. We were a long ways up, and from there I could see the back of the ship's funnel and the restricted space with the storage tank well. The security tape around the well was still up, and I was surprised to see crew members and officers grouped there again. But instead of looking into the well, they were looking up at the funnel.

I wasn't too far away to see what they were looking at. Black, wavy letters were emblazoned across the entire back of the funnel. *Euskal Herria*, whatever that meant.

Graffiti on a cruise ship. *That's interesting*. I wondered if Sam had seen it too.

I looked in front of me to see her starting on the next-to-last element. She'd been a little hesitant at some of the stations, but Alejandro had been murmuring words of encouragement to her, which appeared highly motivating, particularly when it involved him touching her arm. The two of them were laughing, and I realized she wouldn't be noticing anything other than him.

I turned my attention back to the course and moved easily through the final elements. The last one was a zip line, woven around one side of the ship and out over the water before it turned back in. The views from up here were stunning, open water for miles, and in one direction we could see the coast of Spain. The instructor encouraged everyone to take their hands off of their harness and swing free on the zip line. The line was designed to slow everyone down automatically at the end, and we each made a soft landing the final platform. It was larger than the others, with one set of stairs leading down to the deck, and another one leading up.

Once we were all on the platform, Harry said, "Anyone who feels like they've had enough can take the stairs down here. Those who want a little more of a challenge can go head up the stairs to the more advanced course. Any takers?"

I raised my hand, and Alejandro and Valeria nodded enthusiastically. The Marchands thanked him but no, they didn't need to do anymore. Tatiana nodded. The bored look hadn't left her face, and she hadn't broken a sweat. Harry looked at Sam.

"No, thank you."

Valeria touched her arm and whispered something into her ear.

She smiled. "OK, I'll try it."

Harry led us up the stairs to the higher starting platform. We were now about a hundred feet above the deck, with a more difficult set of obstacles that would require a little more strength and a lot more balance. Neither would be a problem for me. I'd been a good athlete in high school and college, making up for any lack of talent with a dogged, unrelenting competitiveness. I was also in good shape from my workouts, and confident the course would be no problem.

The advanced course started with another rope bridge, this one a little more challenging than the first one in that it had a single, thin rope instead of two thick ones. I went first and made it across in a few seconds. Tatiana followed me, crossing a little bit more quickly than I had.

As I stepped out onto the second element, I heard a crack of thunder and looked up. I hadn't noticed it happen, but the sky had grown much darker than when we'd started. The wind had picked up as well, and while the ship was baffled to prevent much rolling during waves, from this high up I could feel a little bit of a movement to the stations, and some of the ropes and ladders were starting to sway. I looked over to Harry and saw him look up at the sky, and then reach for the radio on his belt.

The next element was a cargo net. It was set up vertically and required a fair amount of upper body strength to hang on while crossing it. I timed myself at twelve seconds. Tatiana followed. Ten seconds.

We moved to the third element, the "Centipede," which was a set of wooden beams that were each attached from above on both ends. The beams would swing as you put your weight on them, and then more as you walked across them to the next one. The wind was making the beams swing back and forth on their own.

I heard the scratching sound of Harry's radio and turned to look. He held it up to his ear for a moment, listening, and then put it back on his belt, turning to those of us on the course. "Everyone, I'm afraid we're going to have to cut our course short today." He had to shout, as Tatiana and I were already a ways from him. "We're going to get some rain, and there is the possibility of lightning. Please come back to the starting station and go back down the stairs."

Sam and Alejandro had just started the second element and turned to go back. Valeria was still on the first platform and headed down the stairs to the deck.

I looked in front of me. Seventeen elements to go. Some of them looked interesting and a little more challenging. We were completely hooked in, no chance of falling no matter how windy it got. I looked behind me at Tatiana.

She raised an eyebrow. She might as well have thrown a gauntlet in my face. I turned back and finished the element I was on. I'd just gotten on the next platform when Tatiana stepped out onto the swinging beams.

Harry yelled at us again, this time sounding fainter as we were moving further away from him. "Dr. O'Hara, Miss Peshkova, please come back to the first station. Our primary concern is your safety."

Tatiana was in the middle of the element behind me, so I could no longer go back, which I didn't want to do anyway. We were securely hooked in, and I was sure they were being extra cautious. I ignored him and stepped out to the next element. It was similar to the last one, but instead of swinging beams it was a series of square wooden platforms. There was a slack cable above, helping to provide some stability while moving between them.

"There will be an opportunity later in the cruise to finish the course." He kept trying to call us back, but it was getting harder to hear him above the howling wind. Some of the rigging was slapping against the ship, and I could hear what sounded like sliding deck chairs. I looked down to see the outside decks now filled with scurrying crew members in a rush to bring service items inside and tie down chairs and tables.

We kept going through the elements, climbing up an inclined log, followed by a "Leap of Faith" that required us to jump from the platform onto a trapeze, and then use it to swing to the next platform. I was speeding up, partly because I wanted to increase my lead over Tatiana, and partly because I could now see the storm that was moving toward us. The sky was an enormous wall of dark blue and black clouds that looked endless. I felt raindrops on my face and saw lightning off in the distance. A few seconds later, I heard thunder.

After landing on the platform, I took a quick look behind me. Tatiana was closing the gap. I'd need to step it up.

The next element was another set of swinging pieces, this time round logs that were smaller than the flat beams. The wind was whipping them around but I timed it just right and stepped out onto the first one. I slipped a little on the log's wet surface and hesitated, but heard Tatiana step on the platform behind me, so I moved along to the end of the log. The timing had to be just right to move from one log to the other without falling in between. They were swinging back and forth, and while it took a little more time, it was safest to wait until the next one swung closer before stepping over to it, rather than leap for it.

I made it through five logs, one more to go, and took another look behind me. This time Tatiana hadn't waited for me to reach the next platform, and was only two logs behind me.

Time to ratchet things up. *I'll give you a fucking race.* My adrenaline had kicked in and I hardly noticed the rain now coming down in sheets, or the fact that the thunder was booming immediately after the lightning strikes.

To save time I didn't wait for the last log to swing close to me before I made the long jump onto it. It was soaking wet and I almost slipped off, but I was able to take a few quick steps and jump to the landing.

The next element was a series of round disks suspended from ropes. It was harder than the beams and logs, as not only were the discs much smaller, but they were also less stable, being suspended by only a single rope in the middle rather than one on each end. The first disk swayed and dipped down on one side with my weight as I stepped onto it. The wind was making the next one swing rapidly in circles. I timed it to when it was right in front of me and jumped, grabbing for the rope. I made it, but the small disk was spinning around while it was dipping, and I had to hang on tightly to combat the centrifugal force that was forcing me off of it.

I continued making my way through the disks, all of them dipping and spinning when I landed on them. My arms were having to do a lot of work to stabilize me. My breath was now coming in short gasps, which I could see in little clouds, as the temperature had dropped since we'd started. My fingers weren't working quite as well in the cold but I didn't want to slow down. Tatiana was now on the disk right behind me, not even waiting until I was halfway across the element to start on it.

I made it successfully to three more disks. On the fourth I mistimed my jump and landed on the edge of it instead of near the middle, my foot slipping off the slick wood. I reached for the rope in the center but missed it, falling free and hitting my chin on the disk on the way down. I experienced a momentary sense of panic until I felt the harness jerk me to a stop. I was now hanging by my harness, swinging in slow circles over the deck of the ship.

Ropes courses are typically used as teamwork exercises. They're designed to encourage groups to work together to get everyone on the team to make it to the end. But apparently not in Russia. Tatiana hopped over me onto the next disk, and then to the platform.

The last element was a long zip line. She looked behind at me and smirked, then jumped out onto the line and swung to the end.

Dammit. It was getting colder and my fingers were now completely stiff. It took several tries before I was able to climb back up onto the last disk. I made it to the platform and took off on the zip line. It was longer than the earlier one, taking me far out over the side of the ship and above the dark water that was now speckled with white foamy waves. The wind was roaring, and rain pelted me in the face.

When I landed on the last platform, Tatiana had already gone down the stairs and was getting out of her harness. The rain was now officially a downpour and I heard more thunder. Everyone except for Harry had gone back inside the ship, and Tatiana and I were the only passengers left on the deck. She looked at me with a triumphant sneer and turned to walk through the doorway to the hall.

I took off my harness and handed it to Harry. "Thanks, that was fun."

He looked like he wanted to say something, but just turned to hang the harness on the rack.

I stepped through the door, my shoes making squishing sounds as I walked. My clothes were as soaking wet as if I'd jumped overboard.

I was surprised to see Tatiana still in the hallway. She was with Svetlana. Tatiana was leaning up against the wall, staring sullenly at the floor, and Svetlana sounded like she was rebuking her. As I walked past them Svetlana stopped talking and turned to look at me, her eyes widening. I waved at her affably. She didn't wave back, just looked at me, scowling, her mouth set in a tight line.

On the way to the elevator I passed a few more people, all of them stepping back with frightened looks as I walked by. There were two other passengers waiting for the elevator, and when it came they let me go in first and waved me on, they would take the next one.

Geez…someone's a little wet and everyone freaks out? Whatever. I pushed the button to the fourteenth deck, looking forward to a warm shower and dry clothes.

CHAPTER 11

Sam was sitting on the couch reading when I got back. I was cold and wet, and my muscles were tired, but I felt exhilarated from the exercise. I slid off my soaking wet shoes and left them at the door, starting to the staircase.

"Did you win the deathmatch?" she asked without looking up from her book.

I didn't answer, not wanting to admit defeat. As I walked by her, she looked up. "You know— *Jesse!*"

"What? I'm going to take a shower. Hey, did you see the graffiti someone painted on the funnel?"

"Sit *down.*" She got up quickly and went to the kitchen, coming back with a towel. "Hold this." She put the towel up to my chin and neck and pushed the button to call Ben.

I held the towel on my chin and then pulled it away. It was bright red with blood. I looked down. My neck and lower part of my face were a bloody mess, and my shirt was soaked with it. When I'd fallen and hit the disk, I must have gashed my chin. I couldn't feel it as my face was cold, and I'd mistaken the wetness on my face and neck for water.

I went into the bathroom and looked at myself in the mirror. Looking back at me was a wild hair-framed, soaking wet face, and blood rivulets were streaming down my neck and into my shirt. That explained why everyone in the hallway had seemed so freaked out. I looked like one of the expendable actors from a teen slasher movie, one of the girls who gets her head taken off early on because she leaves the group to go off alone at night into the woods after they all find out there's a chainsaw murderer running loose in the area.

A few minutes later, the ship's doctor showed up at our door. He looked at my face and determined it was not serious, but I'd need a few stitches. I wasn't worried, I knew from experience that head wounds bled a lot but almost always looked worse than they were.

The two of us followed him out of the room and took the elevator to deck four. The storm was still raging outside, but inside the ship it was hard to detect. Cruise ships had extensive roll stabilization systems, and this particular ship would have even more than what was standard in the industry. The doctor put the code into the keypad at the door and opened it. We walked down the stairs to deck three, and past the crew's quarters to the medical services area.

He injected me with a local anesthetic and put ten stitches in the bottom of my chin. They would be barely visible unless I tilted my head back, or someone really short was looking up at me.

I was still soaking wet and cold, so when he was done I went back to our suite to take a shower. The doctor had advised me to keep the stitches dry, but that wasn't going to happen. I'd learned from previous experience with stitches that the main risk was infection, which was currently outweighed by my need to get clean and warm. I took off my clothes and got into the shower, noticing again the fingerprint bruises on my arms. I turned the heat up to almost burning to get rid of the chill.

A lot of thinking happens to me in the shower. Something about the isolation and the flow of the water gets my brain going. It was in overdrive right now, spurred by the exchange I'd seen between Tatiana and Svetlana in the hallway.

The Russians' constant arguing seemed too excessive to be just about fucked-up family dynamics. At least, I didn't think so, though I wasn't an expert on Russian culture. But even if it was, there was the backpack Boris gave to the crew member, and then his extreme reaction when I'd followed him. Why would he care, unless he was doing something he didn't want other people seeing? And it seemed like a big fucking coincidence that Boris was taking pictures near the funnel the day before it got tagged. On the other hand, he didn't strike me as the graffiti type. It seemed way too childish for him.

I touched the bruises on my arm. No, nothing childish about this guy.

He also hadn't been with Svetlana and Tatiana when they'd reboarded in Cadiz. I doubted he was back on the ship at this point. I hadn't seen him since yesterday morning, and the ship was small enough that unless he spent the entire time in his suite, I would have seen him.

Everything I'd observed could have had a simple explanation. They could just be three grumpy people, and Boris could be running some kind of business on the side. The man overboard could be completely unrelated, a drunk passenger or a depressed crew member. But I was starting to get the tingly feeling I got at the beginning of some of my financial investigations. If there was something illicit going on, my discovery of it would usually start off like this, with a few things that seemed odd, but could have normal explanations. There'd be a name in an accounting ledger that I hadn't seen on any other documents. Or there would be some significant sum of money that wasn't obviously tied to any part of the business. Minutiae like that would be missed by people not in possession of near-perfect recall. But these kinds of details would stick in my brain and I'd be compelled to make sense of them. Once that happened, I'd start digging.

I felt the need to do some digging now. It might turn out to be nothing, but I was trapped on the ship anyway, and it would help pass the time. There was only so much to do on this cruise, and it was a safe bet I wouldn't be allowed on the ropes course again.

Boris would be problematic. Even if I wasn't worried about him taking my head off, I couldn't spend the entire cruise following him around. And I'd already alienated the security officer.

It was time to bring in reinforcements. I turned off the water and stepped out of the shower. I wrapped a towel around me and walked to the nightstand next to my bed.

Another benefit of a high-end luxury cruise was unlimited access to the ship's VSAT satellite communication system. I picked up my phone from the nightstand and called my other best friend, Gideon.

I met Gideon Spielberg (no relation, as far as I knew) at Northwestern when we were both undergraduates. He was a total geek, a brilliant one, and hacker extraordinaire, and we bonded over our mutual introversion. We started off as good friends, which led naturally to dating. By the time our junior year ended we were a couple, and eventually things got serious enough that he brought me home to meet his family. His mom found out I was living alone and I ended up spending Passovers and high holidays at their house in Chicago's Skokie suburb.

Gideon was also the resident drug dealer on campus, primarily marijuana and ecstasy, the proceeds from which greatly supplemented his monthly student stipend. His primary customer base was well-off suburban yuppies because "they have more money than college students." I also thought he didn't really want to play a part in anyone flunking out of college because of a drug problem.

I loved him, and expected that at some point we would formalize our relationship and move in together. This fantasy came to a screeching halt shortly after our graduation ceremony. We were sitting up in his apartment talking, just starting on a bottle of good whiskey, when he got unusually quiet.

"Gideon, what's up?" I said, filling our glasses.

He said softly, "Jesse, I have to tell you something."

I looked up.

"I can't date you anymore."

I thought he was kidding and started to make a joke. But his face was dead serious. "What? Why?"

"It's not you—"

"Oh, great. *Seriously*, Gideon? You're going to give me that 'it's not you it's me' crap? Save it." I could feel tears welling up, and I threw my drink on the floor and got up to leave.

"Jesse, I'm gay."

That stopped me. All of a sudden, a million things made more sense. Our lack of connection in the bedroom, for one. A little part of me had been relieved, as I'd just assumed there was something wrong with me.

I was devastated, but we remained close friends even as I went off to graduate school. Gideon had been offered a full ride to MIT to do a PhD, but he turned it down, instead taking a job with the Chicago PD in their Special Investigations Unit. He worked in the cybercrimes division, responsible for identifying and breaking pedophile rings.

As many of the criminal rings crossed state and country lines, Gideon had access to a large number of restricted national and international databases and systems. Some he accessed using official channels, some less official, and some borderline illegal. His work regularly resulted in huge wins for the department, so his supervisor left him alone to do whatever he needed to do to get results. I'd made liberal use of this situation over time, and he was my go-to for anything technical or information-related.

Other than doing the occasional favors for me, Gideon was strict about illegal hacking, and lived by a self-imposed rule to limit himself to using his skills to catch criminals. Not because of any deep-seated compulsion to follow the rules, but he knew that if he got into the habit of hacking for personal use, he'd end up doing it continuously, and he'd inevitably get caught.

As far as I knew he only violated his rule one time. It happened when he learned there would be no legal consequences for the men in Kresge Hall who had almost raped Sam and put me in the hospital.

While I'd been recovering after the attack, he was a regular visitor, and when I was discharged he stayed at my place until I was completely healed. We were at my house on the couch when the DA called to inform me they wouldn't be pressing charges. Everyone knew this wasn't the first time those four guys had stalked and attacked a woman. The university's campus security had done the right thing, turning over this and similar cases to the local DA almost immediately. But the attackers had been careful to leave no evidence or witnesses each time, and as each event boiled down to a she said-they said situation, the DA never had enough to bring a case against them.

"So that's it," I'd said, putting down my phone. I hadn't really expected anything different. I wondered who they were going to attack next.

"No, it isn't." Gideon's voice was flat.

He was the sweetest man I'd ever met, but there was a side of him that came out at his job when he was chasing pedophiles. I was seeing it happen with the four rapists. There was cold fury in his eyes.

"What are you going to do? You're not going after them, are you?" I didn't think that would end well. Gideon was six feet and 190 pounds, but no match for four large men.

"Yes, I am. My way."

His way meant scorched earth, electronic style. Gideon was skilled at penetrating criminal enterprises, some very sophisticated, and getting into the rapists' electronic lives was child's play for him. By the time he was done, I almost felt sorry for them. He was a one-man electronic army of vengeance, his retribution biblical in proportion.

He started with their school files. All of a sudden, their records indicated they were failing all of their classes, and their student IDs and meal cards wouldn't work anywhere. This was mostly an annoyance, but it was only the beginning. While they were sorting out their school records, he invaded their social media and email accounts. This is where his creativity came into play. Through a series of pictures, messages, and postings, some released "accidentally," Gideon displayed to the world their horrifying secrets. The fact that they weren't true didn't matter.

It started with a leaked report from the campus clinic that showed one of them had an enduring case of genital herpes he'd been hiding, knowingly giving it to every woman he'd been sleeping with. His love life predictably dried up, and some of the women he'd exposed threatened legal action.

Another had been engaged in a year-long stream of rapturous communications with his young love. His really, *really* young love. So young as to be illegal in every US state. Given that he tracked pedophiles for a living, this was an easy one for Gideon to put together. He'd seen enough communications from them to inject a real aura of authenticity into the messages.

A video was posted that caught the third being intimate with a sheep. Videos like this, obvious fakes, weren't uncommon on the internet, but this one was a masterpiece. Gideon had worked one summer on the crew of an animated film and learned the technical aspects of motion capture. In this case, he reversed it, taking real film and pictures of the rapist and applying a virtual motion capture in the other direction, accompanied by audio of the guy's real voice. The result was a truly authentic looking and sounding video, and short of analysis with specialized equipment, undetectable as a fabrication. To top it off, Gideon added musings from the guy comparing sheep versus goats and horses as partners. The overall scenario was convincing, as he'd selected this humiliation for the guy who already had a reputation as a complete horn dog. It wasn't that big of a stretch for people to think he might be trolling barnyards on otherwise dateless nights.

Pictures and messages surfaced that showed the fourth asshole with a swastika tattoo and in the company of a local group of neo-Nazis.

"That will hurt," I said, admiring Gideon's handiwork.

"That one's actually true. I went into their backgrounds to see what kinds of phony secrets would be plausible for each of them, and found a real one. He's a member of that group. Or, you know, was."

He destroyed their credit ratings. Not something they might

notice right away, but it would be evident after graduation when they tried to buy a car or a house. At that point they might try to take a trip somewhere, to get away from it all. If so, they would be surprised at the airport to learn that they were on the TSA no-fly list.

Trying to sort all of this out and defend themselves was complicated by the fact that Gideon infected their phones and laptops with his own version of ransomware. Each of them received an email notification that unless they paid $5,000 within forty-eight hours, everything would be wiped from their systems, including all of their files, contact information, and pictures. They all paid up. Gideon had the money put into an account that distributed it anonymously to a local battered women's shelter, then he wiped their systems anyway.

This was all very illegal, and he would have been fired and charged with several felonies had he been caught. But he left no discernible trace, certainly not to anyone at CPD, where no one had anywhere near his technical skills. And no one in law enforcement was that eager to jump in and investigate on their behalf.

Gideon had my back, and I was glad he was my friend. Among other things, he would really suck to have as an enemy. I love him like a brother, which I guess is a good thing as it's my only option at this point.

I hadn't spoken to him since we'd left port in Barcelona. He picked up on the first ring.

"Hey! What's up?"

"Hey. Would you mind looking up something for me?"

"Sure. Where are you? How's the trip?" He knew about my aversion to being trapped in groups, people in general, and coliform bacteria.

"We're getting close to Bilbao, and it's great. There's a guy—"

"*Whoa!* 'It's great'? Who are you, and what have you done with my girl who hates crowds?"

"There's a guy on the ship we're looking into. Can you see if you can find anything on a Boris Alekseev? He's Russian. Carries himself like he might be current or former military."

Gideon and I had worked together on a number of investigations, and by now he was accustomed to my focused brevity. He changed gears immediately to solution mode. "Sure thing. But I thought this was supposed to be a vacation. Sounds like you're up to something."

"Just killing time. Thanks." I thought of one more thing. "Can you get a hold of the crew list?"

"No problem."

"Great. Later."

We hung up, and I finished dressing and joined Sam downstairs. "Want to grab an early dinner?"

"Sure." She grabbed her bag.

I opened the door to the hallway, where the security officer Ballsy was standing by our door.

"Miss O'Hara, may I please have a word with you?" His tone indicated that it wasn't a request. He looked at Sam, then back at me. "Alone?"

CHAPTER 12

Sam went on ahead to the restaurant, and I gestured Ballsy into our suite. I could tell he was uncomfortable, probably preferring to be on his own turf.

He stood stiffly just inside the door, and didn't waste any time getting to the point. "Miss O'Hara—"

"It's Doctor O'Hara." Unless I was in a courtroom, I didn't usually care about that, but with this schlemiel I felt the need to assert myself.

"*Doctor* O'Hara, you came to my office saying you'd seen something in the storage tank well." He looked at me with his thin eyebrows raised.

I waited. I had no desire to make things easy for him.

"We found something there." He paused again for me to talk, and when I didn't, his face reddened. "I want to know what you were doing near the funnel, and how you managed to see something the crew missed."

"What was the crew looking for?" It was probably related to the Charlie code, and I was dying to know what it was. It was either drugs or explosives.

"That is not your concern."

"What did you find? Was it drugs?"

He smirked. That meant I was wrong. It wasn't drugs, so it must have been explosives. Maybe the Charlie announcement was related to a bomb threat. If so, no wonder the captain had been so mad at Ballsy. He'd given the all clear for a bomb threat when the explosives were still on board.

Ballsy raised his voice, trying to sound more commanding, but it came out as a whine. "I am the one asking the questions. Again, what were you doing at the funnel, and how were you able to see something the rest of the crew had missed?"

"I have a good eye for details."

A nasty sneer crossed his rodential features. "That is unlikely the reason. You have been acting suspiciously, and you will forgive me if I do not believe you. You must understand, you are in a serious situation here. Lying to me is a very bad idea. I can make your trip much less enjoyable if you don't cooperate."

Well, that escalated quickly. The stupid little ratfuck not only thought I was involved in whatever security issue was going on, he was threatening me. I needed to put a stop to this shit right away.

I'd gotten a quick glance at his office before he'd shut the door in my face, which gave me more than enough to let him have it. I looked up at the ceiling dramatically.

"Your office is a ten-by-seven-foot windowless room with two file cabinets, a desk, three chairs, and a clock on the wall that is fast by four minutes. At the time I stopped by your office, to give you what turned out to be useful information, you had four open folders on your desk and a stack of another one hundred and ninety or so of them. I'm guessing those were the dossiers you created on the passengers before we boarded, no doubt put together based on the information we'd given you during the rectal cavity search you called a 'pre-trip vetting.'

"Based on the packets of the Prilosec knockoff on your desk, you have a peptic ulcer, which is a little strange, as while you feel the need to color your thinning hair, no doubt in an effort to hide the gray, you're not that old. You're five foot six and wear lifts, meaning you're probably closer to five foot four. You suffer from both terminal bad breath and excessive sweating, and in a surprise to exactly no one, you're currently single." I'd seen a few pictures on his desk, all of him either alone or with two people who were probably his parents. If he'd actually managed to get a woman to date him even one time, he'd no doubt have taken a picture of it and put it up for everyone to see.

The smirk had left his face, replaced with a mix of shock and fear that he was working hard to hide.

"Now, do you want to tell me what you found in the storage well? It would be a nice gesture, given that I've already helped you find whatever it was you were looking for."

He reached for the door and opened it, likely wondering what else I might discover about him if he stuck around. "This is not over. We will be watching you," he said, glaring at me, trying to be authoritative but sounding more like a petulant child.

"Me too." I couldn't help myself and made the "I'm watching you" signal with two fingers pointed at my eyes and then to him. I was rewarded with a horrified look, and he quickly left the room, slamming the door behind him.

Terrific. What an enormous waste of time. I felt far less safe on the ship knowing the head of security was focused on me instead of whoever it was that was planting bombs. Not to mention this guy was the walking sequels to *Dumb and Dumber: Dumberest,* and *Even Dumber Than That.* I waited a minute to give him a chance to leave our floor, then headed out to join Sam.

CHAPTER 13

"What happened?"

"In a nutshell, Ballsy thinks I had something to do with the backpack they found in the well. I'm now a suspect."

I could see "uh-oh" written all over Sam's face. She knew my reaction to abject incompetence.

We were sitting at the sushi bar in Little Tokyo, a smallish Japanese restaurant on deck seven, with a ten-seat bar and a few tables. We'd ordered *omikase*, the chef's choice meal. Unlike typical chef's choice tasting menus, Japanese *omikase* was whatever the chef felt like making at the moment. It could change on the spot, and the chef would keep making and serving individual dishes until you told him you were done. If you didn't pay attention, you could rack up quite a bill, which wasn't an issue on our all-inclusive cruise. In addition to whatever our sushi chef, Reo, would make for us, we had a server from whom we ordered drinks and sides. They had Sapporo on tap that I couldn't turn down, and Sam got a bottle of cold sake for us to share. It was clear and clean. We'd get to the cloudy sweet versions later in the meal.

"Did you tell him what you'd seen with Boris?"

"We didn't get to that."

Sam sighed. This wasn't the first time my personality had gotten in the way of effective communication. But I wasn't going to take the rap for this one.

"Look, this time it wasn't my fault. The guy's a grade-A asshole. I tried to help him."

"Did you at least find out what was in the backpack? Was it related to the security alert?"

"I think so. Based on his reaction, I think it was explosives, not drugs. But I'm still not sure if it was the same backpack Boris gave to the crew member. And we don't know if the Charlie code was related to a bomb threat." I put a piece of scallop sushi, *hotate*, in my mouth. "Maybe you can see if you can confirm that with one of the crew. Use your special powers."

"Of course, but if there's a chance explosives are on board, don't you think you should at least try again to work with the security officer?"

"I think he's more interested in being in charge than actually doing his job. And you know how I feel about people who put their egos ahead of their work. I'm done trying to help him."

"Even if it means we might be in danger? You said they gave the all clear before they found the backpack. It looks like the security officer might not be up to the job."

No kidding. We were *less* safe with that asshat in charge. "Sam, I don't know what you want me to do." Maybe another man overboard would be a good start.

"Do your thing. You know, be insanely focused and determined to get to the bottom of things." Sam wanted me to relax on our vacation, but not at the expense of the ship blowing up.

"It's going to be difficult. Ballsy has me under surveillance. And if it's related to Boris, we already know how he feels about being watched."

Despite my conviction that I wouldn't be working with Ballsy, I wasn't exactly sure how to proceed. The ship's crew were tight-lipped about the alerts, and even with Sam's special powers, it was unlikely we'd be able to get much out of them. They may have found a bomb on board, but they weren't talking about that either. And we didn't know anything about who had gone overboard and died. Not to mention that I'd already been attacked by one of the suspects.

Getting to the bottom of things would be challenging, but with Ballsy on my back, it might be impossible. Regardless I had no intention of trying to work with the little vermin, so I changed the subject. I'd figure it out somehow.

"I've got Gideon looking into Boris, and he's getting me a crew manifest. By the way, did you see the graffiti on the funnel when we were up on the ropes course?"

"No, I was too busy trying to avoid falling to my death."

"Sure you were." *More like thinking about Alejandro's manly dimples.* She ignored my tone. "Really? Graffiti?"

"Yeah. It said *Euskal Herria.*" I spelled it for her. "Do you know what it means?"

"It's Spanish for 'Basque Homeland.' It's often a moniker of the ETA."

I thought about that while Reo placed the next dish in front of us, a piece of sea bass cooked within the inner lining of cedar tree bark that was sitting on top of a small dollop of clear rice oil. The oil was sublime. I wondered how many rice grains it took to make a tablespoon of the stuff.

While we were was eating, I heard familiar loud voices. The four Aussies who had tried to join the ropes course were wandering into the restaurant and coming to join us at the bar.

One of the women took the seat next to me, nodded, and said, "How ya going?"

"Great, thanks."

In my experience with Australians, albeit limited to a few interactions during Octoberfest in Munich and one short trip to Sydney right after college, I'd found them to be fun and friendly, with a unique zest for life that I envied. This group didn't disappoint, and it was nice to be around some people closer to us in age than the other passengers, even if they were very wasted people. I wondered if they were traveling on family money or their own.

We did introductions. Jack, Mason, Olivia, and Grace. Jack looked familiar.

"Hey, are you Jack Wilson and Olivia Johnson? From Elemental?"

"Yeah, that's right."

Definitely their own money. Jack and Olivia were the founding partners of Elemental, a multibillion-dollar software company. I recognized them from the Forbes list Sam and I had consulted to settle a bet about the locations of the world's billionaires. I'd won the bet, and Sam had to watch four movies of my choice without making any snarky comments. This was a difficult bet to lose, as film was one area we didn't have in common. I like awesome comedies, and Sam watches boring art films. Me winning meant we culturally enriched ourselves with viewings of *Monty Python and the Holy Grail*, *Caddyshack*, *Airport*, and *The Heat*. Sam, to her credit, was gracious in defeat, and I even caught her giggling a few times in spite of herself.

The Aussies ordered a round of drinks. The single round for the four of them included beers, shots, and a couple of bottles of sake to start. Enough to last most people an entire evening. The six of us chatted amiably as Reo set their drinks on the bar.

The cruise was a break for Jack and Olivia. They'd been working nonstop for several years while their company experienced explosive growth. And while it was wildly successful, they needed a vacation, and were taking this trip with their best friends to get away from things for a while and recharge.

In addition to being fun and friendly, they were loud and profane. "That ropes course looked like a fuckin' beaut. Too bad about the weather," said Mason.

"She finished it," said Sam, sounding a tiny bit proud.

"Good on yah, then." He examined the bandage on my chin. "Fuckin' rough, was it?"

"Not so bad. A little windy."

At that moment Ballsy walked by. The sushi bar was near the front of the restaurant and the opening to the atrium. He stopped at the entrance, looking in, and unsuccessfully trying to look like he wasn't watching us.

"Can we help you, mate?" Jason asked him.

Ballsy pretended like he didn't hear him, and I gave him the "I'm watching you" two fingers to the eyes gesture again. His eyes widened, and he walked on.

"Maybe he doesn't like Aussies," offered Olivia.

"What's not to like?" I said. "I mean, other than you eat your fucking national animal."

"*Hah*! Good one." They all laughed, probably because it was true. "Kanga" was sold at most grocery stores and butcher shops in Australia.

We were having fun, but I could see out of the corner of my eye that sentiment wasn't shared by everyone. A couple was sitting at one of the tables, the man making a point of frowning over at us every time someone swore, which between me and the Aussies was often. He called over the server and said a few things. She looked uncomfortable but nodded. A moment later, she came over and whispered in Reo's ear.

He looked at Jason. "Sir, may I ask you and your group to be a bit quieter?"

"Ah reckon you can ask." Jack looked behind him at the scowling man at the table. "She'll be right." He got up and walked over to their table, leaning down and saying something to them that caused the man to scowl and the woman to look away in disgust.

Jason smiled and sauntered back to the bar.

"What'd ya tell 'im?" Mason asked.

"I told the figjam he could fuck right off, but his wife was welcome to join us if she wanted to have some fun."

I saw Reo stifling a smile.

Sam leaned over to me and asked quietly, "Figjam?"

"It's an acronym for 'fuck I'm great, just ask me.' It means they think he's a self-important ass."

Sam looked over at the table. "Spot on, it seems."

Jack and company were not interested in eating, and went through several more rounds of drinks. It never failed to astound me how much

Aussies could drink, and I said as much.

"Ah reckon we're the best drinkers in the world," said Mason.

I wondered and pulled out my phone. "Nope," I said, scrolling through the World Health Organization's website. "It's Belarus. They drink more per capita than anyone in the world. Over seventeen liters each year per person." I looked through the list. "You guys barely crack the top ten." Australia was number ten, the first nine on the list dominated by eastern European countries and France. In a shock to no one, Russia came in at a solid fourth. "America is down at forty-eight."

Mason snorted. "Rubbish. Seventeen liters per year? We're going to drink that much tonight. And they're probably just putting away bullshit beer in Belarus. What about hard liquor?"

I re-sorted the list. "Nope. South Korea leads everyone in hard alcohol consumption."

There were head nods and murmurs of understanding from the group.

"Makes sense. Poor bloody bastards," said Jack.

They all raised their glasses in a toast to the South Koreans.

They finished their drinks, round three by my count. I think they were right about putting away seventeen liters in one night.

Jason downed his last beer in one long gulp. "Hey, Reo, some roadies, yeah?"

They were bar hopping and wanted something to tide them over until they made it to the next establishment. Reo obliged them by putting four large cans of Kirin on the counter that would hopefully last them until the next bar, which was four doors down.

"We're off. Wanna join?" Jack asked.

I looked at Sam, who shrugged. We were done eating, and it might be fun to hang with them for a while.

"Why not. Where to?"

"Ice skating!"

I couldn't imagine that ending well, and I already had my set of stitches for the trip. "Maybe some other time."

"Right then, cheers."

We waved goodbye and watched them walk unsteadily out of the restaurant.

"What do you think the over/under is on them requiring medical services tonight?" I asked Sam.

"I'm not taking that bet." She put her empty glass on the bar. "I'm stuffed. Want to poke our heads into the casino?"

I wasn't a gambler, but agreed to check it out. We thanked Reo and walked out to the atrium, and then down the central staircase to the casino.

The casino was one of the star features of the ship, and took up almost the entirety of deck five. There were a number of slot machines, fifteen blackjack tables, four craps tables, a roulette wheel, and three separate areas for baccarat. In the center of everything was a round, mirror-backed bar with leather covered stools. It was still a little early for gamblers, and there were only about thirty people in the space.

I was glad Ander wasn't there. I wasn't surprised, as he didn't strike me as the gambling type. But I was relieved. I was a little wasted after a futile attempt to keep up with the Aussies' drinking, and far enough along that I'd make an ass of myself. And while making an ass of myself was inevitable over the course of the trip, I was hoping to delay it until I'd had a chance to get to know him better.

The Marchands were playing blackjack, they saw us and waved. I saw Ballsy standing off to the side near the entrance, looking into the casino toward the blackjack tables. He glanced at us briefly and scowled, but then turned away. Apparently I wasn't his target for the moment.

Sam wandered off to one of the baccarat areas and I went to the bar and ordered a Jameson. My drink came right away, and as I was taking the first sip a man sat down on the seat beside me.

"You look like you could use some company." American by the sound of it. He was in his forties, casually dressed in black linen slacks and a white short-sleeved dress shirt. Like most of the men on this cruise he was sporting an obnoxiously large watch on his wrist.

"Looks can be deceiving." I didn't look at him.

"What are you drinking?" He sat down next to me, the smell of his noxious and no doubt expensive cologne wafting into my nostrils.

"Bitterness and regret." I continued to maintain no eye contact with him.

"Hah! A lady comedian."

I spent a fair amount of time in bars, and while I'm not exactly beautiful, I was used to getting hit on when I was alone. This guy wasn't taking the hint that I wasn't desperate for his company.

"Is it miss, or missus?" he asked, leaning in closer.

"It's doctor." Being able to say that might be the single most useful aspect of getting a PhD.

"Can I get your number?" So much for sitting at the bar. I got up to leave.

"Six," I said as I walked away.

"I'm Phil," he called toward my back. "Suite 807 if you want some company later." It never ceased to amaze me how attracted some guys were to my utter lack of interest in them.

I heard the scratching of a radio and turned to see Ballsy answering a call. The exchange was brief, and he left the casino quickly. Something had happened that required his immediate attention. I wondered if someone had spotted a mousetrap.

I joined Sam at the baccarat table. Baccarat had always seemed mysterious and exotic in Bond films, the game the sole purview of the rich and glamorous. But it's really not much of a game. Baccarat players don't actually have to *do* anything, merely place bets on card hands played by the dealer. I suspected the game attracted the *hoi polloi* primarily because the games are usually very high stakes, so rich gamblers are assured to not have to rub elbows with the unwashed masses.

Sam played while I sipped my drink. The game was mind-numbingly boring, so I said good night and left her to it. On my way out I passed the Marchands. They were happy and smiling. In front of them was a huge stack of chips. They'd won big. Good for them.

It was midnight by the time I made it back to our suite. I stepped out onto the balcony. The water was calm; we'd left the Atlantic Ocean with its storms behind for the quiet waters of the Bay of Biscay. Tomorrow we'd dock in Bilbao, our first stop in Spain's Basque Country.

I'd done some reading about it prior to our trip. It was a peculiar and singular region in Spain, steeped in ancient culture and in many ways one of the most unique places on Earth. I was looking forward to it. I liked peculiar things.

DAY 5

CHAPTER 14

We were having breakfast on the pool deck, sitting at a small table near the railing. Sam had gotten back very late, but as always was radiant in a neon orange bikini, her large hat, and designer sunglasses. We were drinking coffee and looking out into the water as the ship turned slowly from the Bay of Biscay into the Bilbao Abra, the Bay of Bilbao. The sky was much lighter now, the whitecaps were gone and the water was back to boring smoothness.

"It looks like we outran the storm," Sam said.

"Yeah, I didn't really notice it, other than on the ropes course."

"Cruise ships have an enormous amount of baffling to prevent rolling. Vomiting passengers puts a damper on the fun."

The crew's relief at leaving the storm behind was palpable. A few were busy sweeping up the remainder of the detritus left by the storm, but they were all smiling, and the servers seemed more energetic than usual as they floated among the passengers with coffee and mimosas.

I wasn't interested in the ship's baffling. "So?"

"So what?"

"So, what did you find out last night about the security alert? I'm sure you had more than enough time to work your magic with the casino staff."

She smiled at my acknowledgment of her superior people skills. "Yanis, the baccarat dealer, was very chatty once the table emptied out. The Charlie alert was definitely from a bomb threat. He didn't know anything about the backpack they found, but the dog they brought on board was looking for explosives."

"I assume he didn't find any, or we'd be off the ship by now?"

"We're all clear according to Yanis."

I wasn't so sure. I hadn't seen Boris since the port in Cadiz, and he'd been too worked up when he grabbed me in the stairwell for it to be just about one failed bomb threat. "Did he know anything else about the threat? Did anyone take responsibility for it, like the ETA?" I was thinking about the graffiti on the funnel.

"He didn't say."

"Did he know anything about who went overboard?"

"He thinks it was a crew member, but he's not sure." She looked down at the table, then back up at me. "Look, Jesse, I know I encouraged you to look into things, but do you think we can let it go for today while we're in Bilbao?"

"Sure, OK." It might help to turn my brain to other things for a little while.

I looked around us as the ship slowed down as it approached the terminal. From where we were sitting I could see all the way to the mouth of the bay.

The deep-water port of Bilbao Abra is one of the top five ports in Spain and not far from downtown Bilbao, the largest city in Basque Spain, and one that dates back to the thirteenth century. The bay is bounded on the western side by the Punta Lucero, a set of rolling hills that were cut with a series of roads. On the eastern side was the Punta Galea, the home of the extensive La Galea hiking trails, which wove around the coast's point, just above steep cliffs. To the south on the western side was a large industrial area and port that only partly marred the awesome view.

In addition to sampling the food, one of our target destinations here was the Guggenheim Museum Bilbao. As we were only scheduled to spend one day there, the hiking trails would have to wait until a future trip. One that Sam would be taking without me.

She leaned back on her reclining chair, closed her eyes, and tilted her head up to the sun. "This is heaven."

Heaven for me was more like being escorted to the world's most exclusive comedy club, where I'm met at the door by a shirtless Chris Hemsworth, and escorted to my private table where my two dates, Ryan Reynolds and Robert Downey Jr., eagerly await my arrival. In my version of heaven, I get a seat in the front where Melissa McCarthy, Seth MacFarlane, and Kate McKinnon do their best comedy, then ask me up on stage to do a set with them. I reluctantly agree, and then proceed to bring the house down.

Yeah, I'd been thinking about this one for a while. But I didn't want to dampen Sam's mood. "Yes, heaven."

I looked at my watch. "Are you ready to go into town?"

"Yes!" She sat up and gathered her things while I finished my coffee. We went back to our suite to change, then walked to the elevator. When we got in, I saw her push the button for deck seven, which was not the deck to the gangway.

"Do you mind if we check in on Chaz before we leave?" It wasn't really a question.

When we walked into the suite Chaz was sitting on a large bed with a couple of other rich dogs, around a small plate of what looked like Kobe beef sliders shaped like bones. A few other dogs were scattered around the room, all lounging on soft cushions. Other than the beds, the room looked a whole lot like the bottom floor of our suite, minus the Steinway.

The full-time pet attendant minced over. "Miss Hernandez! I hope you're enjoying your stay."

"It's been wonderful, Gaspard. I just wanted to let you know that we're going ashore for a few hours."

"No problem." He looked fondly at Chaz. "He's an angel! And clearly the most popular among the other dog guests." He reached down to give Chaz a head scratch, and Chaz turned toward him, gently licking his hand.

119

That figures…like mother like son. And Chaz seemed to like everyone but me.

Gaspard leaned in close to us and said conspiratorially, "I think he has a love interest." He pointed to one of the other wealthy dogs, a large one that was sleeping on the floor. "That's Penelope. She's a Scottish Deerhound. Very sweet, but unfortunately doesn't seem to want to return Chaz's affections. He's been following her around all day, but she doesn't take any notice of him."

There's a fucking shock. She's probably terrified that his neuter didn't take, and she might produce a litter of puppies that die young from terminal ugliness.

"Maybe she doesn't realize he's a dog. That would be an honest mistake," I offered.

Sam ignored me and picked up Chaz and gave him a hug. Little Heinrich gave me an obligatory growl, but I could tell his heart wasn't in it. Four days of luxury accommodations will take the edge off.

We said good bye to Gaspard and left the ship, then made our way to the private car pick-up location, where our driver would take us to the center of town and our restaurant.

I looked around the terminal and then stopped. "Sam, do you see them?"

"Who?"

I pointed to the parking lot where Boris was now with Svetlana and Tatiana, all of them heading for a car.

"Something's up. Look how they're moving."

They weren't running, but were definitely moving with purpose. Svetlana and Boris looked like they were at it again, and we could hear a stream of invectives coming from both of them. All three of them looked tense.

Sam knew from experience that when I picked up on things, it usually meant something. But today she wasn't eager to derail our city plans, and I'd already agreed to let things go for the day.

"We have a lunch reservation at one of the best paella places in the city." She started to walk again.

I stayed put. "I know…but something's going on."

"Yes, maybe like us they're suffering from a severe lack of paella."

I wasn't budging.

"We agreed we'd let it go for the day," she said, resignation in her voice.

"Can we just follow them for a bit? They're probably going into town. If so, we're going that way anyway. If not, well, a little detour won't kill us." I didn't add that not figuring out what Boris was up to might be something that actually would kill us. I was fairly certain at this point that it was his backpack they'd pulled out of the storage tank well. And if that wasn't enough to make him suspicious, the fact that he'd disappeared for several days and then all of a sudden reappeared sealed it for me.

"OK, but I'd prefer not to miss the Guggenheim this afternoon."

"Don't worry."

We started walking again and found our driver, Mattin, in the Mercedes Class section of the quay. We got in and I proceeded to wow him with my linguistic skills.

"*Hola.*"

"*Kaixo,*" he replied, a wide smile on his face. "That's Euskara for 'hello.'"

We asked Mattin to follow the Russians. He didn't seem thrown by the request, and without being instructed to, followed them at a discrete distance. I wondered if he was used to his charges tailing other passengers.

Their car, a medium-sized black sedan, headed out of the terminal area toward the center of town via a highway. But instead of going into Bilbao, they turned north, driving past the exit and back up the coast on the west side of the bay.

Mattin was a lifelong and passionate Bilbao resident, and during the drive entertained us with information about the region's history and culture, starting with the language. "Most people here speak Spanish, but Euskara is an official language of the region too, and it is growing in popularity. It is one of the oldest living languages on the planet and is completely unique. Some people call it the hardest language on Earth to learn, and there are a variety of dialects."

We already knew this, and Sam could actually speak a little of it, but we didn't want to dampen his enthusiasm, so we listened attentively.

"The Basque Country includes parts of Spain and France, and its origins go back to ancient times. Basques are the oldest ethnic group in Europe. Some believe we have been here since 5,000 BC."

I'd done some reading before the trip and knew that the genetic makeup of the people here was different than anywhere else in Europe. Scholars believed it could be related to the isolation created by the region's mountains, which deterred mixing from human migration thousands of years ago.

"Bilbao is the largest city in Basque Country, about a third of all of Basque people live in or around this city. It has two names. Bilbao is the official name. The historical name is Bilbo, although we don't hear that much anymore."

No doubt to avoid confusion with Hobbiton and Middle Earth.

"The city is home to some wonderful architecture. Many former industrial areas have been turned into modern spaces, designed by some of the world's most renowned architects and artists. You will see this when you visit the Guggenheim Museum. It is considered one of the most important structures built anywhere in the last few decades. And of course, there is the food. Our cuisine is the best in the world. The very first Spanish restaurant to be awarded three Michelin stars was Zalacaín, a Basque restaurant."

"Best in the world" might not be an exaggeration. Part of the miniscule allure of this trip for me was that the highest density of Michelin-starred restaurants on the planet was in the Basque Country.

We drove for about twenty minutes, past the main port terminal and up the west coast of the bay toward San Mames, a small town nestled in the hills. The Russians' black sedan pulled into a small parking lot and stopped. Boris and Svetlana got out, and headed off on one of the concrete walking trails that ran along the ridge of hills. We pulled off to the other side of the parking lot and watched them walk away. He was carrying a camera. A real one this time, with one of those long telephoto lenses. Apparently his phone camera wouldn't be good enough for whatever pictures he would be taking.

I asked Mattin what sites of interest were in the area, and what someone might want to take pictures of here.

He looked puzzled. "There is not much here. Some views of the bay, but there are better ones. We are above an industrial area. Photographers normally shoot from the other side of the bay or go into town."

We waited, Mattin continuing to regale us with historical tidbits, and Sam pointedly looking at the time on her phone every few minutes. After about a half hour the Russians came back to their car and drove off.

I opened the car door and looked up the path they had taken. "Let's go up ahead and look around."

Sam groaned.

"This won't take long. C'mon, we'll work up an appetite."

She got up with an exaggerated sigh and the three of us started down the concrete path. It led uphill to a vista, from where we could see across to the Punta Galea on the far side, which looked green and undeveloped. As Mattin had said, directly below us was a large industrial area.

"See anything?" I asked.

"Yes," Sam said. "Off in the distance…to the south…I see a restaurant rapidly running out of paella."

"Humor me."

Mattin pointed to the north. "Farther that way is a set of bunkers that were built during the war."

"Can we take a look?" I asked.

Mattin nodded and starting walking. Sam, to her credit, had given in at this point, and offered no objection as we followed him up the path.

We walked for about a quarter mile and came across the first bunker. It was a sturdy-looking concrete pillbox with an opening that was directed toward the mouth of the bay.

"This is part of Bilbao's Iron Ring. It is a set of fortifications that run from here down to south of the city and up to the cliffs on the other side of the bay. It was originally built during the Spanish Civil War to protect the city and the Republic from the Nationalists. The wall failed, and the Nationalists won the war. It happened right before World War Two, and this is when Franco took over Spain."

On the side of the bunker someone had painted *Euskal Herria*, the same thing that had been painted on the funnel on our ship.

"What does that mean?" I asked Mattin. Sam had already told me, but I wanted Mattin's take on it.

"It means 'The Land of the Basque Speakers.'"

"Someone painted that on our ship."

Mattin looked uncomfortable. "It is a phrase that is sometimes used by the separatist movement. Much of the resistance to the Nationalist side came from this region. When Franco came into power he wanted revenge on the Basque people, and enacted many brutal policies. The Basque Nationalist Movement was born because of this. It began a long period of conflict for us. Many people died…" He turned away from us, toward the bay. I wondered if he had lost someone close.

We waited respectfully, looking out over the cliffs, until he continued. "There was a lot of fighting and killing. It is over now. I am glad, because it was a waste. Bombing innocents, terrorism…it gave our country a bad name. We can retain our culture without separating from Spain, and I do not believe that killing each other serves anyone. We are all Iberian."

"So the separatist movement is over?" I thought about Ander's characterization of it being "virtually" over.

"There are a few holdouts who still want a separate Basque country.

124

Sometimes there are protests and a few meetings, but they are not violent. For the most part, we have all moved on."

I wanted to ask him about the protest at the quay when we'd boarded in Barcelona, but he seemed to want to change the subject, so I stayed quiet.

He pointed to the south. "You cannot see Bilbao from here, but it is directly that way. It was a quiet town until the Guggenheim opened. Now we get over three hundred thousand tourists a year, most from elsewhere in Spain, but also France, the UK, Russia. It is crazy, but good for the economy."

We continued to look out across the bay, the port, and the hills.

After a few minutes and seeing nothing that might explain what the Russians were doing, we headed back to the car. We got in and Mattin turned it around to head back into Bilbao. About a mile down the road, I spotted the black sedan pulled over to the side. As we drove by I could see Boris watching us through his window.

CHAPTER 15

We'd done our restaurant homework and had Mattin drop us off at La Barraca for our paella experience. There were two La Barraca restaurants in Bilbao, and we'd chosen the one on Calle de Bertendona. It was off the beaten track, and catered more to locals than tourists. Mattin would be back in the area in an hour and a half to wait for our call to take us to the Guggenheim.

The inside was small and intimate. Fifteen tables were surrounded by pale orange stucco walls and several black-and-white photographs of streets and buildings, presumably Bilbao from a few decades ago. Sam had made reservations weeks earlier, which was a good thing, as the place was packed. But even though we were late, the reservation along with a *soborno* she slipped to the host secured our table.

There were fourteen different paellas on the menu. We ordered two of them, paella de marisco (seafood) and paella de carne (meat), along with a bottle of txakoli, a regional young white wine. The paella would take a while, so we relaxed.

"What do you think they were doing on that overlook?" I asked, sipping the txakoli.

"Views? Exercise?"

"But there are better views, and they didn't look like they were having much fun exercising."

"Russians don't look like they're having fun at anything." Sam believed that being unhappy was a Russian's genetic birthright. She'd expressed similar sentiments before.

"What do you have against Russians?"

"Nothing."

No way it was nothing. Sam generally found the positive in everyone. "Really?"

"OK, I dated one once, in college. It started to get serious, and he took me home to meet his family. They were awful. I spent an entire weekend with a bunch of people who did nothing but drink and complain. And they never smiled. Not once." Definitely not something she was used to.

"Kind of harsh, don't you think? Indicting an entire country because of one family?"

She was saved from responding by the waiter. He set two large shallow pans in front us, each filled with yellow rice that had been baked with succulent proteins. We dug in.

Really good paella results from a sofrito base and depth of flavor developed over time, and a perfectly formed socarrat, the crispy bottom rice layer of authentic paella that is caramelized and toasted. This makes the difference between paella and rice casserole. These paellas were perfect. The seafood dish tasted like none I'd ever experienced, with monkfish, clams, mussels, peppers, prawns, lobster, and a few things I didn't recognize. The meat paella was less exotic but no less tasty, with chicken and rabbit, along with some local vegetables.

I took my jacket off when the food arrived. Big mistake. I was wearing a capped sleeve t-shirt that exposed my bruised upper arms. The marks were still prominent, having turned bright shades of red, purple, and yellow, and clearly in the shape of fingers. Sam looked up from her food and gasped. "Is that from Boris? From four days ago?"

I looked away.

"Jesse, I think you need to stay away from him. He seems dangerous."

"I thought you wanted me to get to the bottom of things?"

"I want you to be safe. Will you promise me you'll be really careful, at least with Boris?"

I nodded noncommittedly.

"I mean it. He looks like trouble, and the fact that he would practically attack you for following him means whatever he's doing, he's very serious about it."

"That's what I'm worried about. Based on my discussion with Ballsy, and the fact that we received a bomb threat, it seems likely it wasn't drugs in the backpack they found. That only leaves some kind of explosives. If so, what if he tries it again?"

"We're not one hundred percent sure it was Boris's backpack, are we?"

"No, but it seems like a big coincidence, doesn't it? He gives a crew member a backpack, takes pictures of the storage well, we get a bomb threat, and then they find a backpack in that storage well. Then there's a team of officials with a bomb-sniffing dog on board."

Sam had stopped eating and continued to look at my arms. She looked like she wanted to say something else, but I didn't give her a chance. "There's no way that little shmendrik Ballsy is going to figure out what's going on. I don't have a choice at this point." My library of insults included a fair number of Yiddish ones I'd learned from Gideon's grandfather. I had great respect for the Jews' erudition around personal insults. Like the Inuit and their many words for various kinds of snow, the Jews had scores of words for loser. And it was interesting that so many started with "shm." Shmendrik, schmo, schmuck, schlemiel... I would have to ask Gideon about that later.

Sam was clearly shaken by the look of my arms. "Maybe you could talk to the captain. It's his ship."

"And tell him what? That I saw a passenger and a crew member talking? And that the passenger *might* have given the crew member something that looked kind of like what they took off the ship? I know there's something up, but I doubt that's enough for him to do anything. And besides, he doesn't know me. He'll just tell me to take it to the security officer, even if that security officer has already screwed up."

Sam didn't argue with that. I wasn't long on patience anyway, and having to slog through things I'd seen, and the obvious implications, with other people who were slow to get it was a maddeningly tedious exercise for me.

I continued. "What really confuses me is the ETA graffiti on the funnel. Boris isn't Basque, or even Spanish. Why would he be involved with the ETA? Not to mention we've been told there is no more ETA. But it's another coincidence." I didn't believe in coincidences.

There was nothing more to do at the moment, so we returned to our food. We managed to finish everything, which I think surprised our waiter. One thing Sam and I have in common is that despite being fairly trim, we can both put it away like champs.

"Uh-oh..." I said, looking at my watch. Between the paellas and the txakoli, the afternoon had gotten away from us. "It's three thirty. We have to be back at the ship and boarded by five."

"That doesn't seem like enough time to make any kind of reasonable trip to the Guggenheim." Sam tried to pout but was too full of paella and wine to pull it off. She signaled the waiter, who brought our check.

"I'm sorry," I said as we walked out. "I know you were looking forward to that."

"That's OK. This trip was for you anyway. I can come back another time."

We found Mattin on the side street where we'd left him and he drove us back to the terminal. As we approached the ship, we were surprised to see the couple that had joined us in the ropes course being led down the gangway by Ballsy. They were in handcuffs.

"Isn't that the Marchands?" I asked Sam. They'd seemed nice, and it was hard to imagine them as criminals. For one thing, they were both at least in their sixties.

We watched them as they were taken to a waiting police car. Once they were in the car, Ballsy closed the door and waved the driver on. He turned and headed back to the ship, passing right next to us. He didn't say anything, and I couldn't tell if he was even looking at us through his mirrored sunglasses.

***

I was lounging on the couch and Sam was getting ready to visit Chaz the Impaler. We were both full and wanted to skip dinner, but agreed to meet later for a nightcap. While we were talking there was a polite knock on the door. I got up and opened it.

"Hi Ben."

"Hello. I am sorry to bother you. The captain wanted to let you know that we have a slight change of plans to our itinerary. We are going to be staying in Bilbao for an extra day."

"Why?" I hadn't realized cruise itineraries were so fungible.

"There are some very minor mechanical difficulties. Nothing to worry about. It should be fixed soon. You are welcome to go back ashore as long as you are back by five p.m. tomorrow evening."

Ben's eyes had bags under them, and he looked a little disheveled. I wasn't surprised. We'd already had to skip several ports, they'd pulled a body out of the water, sequestered us in our suites during a security alert, and now they were messing with the schedule again. I was sure the staff were getting shit from some of the passengers. These people weren't used to not getting exactly what they expected and paid for. But being stranded in Bilbao for one more day was fine with me. We'd spend one more day off the ship, Sam would be able to see the Guggenheim, and I would get to try another Basque restaurant.

"Also, Mr. Ibarra has extended an invitation for Dr. O'Hara to meet him tonight in the deck four bar. He has suggested nine thirty. Should I tell him that you will join him?" He smiled, clearly titillated at playing matchmaker.

I looked at Sam. She nodded enthusiastically.

"Sure."

"Very good." He turned to leave.

"Ben, hang on a second."

He stopped and turned around.

"Do you know why the Marchands were arrested?"

He hesitated, looking behind him and then back at me. "Drugs were found in their room," he whispered.

"You're kidding."

He shook his head and sighed. "Unfortunately, it is somewhat common on cruise ships. One might think that with this clientele, it would not be an issue." That was debatable. I didn't think the rich were any more scrupulous than the non-rich. Possibly even less so. But I didn't say anything. He gave one of his little bows and left.

I turned to Sam after he left and closed the door. "Is that true? Is drug smuggling really that common on cruises?"

"Yes. It's not that surprising, really. These ships travel all over, often from countries that supply drugs to those that buy them. Crew members' salaries are low, and they can make as much in one drug smuggling trip as they make in six months of work. Passengers are often used as mules."

"Don't the Marchands seem a little long in the tooth for that kind of thing?"

"That might be what makes them attractive as smugglers. Last year, a couple in their seventies was arrested for transporting twenty kilos of cocaine on a cruise."

"No shit. But how do they do it? You said all of the bags were searched when we boarded."

"Yes, but sophisticated drug organizations know how to defeat them."

It didn't surprise me that the Marchands had gotten caught. They didn't come across as sophisticated drug smugglers. But this was making me rethink things. "Do you think maybe the backpack they found was full of drugs? And the security alert was about that?" Despite my interaction with Ballsy, I wanted to believe that was true. Drugs were less hazardous to our health than bombs.

"Those kinds of alerts are usually reserved for more dangerous kinds of security issues, and Yanis said there was a bomb threat. I also don't know why they would keep us in our rooms while they were looking for drugs. But, maybe. It's also possible the bomb threat was a hoax. It wouldn't be the first time."

If so, that would make things a little less worrisome. Given Ballsy's spectacular incompetence, I liked the idea of not relying on him to prevent something that could kill us.

Sam smiled and raised an eyebrow. "Should we decide now what we're doing tomorrow? You might be busy later. That is, if you can set your investigation aside for a few hours."

"Guggenheim?" I offered.

"Definitely. And I'll find us a place for lunch."

"OK."

She turned to leave, calling over her shoulder, "Have fun tonight."

CHAPTER 16

It was after nine, and as I was getting ready to meet Ander there was another knock at our door. I opened it and was surprised to see Svetlana. She walked in without me inviting her and sat down on one of the Mario Bellini chairs.

Since she was Russian, I assumed she would want a drink, so I poured us each a glass of Jameson. The concierge had gotten the same message as the pub bartender and had left several bottles in our suite. I sat down on the couch across from her.

Svetlana took a sip and winced, putting her glass down on the coffee table. I guessed Jameson couldn't compare to skull-bottle vodka.

"You are famous Court TV investigator."

This is why *Jeopardy* never took off in Russia, their inability to speak in the form of a question.

"Yes."

I waited for her to continue. When she didn't, I prompted, "Did you enjoy your trip to San Mames?"

She looked around the room, still not in any rush to say anything else. This wasn't looking like a social visit. I got the feeling she didn't do many of those.

I pushed on. "Is Boris threatening you?" I couldn't imagine her feeling threatened. She had a toughness about her, and I'd seen her right hand in action. But she and Boris were fighting about something that looked serious, and I wasn't sure why else she'd be having this much of a problem with someone she wasn't related to. And I'd seen his anger up close and personal.

"You come to bar tomorrow, meet granddaughter."

Huh. Not what I was expecting. I wasn't sure why she wanted me to meet Tatiana, who I'd actually already kind of met. That is, if you could call getting run over on the ropes course "meeting." Or maybe "meet" was a poor translation of something else. But she had completely ignored my question, and I was still curious about what was going on with Boris, which now looked like it could be related to drugs. I hadn't heard back from Gideon and knew little else at this point other than his name. Maybe I could find something out about him from Tatiana.

"Sure. But why do you want me to meet with Tatiana?"

She looked down at her hands, then back up at me. "Granddaughter is twenty. You are…twenty-five, yes?"

Thirty, but who's counting. I nodded.

"Is difficult on ship to be only young person."

OK, now this was making more sense. Svetlana had dragged Tatiana along on this trip, and then realized she'd stuck her on the senior's cruise for ten days with no one within three decades of her own age. And maybe she was worried if they spent too much time together, she'd end up slapping her too. Either way, I wanted to know more about what was going on and was happy to add an activity to this trip other than eating, avoiding Osama Bin Chaz, and drinking. The latter was normally not an issue, but ten days of free alcohol could be dangerous even for me.

I nodded. "Sure. How about we meet at the pub on deck four. Tomorrow at eight?"

"*Da.*"

She left her drink unfinished and got up to leave, smoothing her skirt and giving one long look around our suite. She looked tired, but there was also something very resolute about her. She turned and walked out of the room, not bothering to close the door behind her.

"Bye," I said to the open door.

I sat there thinking, then remembered my meeting with Ander. I hurried upstairs to brush my teeth, put on a clean T-shirt, and run a brush through my hair. I headed to the stairwell and skipped down them two at a time. I came out on deck four, and as I was walking to the pub I heard a very loud, "Jesse! *He-ey!*".

It was Trish Henderson. She'd was shouting and waving over the railing from two decks above up to get my attention. The "hey" actually came out as two syllables, her voice cutting easily through the din of the multi-level atrium.

It occurred to me that her husband probably didn't start out as a loud guy, but had suffered severe hearing loss after living in close proximity to her.

Her hand was waving madly at me, and people were looking at her and then at me. I quickly gave a small wave back.

"Let's do lunch!" at ninety decibels, accompanied by one of those "call me" signs, followed me into the pub.

Ander was already there and smiled as I took the seat next to him. He was dressed more casually than he had been at dinner. Replacing his plain suit and tie were jeans and a black long-sleeved T-shirt that somehow made his dark eyes even darker and his teeth whiter. *Damn.* He wasn't just nice looking. He was hot.

In *Matrix*-like fashion, Enzo made our drinks appear in front of us, a heavy shot of whiskey for me and what looked like a glass of Ander's cola/wine drink.

"Thank you for coming down. I hope it is not too late?"

"No, not at all." We clinked glasses and drank.

"How was your day? Did you enjoy Bilbao?"

I shared with him our tour of the hillside, leaving out the part about Boris. For some reason I found myself not wanting to share that with him yet. "How about you? How are you finding the cruise?" I suspected that, like me, he wasn't much of a shopper, and I couldn't really imagine him getting a spa treatment. Maybe the surfing simulator? At the very least, he'd totally rock a bathing suit.

"It is not what I am accustomed to, but it is pleasant. I am trying not to spend all of my time eating." He patted his flat stomach. "You?"

"To be honest, I'm not sure I can stand seven more days of this."

"Why? Most people would love to be here."

"I don't know…I'm not used to being around this many people for this long. But it has been more exciting than I thought it would be."

He raised his eyebrows, encouraging me to go on.

"Well, there was the body they pulled out of the water yesterday. And whatever it was that they kept us in our rooms the first night."

He nodded. "I know about the body. It was a crew member."

So it was a crew member. I wondered what else he knew. "Did you hear about the couple smuggling drugs on board?"

"Yes, I understand it is common on cruises. The money is compelling. I heard they were paid over one hundred thousand euros to smuggle cocaine."

I gave a low whistle. For that kind of money I'd think about doing it myself. "They don't exactly look like the type."

He nodded. "I think that is part of the scheme. But they are probably working with a crew member. It is a hard thing to do this alone."

"You know a lot about this. From experience?" I smiled at him.

"I teach law, so legal matters that occur around me are interesting."

Right, I'd forgotten about his teaching. And I knew from our previous conversation that he had an inquisitive streak, like me. It was part of what had attracted me to him. I asked, "Have they identified any crew members working with them?"

"I do not know, but I am sure the ship security officer is looking into it."

"Right, Ballsy. He's a busy man on this cruise." I didn't want to insult him in front of Ander. They might be friends. I hoped not.

"*Balasy*," he corrected me. "It is a Basque name, not very common. It means 'flat footed.'"

That figured. I changed the subject, wanting to learn more about him. Not something that happened often. "What is your life like when you're not on a cruise ship?"

"It is not like this." He laughed.

I usually found it annoying when people laughed too much, but it didn't bother me with him. He talked about his life as a professor, and what it was like growing up in the outskirts of San Sebastian. He wasn't committed to talking about himself the whole time, and soon moved the conversation back to me. He wanted to know what it was like living in Chicago, and my various careers. It was easy to talk with him, and I liked that he was equal parts listener and talker, although it felt strange to talk about myself. It had been a long time since I'd shared anything meaningful with anyone other than Sam and Gideon.

I told him about our trips into Seville and Bilbao. When I got to the description of our paella lunch, he leaned forward, his eyes glittering. Food was near and dear to his heart, and he was justifiably proud of his homeland's cuisine.

"Are there many Basque restaurants in the US?" he asked.

"No, unfortunately. But I travel often to Seattle, which has one of the best." I told him about Harvest Vine, a small tapas-style restaurant that had been established by a chef trained in San Sebastian.

He was doubtful. "It is hard to believe they could create authentic Basque food, and even if so, the atmosphere would be hard to reproduce. Food is about community here. It is the center of life."

I pulled out my phone and showed him some pictures. "These are from a cooking class they held last year. It's a small, intimate place." I scanned through the photos showing people eating at the counter right next to the kitchen.

He looked at them politely, and then did a double-take. "Wait… please go back…"

I scanned back a few pictures.

"Are those percebes?"

"Yes, from your coast."

I could tell he was impressed. Percebes are goose barnacles, a regional delicacy not often experienced or even heard of elsewhere.

"Do you also have txokos?"

I looked at him blankly.

"Cooking clubs. Social groups who get together to cook, share recipes, eat, and talk. They are very popular here. Historically they have been men-only, but now many allow women. Maybe if you come back, I can take you to mine."

If I come back… I surprised myself by thinking I might want to do that.

Our discussion flowed easily to other subjects, eventually moving to our academic backgrounds and careers. Ander worked full time as a professor, and also had taken over managing his family's small pig farm. He explained that the traditional Basque pigs, Euskal Txerri, were better suited for small family operations than large production facilities, and that the small family farms in the region were keeping part of their culture alive by raising those pigs.

"Full time teaching and pig farming. You must work all the time."

"There are many Basque idioms related to hard work and perseverance. I suppose it is in my DNA."

Our conversation predictably moved to family. Ander was the oldest of four brothers and one sister. His folks still lived in the house he grew up in, and his siblings lived close by. He had nine nieces and nephews, and while unmarried, he was interested in starting a family at some point.

It was inevitable that he'd get around to asking me about my family.

"My dad lives in Crest Hill," I said.

"Is that near Chicago?"

"It's about an hour away."

"So you must see him often."

"Not really." The last time I had any contact with my dad was when he'd called and heard me answer the operator's, "Will you accept a collect call from Statesville Correctional Center?" with, "Fuck no."

"That is too bad."

No, it wasn't. I finished my drink and motioned to Enzo for another. Ander wasn't getting the hint. "When was the last time you saw him?"

The last time I saw my dad was during the sentencing phase of his trial. This was the part where family members and friends of the convicted shared redeeming qualities in the hopes of a lighter sentence. The parents of the young woman he'd killed were sitting in the front row, looking at me stonily as I took the stand. If they were expecting to have to listen to what a terrific guy my dad was and why he didn't really deserve to spend a lot of time in prison, they were disappointed.

The courtroom grew silent as I described in vivid but unemotional detail what it was like growing up in a house with a self-absorbed, philandering drunk as a father. How he'd gradually sucked the life out of my mother, who, in addition to working a full-time job to make up for his serial unemployment, had spent considerable energy trying to keep things at least appear normal in our house. Who, night after night, cooked and set a dinner table for four around which she, my little sister, and I sat in tense silence waiting for him to show up, because he'd said he "really will this time." Who would offer explanations for him, like, "He's on a work trip," when we got up Christmas morning to no dad.

I shared with the courtroom about the weekend he'd brought home a cocker spaniel puppy. My sister and I were thrilled. We named him Mugsy, and spent the weekend taking him for walks, feeding him, and watching him take naps, while planning for longer hikes when he got older. Dad left after he dropped off the dog Friday night. He came back on Sunday and took it away.

We never saw Mugsy again. I learned later that it was his girlfriend's dog, and they'd needed someone to watch it while they went away for the weekend.

None of this would have any impact on his sentence, but what I said next definitely would. I told the court he regularly drove drunk, often with me and my sister in the car. He'd gotten pulled over a few times, too few times, but he always wore suits and ties and was a smooth talker. He didn't look or sound like what people imagined an alcoholic to be like, and had managed to avoid any serious consequences.

I talked steadily for over an hour, telling the court it was astounding that he hadn't killed anyone before now, and unless he was locked up, I was sure he'd do it again.

Nearing the end, I turned to look directly at him. "You killed my mother, you epically worthless piece of shit. Enjoy fucking prison."

There were small gasps of surprise in the courtroom. Most of the people had known about the young woman in the other car that he had killed. A lot of them weren't aware that my mom had been in the car with him too.

I got up and left the courtroom, looking straight ahead as I walked out.

I learned later they'd given him fifteen to life. Not enough in my opinion, but poor parenting and philandering weren't crimes, and that was the max sentence. The fact that the woman who was killed was the daughter of a state senator probably had more to do with him getting the max than him being a shitty father and husband, but I liked to think that I at least played a part.

After my testimony, I stopped by the liquor store on my way home and picked up several bottles, then drove back to our empty house. It was dark and quiet. My younger sister had gone to live with my grandmother in Cleveland. I was eighteen and left to myself.

I sat on the couch and shut off my phone, opened one of the bottles, and turned on the TV. I stayed on the couch and drank for three days. On the fourth day, I packed my things and went off to college.

I didn't think Ander could relate to any of that, so I just said, "It's been a while," and changed the subject. "What attracted you to law and economics?"

"As far as economics, well, that is what makes the world go around. And law is the basis for a civilized society. I like order, keeping things in their place. Law is what allows us to keep order. You must feel the same way, yes? It turns out we are both involved in the law."

My experience with the law had been more about the intellectual exercise of investigating corporate fraud rather than keeping order. That and a few episodes of breaking and entering, most while I was a minor. But I nodded.

As was his way, he continued asking about me. It was nice being with someone who was both interesting and interested. "What about you, what made you choose financial investigations?"

It didn't seem like my dead career would be much of a highlight, and I assumed he'd seen my last court appearance on YouTube, along with everyone else. Instead I talked about my various employment attempts, and how working for myself seemed like a good option, given my unique people skills. Even so, I half expected him to rethink any interest he had in me after learning about the sheer number of people and organizations I'd alienated over time.

But he surprised me by laughing out loud. "*Bihotzean dagoena, mihira irten.*"

I looked at him blankly.

"It means, 'What is in the heart, comes to the tongue.' What is the English phrase…'suffer fools'? That is not something you are suited for."

I really liked how he found humor in the things around him. He seemed serious and intelligent, but also very happy. An odd combination. "You have a very positive outlook on things." One thing we didn't have in common.

"It is emblematic of the people in this region. *Zoriontasuna da eduki gabe eman dezakegun gauza bakarra.* 'Happiness is the only thing we can give without having.'" He paused, looking at me a little more closely. "You are different from other women I have met."

I'd only heard that about a thousand times.

"You are very smart. And there are things that are more important to you than how you look."

"Ouch."

"No, no. I do not mean that in a bad way. I am sorry. It is difficult for me in English…" He appeared to be searching for words, then just said simply, "I like the way you look. And I like you."

Lots of guys didn't give me a second look, as I didn't dress the part. The ones who did wanted me for my brain, unfortunately often because they were deficient in that department. Ander wasn't. And while we were very different, he seemed a kindred spirit in some key aspects. I liked him too.

He looked up at the clock above the bar, and I followed his gaze, surprised to see a few hours had gone by.

"*Adiskide onekin, orduak labor.* 'With a good friend the hours are short,'" he said.

I wondered if he was friend-zoning me, but he asked if he could walk me to my suite. We walked out of the pub and I felt an electric jolt as he gently put his hand on my back.

We stood close together in the elevator, which arrived at my floor in what seemed like zero minutes. I stopped at the door of my suite and turned around to face him.

He said, "Thank you. I hope we can do this again." He learned forward and kissed me gently.

I was immediately reminded of how long it had been since I'd been with anyone, and found myself responding quickly. I wondered if I should invite him in, but he pulled away, saying "Would you like to have dinner with me tomorrow night?"

"Yes," I answered, probably too eagerly. I guessed nothing was going to happen tonight, which was fine. I wasn't loaded, and still found him attractive and interesting, so he was probably worth the wait.

He smiled and gave my hand a squeeze, then walked toward the elevator. I watched him until it closed. I turned and opened the door to the suite, barely avoiding smacking Sam in the face, who'd been up next to it listening.

"Busted," I said.

She gave me a grin that wasn't at all sheepish. "Do you want me to clear out of the living area so you can invite him in?"

"No, thanks. We have a dinner date tomorrow night." I realized in that moment I'd completely forgotten about meeting Tatiana, but my curiosity about the Russians would have to wait. I had my priorities.

Sam looked at my still-flushed face. "You like him," she said, beaming. "You should go for it. You know there's only a week left on this cruise." She looked at me intently. "Not to put too fine a point on it, but going this long just isn't healthy."

I believed her. Sam was the healthiest person I know. And whether or not Ander was Mr. Right, he definitely qualified as Mr. Right Now.

DAY 6

CHAPTER 17

The next morning I got up with a little extra spring in my step. I was psyched about my date with Ander, and wondered where that might lead in the remaining days on the ship. I was also energized about ramping up my efforts to investigate Boris now that he was back on board, even though Ballsy would be a complication. I'd seen him attempting to stealthily tail me since he tried to interrogate me in my room. He wasn't exactly cagey; I half expected to see him hold a plant up to his face to hide behind it, *a la* Inspector Clouseau. He was a bumbling fool but I'd still need to be careful.

Because of my date with Ander, I'd have to let Svetlana know we'd need to move my meeting with Tatiana to the next night. It seemed a small price to pay for getting lucky and breaking my sex-fast, which I realized was now at three months and counting.

Not only that, but Ander was the kind of guy I could envision having a relationship with. My last real one had been with Gideon. Eight years ago. *Yikes.* But I didn't want to get ahead of myself. Two dates in was a little early to start thinking about that.

I dressed and went down the stairs to the living area, where a pot of freshly made coffee and a breakfast spread had been left discretely by Ben. Sam was already there.

"You look chipper," she said as she poured and handed me a cup of coffee. "I told you meeting people would be good for you."

"It's not that."

She raised an eyebrow.

"OK, it's partially that. But also something else." I told her about Svetlana's visit. "She's going to introduce me to Tatiana. I might be able to get something out of her about Boris. Even if he wasn't involved in a bomb threat, he might be part of the drug smuggling."

"She wants you to be a babysitter? Doesn't really sound like you."

"My relationship to humanity is complicated."

Sam, to her credit, didn't touch that, instead just looked at me over the rim of her cup while she drank.

Looking at my watch, I saw that it was already ten thirty. "Are you ready to go into town and see the Guggenheim?"

"Yes! I'll see if Palben can join us." She reached for the Ming salt shaker on the coffee table and pushed the button to call Ben.

"Palben?"

"Yes, remember? He's the one who gave me Boris's name. He said we would give us a behind-the-scenes tour of the Guggenheim."

"Right." I headed up to my room to get ready and heard Ben show up at our door in less than a minute.

When I came back down Ben was gone and Sam was ready to go.

"Is Palben joining us?" I asked her.

"No, the executive crew is in some kind of special meeting. We're on our own."

She'd done some quick research and had made a lunch reservation at a restaurant near the museum that looked good, The Etxanobe Pantry. We left the ship and Mattin was waiting for us at the terminal. It took less than a half hour to get there and he dropped us off at the front door. The street was busy, full of restaurants and shops, many of them modern looking but set within what looked like very old stone structures.

The restaurant interior was classic, with white linen tablecloths and minimal ornamentation. It was packed, like every other place we'd seen in Bilbao. Even with our reservation I saw Sam slip the hostess a *soborno* and we were promptly seated and given menus.

146

All of the food was organized into tasting selections. We ordered the gastronomic menu, which was the chef's daily suggestion of dishes, along with a bottle of regional Rioja. I wasn't a huge wine drinker but was starting to get very comfortable with the regional offerings.

Mattin had done most of the talking on the way over and Sam was impatient to get to the good stuff. "How was your date?" I hadn't yet given her the low down, wanting to keep the details to myself for one night.

"Great. I like him. And he seems to like me."

"What's not to like?" she said, smiling. "What did you learn about him?"

"Lots of things. He comes from a tight family, he likes to climb mountains, and in addition to teaching, he runs a pig farm."

"A pig farm? Really?"

I nodded. "And he's curious, and pays attention to things. Like, he had all the details about the Marchand's drug smuggling. He said they were paid one hundred thousand euros to bring twenty kilos of cocaine on board."

Sam frowned. "One hundred thousand euros? That's a lot. That elderly couple I told you about, the ones who got arrested last year for smuggling some cocaine onto a cruise ship? They were paid one tenth of that."

She was right…that was a lot. I didn't know the street value of cocaine, but that amount of money would definitely cut into a drug supplier's profit margin.

We'd emptied our glasses and Sam reached for the bottle on the table and refilled our them. "What else did he say? Did he know anything about the body they pulled out of the water?" Her interest in my date was momentarily taken over by her concern about the curious goings-on that had been taking place on the ship.

"He said it was a crew member."

"Does he know who?"

"He didn't say." We were interrupted by a small team of waiters

MURDER ON THE SPANISH SEAS

with our meal. It was a remarkable array of small plates, and we put our discussion on hold while we focused on the food, which did nothing to controvert the notion that the Basque Country was home to the world's best cuisine.

We started with the lobster carpaccio, followed by a cold anchovy lasagna that tasted better than it sounded. Next was the omnipresent rice dish, in this case some kind of creamy mushroom risotto. The main seafood dish was fresh bass with roasted potatoes, and then for the finale, Euskaltxerri rib with a beet reduction. The pork rib was one of the more famous dishes in the Basque Country, often served as a pinxto. I wondered if this pig had come from Ander's family's farm. Whether or not it had, the entire meal was astounding. And filling. Even with the small portions we were stuffed and skipped desert, settling for iced espressos. We paid our tab and left.

Mattin was waiting by the curb to take us to the Guggenheim, but it was less than a half mile away and it was sunny out, so we told him we would walk and call him when we were done. As expected, he was fine with the change in plans, and drove away with a smile and a wave.

We walked down the street and turned on to Heros Kalea, one of the major throughways in Bilbao, slowing frequently to avoid groups of people on the sidewalk. As usual, my head was on a swivel, taking in everything around me. The street was a mix of old and new construction, bracketed on each side with buildings that were four or five stories high, with shops underneath and apartments above them. Many of the shop signs displayed a distinctive blocky lettering that seemed common in the city.

We kept our conversation going while we walked, which consisted primarily of Sam grilling me for more details about Ander. When we reached Abandoibarra Avenue and the stairs that led down to the museum, I stopped. Looking pointedly toward the museum, I said, "Sam, hang on."

"What is it?"

"Do you remember when you were at the quay, when you boarded in Barcelona? The group of men who were causing a problem?"

She nodded.

"Don't turn around, but I think I see one of them. He's been following us since we left the restaurant."

Sam looked a little skeptical but knew better than to question me about anything I'd seen. "What should we do?"

There wasn't anything to do about it at the moment, so I said, "Let's keep going."

It was hard, but we did our best to avoid looking behind us as we walked down the stairs and toward the museum entrance. It got a lot easier not to look back when we got to the plaza at the museum's front entrance and were faced with one of the most spectacular structures I'd ever seen.

The Guggenheim complex was massive. It was built in line with the city's main avenue, the Calle Iparragirre, and was situated next to the Nervión River that bordered Bilbao on the east and north sides. The main building was organically shaped, the exterior constructed with reflecting metal and glass and vaguely reminiscent of a huge ship, if that ship had been designed by Salvador Dali. The metal cladding on the outside didn't take away from the waving, live nature of the structure, which looked in some places to be in the act of melting. In the courtyard was a ten-meter-tall metal spider, not far from a reflecting pool, in which a sculpture of small stacked boxes rose up out of the water. We admired the architecture, wordless, for a few minutes before we went in.

The inside of the museum was as audacious as the outside. The large open vestibule was flooded with light that originated from a skylight at the apex of the central hall ceiling, fifty meters high. The space was defined by sweeping angled columns that ran sinuously from the floor to the various levels. I could see why architects had recently named this place the most important architectural achievement of the last thirty years.

The museum carried a number of standing and rotating exhibits, a total of twenty spread out over three floors. Too many for one afternoon, so we picked three of them to focus on: the Masterpiece, Lygia Clark, and Kadinsky exhibits, which included a lot of Sam's favorite artists and gave us a mix of classic and contemporary styles.

Sam had gotten her MFA from Northwestern in visual arts. Unlike a lot of artists, she didn't need to sell her work to make a living, and wasn't all that interested in making a name for herself. She just loved art. Inspired by the eclectic mix of faculty at Northwestern, she had an appreciation for all genres and dabbled in a variety of media herself. She was supremely talented, and probably could have supported herself with it had she needed to. But instead, she characteristically used her resources and assets to support the community. She believed strongly in helping developing artists, and in addition to the rent-free studio space she provided for them at her home, she organized and underwrote a yearly auction in which artists in her community could showcase their work. The event was a hot ticket item. Sam's very wealthy grandparents were well known for their philanthropy, and in addition to their name, and Sam's personal charm that was at least regionally famous, her own creations were in high demand. She started many but finished few of them, and always put the ones she did complete in the auction. There were often bidding wars for her pieces, and whatever they sold for was donated back into the community for supplies and, in the case of high-ticket items, scholarships.

I learned a lot about art from being around Sam. She took me to various shows and galleries, and taught me the go-to phrase to use when looking at art next to snotty art people. "Yellow is such a difficult color to work with," never failed to elicit knowing nods from other art-lookers.

As we moved through the exhibits, I continued to scan the crowd for the man I'd seen following us. He didn't seem to be around, and by the time we finished the first exhibit, I allowed myself to relax.

To the extent I knew anything about art, I liked surrealism, and was happy to see a few pieces by Dali and Yves Tanguy. Sam gravitated toward abstract impressionists like Lee Krasner and Rothko, whose art looked like someone took some paint and threw it on a canvas.

"I could do that," I said as we were looking at Rothko's "Untitled."

She sighed. "But you didn't." We'd had this exchange before.

When we'd seen as much as we could handle in one afternoon, we walked outside. It was still warm and sunny.

I looked over at the river and a wide brick path that ran alongside it. "I'm not ready to go back to the ship. Want to walk along the water?"

"Sure, I think this path goes to the Palacio." In response to my questioning look, Sam said, "The Palacio Euskalduna is a huge conference center and cultural space. It was built about twenty years ago over what used to be the old shipyard."

We wandered down the path along the river. After ten minutes or so we could start to see the top of the Palacio. She wasn't kidding, it was enormous, and as we got closer I could see it had been built in the shape of a ship. There were large banners hanging from the sides of the building and on the light posts in the plaza areas, all advertising the latest event: *Gastech: A Cleaner Energy Future.*

We tried to walk around to the front of the building but were blocked by a crowd. About a hundred protestors had crammed into the plaza, obstructing the entrance and spilling out onto the grass. Most of the people were calm, but a few pockets of people were more agitated, shouting and carrying signs in what I was starting to recognize as Euskara, including *Euskal Herria* and *ETA.*

We didn't know what was going on, but didn't like the looks of things, and called Mattin to pick us up. After a few minutes, he called back, saying that the police were redirecting traffic away from the Palacio and it wasn't safe there right now. We agreed to meet him back at the Guggenheim and began walking back up the path.

When we were about fifty yards away from the Palacio, I heard a loud *boom,* followed by yelling and a few screams. We stopped at the sound and turned around. We could see a small plume of smoke rising from the rear of the Palacio, and people were running away from the building, most of them from the front but a few coming from the back. We fast-walked the rest of the way to the Guggenheim parking lot, where Mattin was waiting for us.

"Mattin, did you see the smoke?" I asked as we hurriedly got into his car.

"Yes. The police were already not letting any drivers through to the Palacio because of the protest, before the explosion." He quickly pulled out of the parking lot and drove us away from the area, toward the port.

We were all tense and remained silent until we were a few miles away from the Palacio.

"What's happening?" I asked him finally, after my heart rate started to slow down.

"I do not know. The only event right now at the Palacio is the Gastech Conference. It is the largest conference for gas energy products in the world. The conference is held in a different city every year, and Bilbao won the bid to hold it this year. All of the big shots in gas energy are here. It brings a lot of money into the city."

That explained the crowded restaurants, but not the demonstrators. "What exactly are they protesting? They seem really angry about clean energy."

He thought for a minute, his brow furrowed. "Natural gas is one of our primary industries. We have the large plant in the industrial area you saw when we were up on the vista. It provides a lot of jobs and brings money into the region. There have never been any safety violations or accidents. I do not know why people would protest this."

"Are protests around here common? Do they ever get violent?" What I really wanted to know was whether or not we should expect more explosions. This was the third protest we'd seen in six days, and I didn't know if this was the norm or if we were in the middle of a major uprising.

"People here are politically active, but there has been no real violence for over a decade. If that was a bomb, it is highly unusual for this kind of thing to happen here. It is probably some kind of industrial accident. The Palacio is a very large center, and holds many kinds of meetings and events. And they are in the process of building an extension, so there is a lot of construction equipment and electrical machinery around right now."

That made sense. And it wasn't *that* big of an explosion, not enough to hurt anyone or do any real damage. At least, it hadn't looked like it. Mattin might have been right about it being an industrial accident.

Unfortunately, I didn't think so. In the Guggenheim there'd been no sign of the guy who'd followed us from the restaurant, but I'd seen him one more time. He'd been one of the people running from behind the Palacio, from the direction of the explosion.

CHAPTER 18

When we got back to our suite, there was a message waiting for me, leaning up against the Ming call button. I opened the cream envelope and read that something had come up and Ander wanted to postpone dinner until the following night. I'd been looking forward to it, and was a little disappointed, but at least now I wouldn't have to change my meeting with Tatiana.

Sam had a message too. "The Hendersons want to have dinner with us."

"I'd love to, but I value my hearing."

"I think I'm going to do it. They seem like really nice people. And they live in Chicago."

Sam was always collecting people. I expected at some point John and Trish would end up at Friday dinner, and I would need to start being strategic about my seating arrangement to protect my hearing.

I plopped down on the couch while she puttered around, putting a small bag together for her trip to the spa. She was just starting to relax after the explosion at the Palacio, and I didn't want to ruin her afternoon, so I decided not to share that I'd seen the same guy who followed us to the Guggenheim at the site of the Palacio explosion.

"Have fun at the trepidarium," I said, picking up a stray hairbrush and putting it in her bag.

"*Tepidarium*. Are you sure you don't want to come?"

"No, thanks." I still hadn't heard back from Gideon, and wanted to use the afternoon to poke around and see if I could find out what Boris was up to, or even if he was back on the ship. We left the suite together and I walked her to the elevator.

I didn't really know how or where Boris was spending his time, so I decided to take the methodical approach. During the entire time we'd been on the ship, I'd never seen him outside, or near any of the pools, other than his trip to the funnel, so I took the stairwell to deck ten at the top of the atrium, planning to work my way down floor by floor.

He looked like he kept himself in really good shape, and thinking he might spend some time in the fitness area, I looked into the glass surrounding the machines and weights. The room was empty.

One of the two buffet restaurants on the ship was on the same deck, along with a Cartier store. I had a feeling Boris wouldn't be shopping for watches, so after peeking into the restaurant to make sure he wasn't eating there, I made a quick tour around the level and then headed down the central staircase.

The atrium was abuzz with couples and groups shopping, eating, and bar hopping. By now I recognized almost everyone on the ship, and in order to avoid any distracting conversations, put on my best "I'm very busy with something important" face.

He could be spending time in his room, I realized, after going through two more levels and seeing nothing. Hell, he could even be off the ship again. But if he was lurking around, he might be on the lower floors, near the casino or my little pub where I'd seen him before, rather than the fancy shops and restaurants. I skipped decks six and seven and went directly to deck five, to the casino.

There were a lot more people in the casino than there had been the other night. Svetlana was with a group at the roulette wheel, throwing out stacks of red chips worth one thousand euros each. She seemed to be enjoying herself. Whatever was going on with Boris and Tatiana was not affecting her gambling fun. She saw me and nodded, then turned her focus back to the wheel.

Boris was nowhere in sight, so I left the casino and headed back to the staircase. When I got to the landing between decks five and four, I looked over the side and stopped.

Gotcha.

I could see the door to my little pub on deck four, and just outside were Boris and Tatiana. They were standing close together. He was talking, and her head was down. He was holding her hands while he spoke to her, occasionally looking behind him. At one point, she looked up.

Even from where I was I could see she loved him. I saw her say something to him and he shook his head from side to side. He gently took her hands and leaned over, kissing her on the cheek. Then he let go of her hands, looked around behind him again, and walked away. Leaning against the wall, she watched him go, the picture of misery.

They were lovers. This was why Svetlana had been arguing with both of them. She'd set up our meeting so I could provide some distraction to Tatiana. Not surprisingly, she didn't want her granddaughter dating a man twenty years her senior.

Well, that was one mystery solved. Before I turned to head back up the stairs, I gave a last look around the deck. Across deck four from the pub was the hallway with the door that led to the lower levels, the one at which I'd seen Boris and the crew member talking. The door was open, and standing in the doorway was First Officer Inigo. And Ander. They were talking in the same conspiratorial way as they had on the pool deck the second day on our trip.

Inigo turned and walked through and down the stairs, and Ander followed him. The door closed behind them.

So this was what had made Ander postpone our dinner date, a trip to the crew's quarters? This was the second time I'd seen him with the first officer. *Is Ander gay?* He'd seemed genuinely interested in me, but why was he going downstairs with Inigo? And why hadn't he mentioned knowing him?

If he actually kept our date the next night, I would need to ask him about Inigo. I was starting to like him, and if he was batting for the other team I wanted to know sooner rather than later.

CHAPTER 19

As much as I loved the amazing meals we were getting on this trip, I needed a break from fancy food, so I went back to Joe's Place to get a burger. There were no seats at the bar, so I sat down at a table next to a group of rowdy men who looked like they were having a great time. When the waitress walked over I ordered a cheeseburger with fries and a beer. I debated about whether or not to add a shot but decided not to. I wanted to be clear-headed when I met with Tatiana later.

The men were playing some kind of drinking game. Every now and then they would all clap and shout together. It looked a little bit like Los Chunguitos, the Spanish drinking game that incorporates Flamenco dancing elements, although what these guys were doing bore little resemblance to dancing. They were laughing and taking shots and slapping each other on the backs, and it appeared that none of them spoke the same language. They were using a lot of exaggerated hand gestures, and I could hear bits of accented English along with Spanish and French. There was one other language that sounded like a mix of all of those, I guessed Portuguese. I'd learned during my travels that if I heard a language I didn't recognize, one that sounded like a mashup of several of them, it was usually that.

One of the men banged his fist on the table as he was laughing, causing a fork to pop up. It was heading for my face. I picked it out of the air with one hand and handed it back to him.

"Ahhh!" they all exclaimed at my reflex.

"Baseball," I said as I handed their fork back.

"Ahhh…baseball. American?"

I nodded.

The Spanish-speaking guy leaned over and handed me one of the clear shots they were drinking. I wasn't sure what it was, but downed it. It was strong with a clean taste, like a really good French eau de vie, or Italian grappa. I could feel it warm its way down my throat. "Gracias."

"You join us!" The men all nodded and one of them got up to grab a chair from another table. They moved their chairs to make room for me.

What the hell. These guys seemed fun. I left my mostly empty plate and brought my beer over to their table. From what I could gather from the little English they spoke, they'd met while dropping their wives off at one of the spas. They'd bonded quickly over their mutual love of afternoon drinking, and had gone in search of the closest bar.

We did a quick round of introductions. Benicio was from Spain, Giovanni from Italy, Marceau was French, and I'd been right about the Portuguese, Tomas was from Lisbon. Benicio was from Madrid, and in addition to Spanish, spoke Portuguese and a little English. He tried to explain the rules of the game to me, such as they were. As far as I could tell, they were randomly clapping and drinking whenever they felt like it. The waitress had long ago given up bringing trays of shots, and had just left a couple of bottles of the Orujo, Spain's version of grappa, on the table.

I shook my head as they all chimed in with Benicio's explanation, an impossible mix of Italian, French, and Portuguese. I got up and went to the bar and came back with an armful of highball glasses, then pulled a quarter out of my pocket.

Benicio brightened, "*Il Duro!*" They didn't have quarters, but all had fifty cent euro pieces, which were about the same size as quarters. I explained the rules, and everyone understood enough English to get it except for Tomas, who got the translation from Benicio. Every time you were able to bounce a quarter off of the table into someone else's glass, that person had to drink a shot.

None of them were any good so I ended up not having to drink much. For them it was a different story. I'd been the unofficial quarters champion at Northwestern, and I hadn't lost my touch. I was putting coins regularly into their glasses, requiring them to drink their heads off. They didn't seem to mind.

We were well into our third bottle of Orujo when one of the men looked over at the door and gave a little groan. At the entrance were four woman who I guessed were the wives they'd left at the spa. The women walked over to our table and started talking quickly and loudly. I couldn't keep track, as it was in four different languages, but I got the gist. One by one the men got up unsteadily from the table, waved goodbye to me, and leaned on their wives for support as they staggered out of the bar.

Good times. I poured a shot of Orujo into my glass, only my second of the night. I was settling in to finish it when I remembered my meeting with Tatiana. I downed it quickly, left a hefty tip on the table out of habit, and walked out to the elevator.

CHAPTER 20

Tatiana was sitting at the bar when I walked into the pub. I was surprised but not unpleased to see Svetlana there as well, although she frowned when I walked in. I was late.

"You have met granddaughter, yes?" Svetlana said, obviously referring to my beatdown on the ropes course.

"Yes, hi." I sat down next to Tatiana and put my hand out to her. She ignored me, her head down, looking at the drink in front of her.

Enzo reached for the Jameson.

"Not tonight, Enzo. I'll have what they're having."

He poured me a shot of the skull-head vodka that was on the bar in front of Svetlana.

She raised her glass. "*Na Zdaróvye.*"

The three of us drank. I was a little surprised, as I'd never been a huge vodka fan, but it was good. Or maybe it was just good compared to Orujo. I wasn't sure. "This is good."

"Is Crystal Head. Is from distillery owned by American Dan Aykroyd," said Svetlana.

Tatiana gave what I recognized as the classic Russian snort of contempt. It was a sound that started from deep in her throat, accompanied by a slight back nod of her head, and rolled eyes. I noticed she was drinking from a different bottle. The label had a picture of a rowboat on it.

I was hoping that the three of us would hang out together a little while, to give me an opportunity to draw Svetlana out a bit before working on Tatiana. But Svetlana put down her glass and got up to leave. She and Tatiana had a quick exchange in Russian.

I couldn't tell what they were saying, but based on their tone I assumed it was something along the lines of Svetlana saying, "Be nice," and Tatiana replying, "Fuck off and die." It made me uncomfortable to hear someone talk to their grandmother like that, but I chalked it up to cultural differences.

Tatiana reached for her bottle of vodka and poured herself another shot, then looked at my glass and raised her eyebrow.

"Sure," I said.

She refilled my glass and we drank.

I'd never really paid much attention to vodka. It seemed its best quality was the ability to be mixed with whatever was on hand. But I could tell subtle differences between this one and Svetlana's Crystal Head. The Crystal Head had been slightly sweet, while this one had a more mineral finish. Neither one gave the burn I usually experienced drinking vodka shots. It was almost like drinking water, which I realized could be dangerous.

I watched Tatiana as she poured us each another shot. She had straight dirty blonde hair that went to just below her shoulders, and very blue eyes like her grandmother's, but a little less cold. She was about my height, and I knew from the ropes course that she was in good shape. Her face was set in what appeared to be a permanent scowl.

Tatiana's jeans and sweater indicated that her grandmother's taste in expensive clothes didn't extend to her. The only jewelry she had on was a necklace with a silver locket that looked quite old.

She put her shot down in one very natural looking sip. I wasn't sure I wanted to get into a drinking contest with a Russian, and was glad I'd only had a couple of shots of Orujo earlier. But I wanted to develop some rapport with her, and there was no way after the ropes course that I was going to let her beat me in drinking. I downed it in one gulp.

"How's the trip going for you?" Kind of a weak start, but I wasn't sure what else to say. I wasn't even sure if she spoke English.

She looked at me but didn't answer, and poured us both another shot. She drank hers immediately and I followed suit. She looked down at the bar and touched her locket. I recognized the gesture and the sentiment, as I was wearing something similar. It was the only piece of jewelry I wore, and one I never took it off.

I pointed to her locket. "What's that?"

She drank her shot. "Is from mother."

At last, she spoke. And I was relieved she could speak English. I hadn't seen her with anyone who looked like she could be her mother, so I asked, "She didn't come on the cruise?"

"Is dead."

Merde…there's a conversation stopper.

"Oh, I'm sorry."

She looked at me strangely.

I forged ahead. I was starting to feel a little loaded, and wasn't able to bring much nuance to the conversation. "Your grandmother is concerned about you. Do you know what she's worried about? Does it have something to do with Boris? I saw you talking to him earlier. Is he your boyfriend?"

Tatiana's eyes opened wide in alarm, and she put her glass down and started to get up to leave.

"Hey, wait, look, whatever it is, we don't have to talk about it." I put my hand out toward her in what I hoped was a calming gesture.

She looked at it like it was something infectious but sat back down.

OK then. I tried a more neutral subject. "What kind of vodka is this?"

"Is Five Lakes." Finally, something she would talk about.

"It's good."

"Is from Siberia."

"You don't like the Crystal Head?"

She gave another snort. "Is not true Russian vodka."

I continued to ask her questions, and she continued to answer in clipped, short sentences or not at all. When I asked about benign subjects, like her swimming, or vodka, or the ropes course, she'd respond. But when I got into anything about Boris or Svetlana, she clammed up. After a half hour of this, I finally gave up, and we drank the rest of the bottle together in silence. When it was empty she got up to leave, turning away without saying anything.

"Bye. Let's do this again sometime." I called to her back.

She walked out of the pub without looking at me.

I didn't want her to think I was following her, so thought it best to stick around for a few minutes. "Have a shot with me?" I asked Enzo. I thought it was against the rules for him to do that, but to my surprise he nodded and picked up the vodka bottle.

"No, not that." I'd had enough vodka to last a lifetime. "What do you like?"

He smiled and turned to pull down a bottle from the shelves. Nonino Grappa Monovitigno Picolit. Italian grappa. Very expensive. He poured us each a shot.

"*Alla vostra salute*," he said, holding his glass up.

"Cheers." We clinked glasses and drank.

He declined a second shot, and I decided I was done too, the vodka all of a sudden catching up with me.

It was almost two in the morning by the time I walked out of the pub and weaved my way toward the elevator. The floor looked empty, all of the action at this hour either a floor above in the casino, or in the livelier clubs on the upper decks. It was quiet other than the low hum of the engines.

As I waited for the elevator I heard voices. Boris and the crew member I'd seen before were together again in the hallway, at the door to the lower decks.

That door gets a lot of action.

This time, their interaction was less businesslike. Boris looked mad. Like when he was with Svetlana in the pub the first night, his face was inches from the crew member's and he was angrily jabbing a finger at the man's nose. In contrast to Svetlana's quiet defiance, this man seemed apologetic.

The elevator arrived and I got in it, relieved that he hadn't noticed me. I'd had too much vodka to be up for another confrontation.

When I got to our suite the spiral staircase up to my room seemed daunting, so I sat down on the couch. I leaned back, thinking about what I'd seen, and promptly fell asleep.

DAY 7

CHAPTER 21

The next morning I woke up with my clothes on. I'd never made it off the couch. My head was pounding, but I forced myself to get up and take a shower, put on a fresh T-shirt, and walk up to the pool deck to find Sam and get some coffee.

She was in her usual spot by the pool. As I walked up she looked me over. "Rough night?"

I muttered something unintelligible and signaled a crew member for some coffee. The sun was high in the sky. I must have slept in longer than I thought.

I told her about my meeting with Tatiana. "She's probably still sleeping it off. You wouldn't believe how much vodka we put away last night."

"I don't know, she seems like she's doing all right." She nodded to the pool.

There was a woman swimming laps. Fast ones. As she came to the side for the turn I could see it was Tatiana.

"Shit, is that her? How long has she been at it?"

"She was in there when I got to the deck, so at least an hour."

Fucking Russians. I sat down and drank the coffee, then filled Sam in on the evening and my meeting with Tatiana. I looked around. "Hey, why are we still in port? I thought we were heading back out today."

"It looks like we're going to be here for a little while."

"Why?"

"I don't know. Ben came by and said there was another minor mechanical issue. We're free to roam the city for two more days."

Two more days? "That sounds like more than a minor mechanical issue." Having said that, I was glad to have more time in Bilbao. "Wanna go into town again? I'd love to try out those hiking trails." Some fresh air would be helpful in my current state.

"Definitely. I've already made lunch reservations."

"Hey, we don't have a curfew. We could have dinner out too."

Sam looked away from me. "Um…I hope you don't mind, but I've made some other dinner plans for tonight. Are you OK on your own?"

"Sure," I said, remembering my dinner date with Ander. I looked over to the pool and had an inspiration. "How would you feel about asking Tatiana if she wants to join us for lunch and hiking?"

Did Russians like hiking? I didn't know, but I'd learned nothing of substance from her the night before, and getting her off the ship might loosen her up. After seeing Boris talking to the crew member again, my uneasiness was returning.

Sam was dubious, pursing her lips and looking like she was going to object.

I knew the notion of helping someone would appeal to her, and said quickly, "Look, I know she's not exactly the life of the party, but she's having some problems, and it might help her to get away from her grandmother."

Sam brightened. "OK. I'll change our reservation to three people. It's for an hour from now. Does that work?"

I looked over to see Tatiana climbing out of the pool. "Yeah, it looks like she's done swimming. I'll go ask her." I walked over to the other side of the pool where she was drying herself off.

She saw me coming and flinched.

Jesus, something's really wrong with this one. I put on my best friendly face and said, "Hey, Tatiana. Sam and I are going into town for lunch and a hike. Would you like to join us?"

She looked around. "I will ask."

"Great, if you want to go, meet us at the gangway in thirty minutes." I couldn't imagine why Svetlana wouldn't want her to join us, or why a twenty-year-old would need to ask, but whatever.

She nodded, and I left to rejoin Sam. We left the deck for our suite to get ready.

Thirty minutes later Sam and I arrived at the gangway. My head was finally starting to clear, and something was bothering me. I turned to her and asked, "Sam, how many of these cruises have you been on?"

"I don't know…lots. I go at least once a year."

"Since when?"

"Since I was a child."

"So, at least twenty?"

"Sure, why?"

"In all of that time, how many problems did you see?"

"Like what?"

"Like mechanical problems."

She thought for a minute. "None. There's a reason these cruises are so bloody expensive."

"Or a person overboard?"

"Just the one drunk man I told you about."

"Or graffiti? Drug smuggling? A bomb threat? Ever been confined to your suite?"

She looked at me pointedly. "Where are you going with this?"

"Don't you think it's odd that we're on the most expensive cruise on the planet and we've already had two engine problems? You said that drug smuggling was fairly common, and sometimes crew members commit suicide, but isn't it a little bit of a coincidence that it's all happening on the same trip?"

She considered this for a moment, and looked like she was about to speak, when Tatiana walked up.

Sam smiled at her. "Tatiana, hi! I'm glad you could join us."

Tatiana looked up at her briefly, then she turned to walk down the gangway. Sam looked at me and shrugged, and we followed her and her omnipresent pall of gloom down and over to Mattin's waiting car.

CHAPTER 22

Because we were going to be hiking in Punta Galea, Sam had made reservations at Tamarises Izarra Restaurant ("New Basque Cuisine") in Gexto, a town about fifteen minutes northeast of Bilbao. Per usual, Mattin was a font of knowledge about the history and interesting aspects of the area.

"Gexto was founded in the eleventh century as a fishing village. Now it is one of the wealthier communities in the region. There are a number of three-star restaurants in Gexto, and some very nice historical monuments."

We turned from the southern tip of the bay, heading up north along the east side of the water. He pointed toward the shore. "There is a brick path that runs along the seafront near the beach. It is nice to walk on, and you can also take a self-guided tour of the great mansions from the nineteenth and twentieth centuries that face the bay. It is called the Big Villas Promenade, and there are twenty-nine panels along the way that describe the architecture. Also, if you are going for a hike at Punta Galea, you will be near one of the most famous landmarks, the Prince's Castle."

"There's a castle?" I hadn't seen anything like a castle when we'd entered the bay. Not that I really cared, but I was making an attempt to get my head into our excursion and put the investigation on the back burner for the time being. It wouldn't be hard. Tatiana was with me in the back of the car, and had said nothing since we'd left the terminal, resisting all of my attempts at small talk. I'd need to put Sam next to her on our way back.

"It is not really a castle. It is also known as the Fuerte de La Galea, the Galea Fort. It was built in the 1700s to guard the entrance to the bay. You can reach it from the hiking trails on the cliffs."

We'd made it to through some residential areas, and were now on a more commercial street full of shops and restaurants. Looking around, I said, "Mattin, what's with the signs here? They all have the same weird lettering." I'd noticed it in Bilbao too. Much of the signage looked like everyone was using the same, possibly optically challenged, graphic designer. The letters were blocky and in some kind of weird cursive.

He laughed. "That is *harri*, it is our national font."

"You have a national font?"

"Informally, yes. *Harri* means 'stone.' The font is modeled after seventeenth century inscriptions found on Basque gravestones. It is a point of pride for many here. The original lettering style was designed to conserve space on stone pieces, and for ease of carving. It has been modified a bit, but retains some of the original elements of stone engraving."

What would our national font be, I wondered, if we had one? Rockwell? California? Comic Sans? Definitely Comic Sans. I was still thinking about this when Mattin dropped us off in front of the restaurant.

We were seated outside at one of the six tables next to the sidewalk, giving us a view of the water and the brick path Mattin had mentioned. As usual we ordered the tasting menu so we could try what was in season, along with a basket of percebes to start.

Tatiana had remained silent for the entirety of the car ride. This continued at the restaurant, and she seemed fine letting us order. But when the percebes came, she frowned. "This is what?"

"Goose barnacles."

She looked skeptical, but, to her credit, tried one. Her eyebrows went up and she reached for another.

The waiter suggested we try Ojo Gallo, a red txakoli made in the region that was difficult to find elsewhere. The name was a bit off-putting (literally, "rooster eye"), but it was tasty and went well with the percebes.

"These are amazing," Sam said between mouthfuls. We were on our second basket. "Why don't we have these in the US?"

I'd learned at the Harvest Vine cooking class that they were extremely rare outside of Spain. "They only grow along this coastline. They have to be manually harvested by divers and don't keep long, so they're scarce. I hear they're starting to try to grow them in Oregon."

"I hope so," Sam said. Tatiana was going through them too, and almost looked like she was going to nod in agreement, but stopped herself. *Damn.* I'd never met anyone in my life with as much of a commitment to negativity as this one.

The only thing that kept us from eating the restaurant out of percebes was the arrival of the tasting menu courses. The first one was their version of a common Basque pinxto, the gilda. The plate was small, served with a shot of amber beer. The Basque gilda was a skewer holding a guindilla chile, a green olive, a pickle, and an anchovy, all dressed with olive oil. Very simple, and very delicious. I could see putting a lot of these away in a bar with a lot of beer.

Tatiana gave her snort of contempt when she saw the small portion, and again when she saw the tiny glass of beer. But she'd learned her lesson with the percebes and said nothing. There was a look of wonder on her face when she followed the gilda with the beer. Apparently the notion of alcohol as a flavor accompaniment, rather than as something to be consumed in mass quantities to dull the pain of a wretched existence, was a revelation.

The courses came in waves. After the gilda was a baked oyster with spiced kefir, followed by seared bluefin tuna with tomato and garlic cream, and then a scallop and prawn rice dish. We were treated to the iconic crustacean of the region, the Txangurro (spider crab), and finally the predictable but tasty pork dish, in this case Bellota Iberian pork shank over mushroom stew. As we were eating, I calculated how much time I'd have to spend on the treadmill to work off this meal. I was glad we were going to spend the afternoon hiking.

Tatiana said little, and seemed a little shocked by the meal. I guessed that the food in Russia wasn't anywhere near this level, even with the privilege associated with being part of a loaded family. Like us, she was a good eater, and we managed to get through the meal with no more snorty contempt sounds.

If Tatiana was a good eater, she was a champion drinker. I ignored the waiter's raised eyebrow when we ordered our third bottle of wine. She'd consumed the lion's share of the first two bottles and seemed unaffected.

In response to my look of surprise, she scoffed. "Is only wine."

We finished with coffee and paid the bill. It was a one-hour walk to Punta Galea from the restaurant, and we wanted to spend our time on the cliffs, so we called Mattin, who'd been taking a walk on the beach. He arrived five minutes later, drove for ten minutes, and dropped us off at the Punta Galeako begiratokia, a lookout point and as far as he could go with the car. It was a few hundred yards from Paseo de La Galea, the center of the series of stone paths that wound around the hills and northeast up the coast.

We walked across the grassy areas to the top of the hill where there was a little bench. From there we could see far out into the water and across the bay, to the hills around San Mames where we'd gone our first day in port. I could see the industrial plant and our cruise ship terminal at the south end of the bay.

We left the point and hiked for about an hour on the well-maintained stone path, admiring the view, until we reached a high point on the cliff and a set of ruins just off the trail. There wasn't a lot left of them, and what was there was well-tagged with graffiti.

We walked around the ruins for a few minutes. Sam was interested in the graffiti and took some pictures with her phone. The view of the coast from here was stunning, but I was more interested in getting

Tatiana to talk to me than sightseeing. She was standing on a small rise looking out over the water, and I wandered over to her. "Is this your first time in Spain?" I asked.

She turned and walked back to the ruins.

I knew I was a little deficient in the personal charm department, but this was ridiculous. Maybe Sam could get something out of her on the way back.

We wandered around for a little while, but it was getting late and I wanted to see the Galea Fort while it was still light out. Keeping to the stone path, we headed back, passing our starting point. The trail eventually led away from the hills toward the beach, and then into some residential streets where the houses were walled off from the public.

We were near the fort and walking through its half-full parking lot. Sam and I were next to each other, Tatiana following a few steps behind. I looked around to make another attempt at conversation with her but stopped myself.

Turning quickly back, I moved closer to Sam and said softly, "Remember when we went to the Guggenheim, and I saw that guy following us? He's here." Sam started to turn around and I stopped her, whispering, "Don't look!"

I was sure it was the same guy. He was six feet tall with a thick build and a shiny bald head. He was about twenty yards behind us.

Sam looked worried. "Let's call Mattin."

"Fuck that. I'm getting a picture of the son of a bitch. Keep walking and act normal." I slowed down and pulled out my phone.

When we reached the far edge of the parking lot, I turned suddenly, stared directly at him, and snapped off a bunch of pictures. There was no cover in the parking lot, and he hadn't been able to hide himself. I was pretty sure I'd caught his face full-on.

He was taken by surprise and stopped as I smiled triumphantly at him.

Feeling a little bit more comfortable knowing he knew that we now had his picture, I turned back around. "Let's go. The fort is just up ahead."

Sam shot me a worried look but said nothing. Tatiana was oblivious and continued to follow a few steps behind us. If she was confused about the frantic picture taking, she didn't bring it up. We continued to walk the short distance to the fort together.

Similar to the ruins we'd seen earlier, the Prince's Castle was covered in graffiti. Unlike them, it had retained a lot of its original structure, including the lighthouse, its cylindrical shape rising above the fort's walls. We'd learned from Mattin that the fort had been built to guard Gexto's Nervión estuary, and was one of the best preserved eighteenth century military structures in the region.

The three us of joined a few other tourists at the base of the lighthouse, looking up. After a few moments, Sam left for the other side of the structure to look more closely at a section of graffiti. Tatiana, maintaining her wild success at effectively not communicating, wandered along behind her. I'd given up trying to get Tatiana to talk, and walked in the other direction.

I was looking at the wall on the south side of the fort when I got bumped. I felt a hand grab my ass, then go inside my back pocket.

"Hey!" I turned to see the goon whose picture I'd taken.

He'd grabbed my phone and was running away.

"*Hey!*" I yelled again. My phone had my entire life on it. Without thinking, I started running after him.

He sprinted away from the fort, across the cement walkways surrounding it, and into a grassy area ringed by a low stone wall. He ran toward a gap in the wall and jumped through. I followed him, scrambling down the embankment to the beach. It was layered with cement, and I could hear my pants rip as I fell and slid down on my ass, unintentionally sanding the palms of my hands on the rough surface as I tried to slow my descent. He popped up at the bottom and took off running. It was low tide, and the beach was less like a beach and more of a rocky shore, littered with stones of various sizes and very little sand. It was easy to run on if you could avoid the rocks.

We ran for a few hundred feet, during which I yelled at him continuously, even though I'd exhausted my minimal Spanish early on ("*Una mas cerveza por favor! Dónde está el baño!*"). He was fast for a big guy, and quickly started to outdistance me. As he ran he turned around a few times to see where I was, smiling confidently at the widening gap. As he neared the end of the beach and the short trail that would take him back up to the street, he tripped over a rock and took a nosedive. He sprawled awkwardly, my phone flying from his hand as he hit the ground.

He got to his knees and whipped his head from side to side, looking frantically for the phone. I'd seen it fall and headed toward it. As I did, he turned his attention from the phone to me.

We stared at each other from a few feet apart. I looked at the phone and back at him. A creepy smile started to form on his face, one that didn't make it all the way to his dull brown eyes. He looked around, his gaze coming to rest on a bat-sized piece of driftwood laying on the ground. He stood and strode confidently over to pick it up, then held it low while he walked toward me, moving it from side to side slowly, still with the creepy smile.

Uh-oh. There were no Krav Maga moves that would prevent my head from getting bashed in by a piece of wood. It was time to distract evil Vin Diesel with clever repartee.

"Hey, it's not even an iPhone," I said, watching him walk toward me.

"It's, like, an S3 or something. Seriously, practically a stone age communication device."

He was a little more than a bat length away and moving closer.

"I don't really even think I got your picture. I mean, it's a bummer, as you're incredibly photogenic and all, but I was moving when I took it and I'm sure it won't even come out. And I probably had my finger over the lens." I stepped carefully to where my phone had landed. As I reached for it, he managed a couple of surprisingly quick steps that closed the distance between us, and took a big swing at my head.

My daily Krav Maga training paid off in sharp reflexes that brought my arm up quickly to deflect the blow. It was the only thing that prevented my head from being bashed in. But he was strong, and it was a heavy piece of wood, and I staggered as it made contact with the side of my face. I saw the proverbial stars and everything around me dimmed for a moment.

I was still wobbling as he raised the wood high above his head and moved in to take another shot.

Fuck the phone, he's trying to kill me. I staggered a few steps in an attempt to get away, but at this point I was so disoriented that I couldn't think of where to go, even if I could outrun him. I braced for another shot to the head when I heard shouting.

He heard it too and paused with the bat still raised in the air. We both looked up.

All of my yelling had gotten the attention of a small but growing group of people above us on the cliffs. They'd followed our sprint down the beach from above, and were now pulling out phones, some snapping pictures and a few making calls. Hopefully to the police.

Somewhere in the desolate landscape of his cerebral cortex was a lonely synapse telling Baldy that leaving now might be a better option than hanging around. As satisfying as it would be to beat my head in, it might not be worth spending the rest of his life in prison. He paused, weighing the option of hitting me again and getting my phone, or getting away ASAP to avoid incarceration. In what was likely a rare event, he made the prudent choice. Dropping the piece of wood, he ran down the beach toward town.

I was panting, my hands on my knees and my head throbbing. After I caught my breath, I bent over to pick up the phone and brushed the sand off of it, checking to see if it still worked. It did. As I stood up, I heard faint cheering.

The small group on the cliff was thrilled to see that I'd rescued my phone. I waved and gave a tired smile, then turned around and headed back up the beach to Sam and Tatiana.

They were still at the fort. They'd missed the whole thing, and were wondering where I'd gone. Sam started to give me a hard time for taking off but stopped as she looked me over. My hands were scratched and raw from the slide down the concrete, my pants were torn, and there was a large red contusion on the side of my face. A little blood was dripping from the arm I'd used to block the goon's homerun swing.

I rubbed my hands together, brushing the sand off. "I think I'm done hiking. You guys ready to go back to the ship?"

CHAPTER 23

On the car ride back I explained what happened on the beach. Mattin was mortified and said little. This wasn't the kind of superior tourist experience he wanted for people who came to his city. Tatiana listened but didn't seem to be fazed by it. Clearly having your phone stolen off your body and being almost beaten to death was no big deal.

There was sand in my clothes and in my hair, and I'd worked up a sweat running, so when we got back to the suite I went to my room to wash up. I was still a little dizzy and had a headache that would probably be around for a while, likely from a slight concussion. I popped some Tylenol and took a long shower.

When I came back downstairs Sam was on the Eichholtz loveseat reading with Chaz curled up beside her. I looked around the room, my eyes resting on a familiar mass on the floor that I recognized as the remains of one of my boots. He sneezed, and I noticed a similarly colored piece of leather stuck to his upper lip. The ugly little bastard had chewed up my $200 jump boots and was sitting on my jacket.

"How can he chew anything with those teeth?"

Sam looked up. "Are you OK?"

I nodded. "I thought he was supposed to stay in his pet quarters?"

"I missed him and asked Gaspard if he could spend some time with us." She was staring at the purple bruise starting to take over one side of my face. "I'll get your boots replaced. How are you feeling?"

I didn't blame Gaspard; it was impossible to say no to Sam. I leaned down and rescued what was left of my boots and jacket. "I'm fine," I said, taking out my phone and thumbing through the pictures. There were a few clear ones of bald Babe Ruth. "I want to send these to Gideon. He's got access to a facial recognition system. If this guy has a record, he might be able to identify him."

"Did he say anything to you?"

"A couple of words. They sounded like '*narrassa*' and '*chortalari*.'"

"Probably Euskara. I think he called you a dirty fucker."

At least I could add Euskara to my global cursing library. I texted two pictures to Gideon with my request, and got a thumbs-up emoji in response a few minutes later. Turning to Sam, I said, "He's on it. What happened to Tatiana?"

"She went back to her suite. You know, she is a really nice young woman. While we were waiting for you at the fort, we had some time to talk."

"She actually *talked* to you? About what?"

"Oh, you know…life."

I didn't know. I sat down stiffly on the couch opposite Sam.

"She likes art. We're going to one of the galleries tomorrow together."

I waited for an invitation to join them but it didn't come. I was OK with that. Art wasn't really my thing, and it sounded like they were bonding. Maybe Sam could find out more details about what was going on between Svetlana and Boris, or even why the three of them always seemed to be arguing. Or if Boris was a drug smuggler.

"Hey, what time is it?" I asked, looking around for my phone.

"Just before five."

I got up off the couch gingerly, already starting to stiffen up from the sprint and beach beating. "Let's go. I signed us up for an engine room tour."

Sam stayed seated. "You're kidding. You're in no shape to go anywhere. Besides, I thought they weren't doing those anymore."

Optional engine tours used to be a standard offering on cruise ships. Since 9/11, tours of the engine room, bridge, and kitchen had been discontinued on most cruise lines. But because this was an uber-luxury cruise, and they'd given the passengers a more thorough pre-board vetting in lieu of security cameras, they'd provided the option for a tour of the engine room.

"They are. And don't worry, I'll be fine." I was interested in getting a firsthand look at the mechanical problems that had extended our stay in Bilbao. I went to the door and opened it, waiting for her to join me.

She knew from experience that there was no changing my mind. She got up with an exaggerated sigh. "OK, but I need to be back by six to get ready for dinner with Alejandro and Valeria."

CHAPTER 24

We took the elevator down to deck four and walked to the restricted access door leading to the lower decks. In pre-9/11 times, controlled access areas would be marked off simply with a rope across a stairwell and a "Crew Only" sign. These days, everyone was taking security far more seriously.

There were three passengers and a crew member waiting. I saw the passengers' eyes grow wide at the bruising and scratches on my face. The crew member, either out of courtesy or professionalism, pretended not to notice.

"Dr. O'Hara, Miss Hernandez, I am glad you could join us." She turned to the group. "Let us get started. I am Paloma, Chief Engineer of the *Gold Sea Explorer*. I will be guiding your tour of the engine facilities. This is a special treat, very few get to see the workings of this modern ship and its cutting-edge technologies. Everyone, please take a pair of goggles and a pair of earplugs and follow me."

Finally, an event on this fucking ship that didn't involve being forced to introduce myself. This was a promising start.

Paloma pulled out goggles and small packets of earplugs from a small bag and handed them out. Once everyone had them, she entered the keypad code and opened the door. She stood aside, gesturing us in. When the last person was through, she followed us in and closed the door behind us. I heard it lock.

We walked down the stairwell, past deck three and the crew's quarters, and through another door to a set of stairs to deck two. She led us inside a good-sized room filled with computers and monitors. and a very large screen on one of the walls. This was the central control room, where the engineering staff monitored and managed all of the ship's systems.

Paloma explained that the ship had six engines, each driving a different generator to produce electricity. About a third of it was used to move the ship. This meant the capacity to turn two large propellers through the water with enough torque to reach and maintain speeds of at least thirty knots, equivalent to a little over thirty miles per hour.

A cruise ship is basically a floating resort, and the rest of the power was allotted to the ship's hotel activities. In addition to moving the ship, it needed enough juice to support all of the systems related to those activities, like lighting, heat, air conditioning, pools, spas, clubs and restaurants, and however much power it took to run the surfing simulator.

"Our modern ship was designed to use liquid natural gas, LNG, instead of diesel fuel. LNG is more environmentally friendly, and will soon become the standard for cruise ships."

I recalled the storage tanks in the well behind the funnel where they'd found the backpack. They were likely filled with the stuff.

"You might have noticed the industrial area just up the coast from our terminal. This is the Bahía de Bizkaia Gas regasification plant. Spain is becoming a global leader in this growing industry, and the facility in Bilbao is one of the most modern in the world. The plant has a capacity of almost a half-million cubic meters of gas." She turned to a set of dials below one of the monitors. "This system controls another modern feature of this ship, of which we are particularly proud, the azimuth thrusters. These are special propellers that allow the ship to turn and stop much more quickly than traditional rudders.

"An interesting note, the tragic collision between the *Titanic* and the iceberg could have been avoided had it been equipped with these thrusters, as they would have allowed the ship to turn away from the iceberg much faster."

She didn't mention the unfortunate side effect of depriving us of one Kate Winslet movie, and arguably the best "all of the dead people get together at the end" scene in cinematic history.

Once she was through with her explanation, she gestured toward the door that we would take to the engines. "We are heading to the engine rooms now. Please put in your earplugs. It is very loud and hard to hear, so once we are in there, you will not be able to ask questions. But I will be happy to answer any you have at the end of the tour."

Paloma led us through the door from the control room to another set of stairs, then we went through a door to the first engine compartment on the lowest level of the ship. It was significantly warmer in here, and very loud.

She continued to speak, almost yelling now to be heard over the engines. "Ship engines are heavy, and for stability are located on the bottom of the ship, above the keel. The engine systems are massive and take up several decks. For safety reasons, the engine sections are compartmentalized into a series of separate rooms with sealed doors. In the rare case of fire, this prevents it from spreading. It also prevents flooding, in the event the ship's hull is somehow damaged and water enters the ship."

I'd seen Paloma gesture to one of the crew members in the engine room who'd joined our group, and who was bringing up the rear. I suspected it had less to do with making sure no one got lost, and more to do with making sure no one got too close to sensitive equipment. The crew member's name was Hugo. He was supposed to be watching the passengers, but I saw him spending most of his time staring at Sam.

Paloma led us through a series of rooms, each crammed with machinery, electronics, pipes, and cables. She hadn't been kidding—it was loud in there. She shouted a few more things as she pointed to various pieces of equipment. I found myself thinking of Trish Henderson, whose natural volume would have been a real asset here.

After we went through three of the compartments, Paloma

signaled for us to turn around and head back to the control room. I'd been expecting to see more, and was disappointed to be turning back. Once we got back to the quiet of the control room, she indicated for us to remove the earplugs, and then opened it up for questions.

My hand shot up.

"Yes, Dr. O'Hara?"

"What is the machinery that is below the funnel on deck twelve? And is it LNG fuel that is in the long storage tanks in the well behind it?"

"Yes, thank you, that is a great question. Those tanks are indeed the LNG storage tanks for the ship. And the machinery below it is the backup generator. We have several of those, and for safety they are located in different areas of the ship. Other questions?"

My hand went up again. "Can you explain the mechanical problems we've had on this trip?"

She was less excited about this question but was polite. "The problem was very minor. One of the fuel gauges was not working properly. That is all. It was easily fixed."

I remembered the Norwegian cruise ship that had gotten stuck a few years back. The problem had been leaking oil. Once the oil pressure got low enough, it had caused the engines to automatically shut down to prevent main engine damage, stranding the ship. In our case, there was just a bad gauge, but I could see why they would be careful with it, given what had happened to the other ship. No one had been in any real danger, but it was a major embarrassment to the cruise line for their passengers to have to be rescued.

"Any more questions?"

My hand went up again.

Paloma looked in vain for another option, but the rest of the group was silent. Reluctantly, she looked at me. "Yes, Dr. O'Hara?"

"Did the fuel gauge fail twice? What happened the second time?"

I saw her face redden, momentarily replacing the look of bland affability that seemed to be a required attribute of the crew. "We are not at liberty to discuss that. But I can assure you it was nothing serious."

"If it was nothing serious, why did it cause a two-day delay?"

The other passengers in the group were paying more attention to the discussion, and some were getting concerned looks. When Paloma didn't respond right away, one of them chimed in. "Yes, are we at risk of getting stuck somewhere? How do we know we'll be safe once we head back out?"

Now they were all looking at her and listening intently.

Paloma probably knew she was in danger of causing some unwanted rumors to start, and the last thing she wanted was for us to go back to the rest of the ship and talk about the engine problems and that the crew was hiding something. But she recovered quickly and replied, "This ship is built with state-of-the-art safety systems and multiple redundancies. As you saw, the ship has six engines. If need be, the entire ship can be powered with only two of the engines and one of the two propellers. We also have two emergency generators in case of engine failure, as well as multiple battery backups that would sustain critical systems on the ship for twenty-four hours in the event that the emergency generators themselves failed. As I mentioned, the emergency generators are not all in the same room in order to ensure that if there is a fire we will have at least one operational generator at all times. Redundancy upon redundancy."

She'd used the word "redundancy" several times, possibly to distract from the fact that she hadn't answered my question. I started to raise my hand again.

Paloma stopped me by putting up her hand. "The problem is truly very minor. The reason for the two-day delay is that there is currently an LNG carrier coming into the bay to dock at the regasification plant. Whenever these carriers arrive, the shipping lanes in and out of the bay are temporarily shut down, so there is no chance of any ship getting too close to them. It is an excess of caution, as the tankers are loaded with gas. Were the carrier not coming in, we would have had only a short delay," she said in a way that implied the issue was over. "Are there any more questions?" She pointedly avoided looking at me.

No one else had any questions, apparently mollified at her information about the carrier. I could tell she was still keeping something from us, but Sam looked at her watch and signaled to me that we had to go. Reluctantly, I turned away and started to follow her out of the control room.

I turned around for one last look and did a double take. One of the engine crew members was the guy I'd seen meeting with Boris on deck four, the one he'd given the backpack and money to. I couldn't see his name tag from where I was, so I maneuvered to get closer. As I fell to the back of the group, I got close enough to see his nametag. Gorka.

Now that I had his name, I'd be able to learn more about him from Gideon. That was as long as Gorka wasn't a common name among the crew.

As I caught up to Sam on the way out, I noted Hugo eyeing her again. "Sam, can you see what you can get out of Hugo about the engine problem that caused the second delay? I think he likes you."

She looked behind us at Hugo, who quickly looked away. She nodded. "No problem."

We put our goggles in the bag and headed for the elevators and back to our suite. Once there, we went to our rooms to get ready for our respective dinners. Sam to get beautiful, and me to get at least clean before my date with Ander.

CHAPTER 25

Ander had picked Joe's Place for our date, maybe trying to accommodate a desire I might have for American food. I didn't mind, the place was starting to grow on me.

We met there at seven. He was staring at the bruise on my face, but before he could ask about it, the bartender came over and showed us to a table near the bar.

"Hey, Jesse!" I looked across the room to see Benicio, Marceau, Giovanni, and Tomas waving at me. There were a couple of bottles of Orujo on the table and four rocks glasses, some with coins in them.

Ander looked surprised. "Friends of yours?"

I waved at them. "Yeah, we go way back."

We sat down and the bartender brought over menus.

Ander picked up the wine list. "White or red?"

He was dressed up a little bit more than he had been on our last date, with a sport coat over a white dress shirt and black jeans. I tore my eyes away from his chest and said, "How about neither. This is a sports bar...are you up for beer?"

"OK." He smiled. "Do you have a recommendation?"

I looked over the list and nodded. They had a decent selection of draft beers, and I picked a light lager to start. "You mind if I order an appetizer?" I wanted to check out the ship's version of buffalo wings.

"Not at all. In fact, why don't you order dinner for us? I have never been to the US, and you can introduce me to the best American cuisine has to offer."

I wasn't sure that Joe's Place was the best place to evaluate American cuisine, but I liked the fact that he didn't feel the need to control every aspect of the meal. Before the bartender left, I ordered the wings and the beer.

She came back shortly with our beers and told us the wings would be up soon. I ordered a selection of what I thought was a good range of typical American sports bar food, including wagyu beef sliders, nachos, and potato skins.

We were sitting close together, our chairs almost touching. Ander lifted his glass to me.

"*Topa.*"

"Cheers." We clinked glasses.

"I am sorry about having to cancel last night. I am glad we could reschedule."

I was struck again with how damn good looking he was. I was also experiencing a strange sensation. Happy. That was it. And...content. Did other people feel like this all of the time? I wondered what he looked like under his clothes.

"Uh, Jesse?"

"'Sorry...what?"

"Are you going to tell me what happened to your face?"

I'd rather jump your bones. "I had a run-in with a guy who wanted my phone."

"You were attacked?"

I nodded.

"Where? Are you all right?"

It was sweet that he was concerned. But I wasn't sure how much I wanted to tell him, wondering if I'd sound paranoid about being followed. *What the hell.* I took a sip of my beer and said, "I'm fine. The guy's been following us for a couple of days. He's also one of the men who tried to board the ship in Barcelona. He didn't seem to like the fact that I took a picture of him." I described the chase on the beach and my face as a batting practice target.

"How do you know it was the same man?"

"I have a pretty good eye for details."

"Yes, of course, but how could you be that sure?"

I sighed. *Time to get it over with.* I looked down at our table. Without looking up I said, "There are five tables of four people in our restaurant right now, four tables of two and one of three. Eight people are sitting at the bar, three couples and two men by themselves. Sixteen of the thirty-four people who have drinks are drinking beer and eighteen are drinking wine, all of it but one red. The woman in the pink sweater at the table of four to the right of the entrance has an empty glass, and has been trying to get the attention of the bartender since we sat down. She's got curly dark hair and, judging by her gray roots, she's coloring it. She's wearing designer glasses and a lipstick color that perfectly matches her sweater."

Ander looked around and said something under his breath in Euskara.

"The man to her right at that table—"

He put his hands up in surrender. "OK, OK. I believe you." He looked around again. "That must be a very useful skill."

Huh. That was a surprisingly positive reaction.

I was seven when I learned that I was different, and that it freaked people out. My mom had taken me to a bookstore for the first time. She let me pick out two books to buy, and I was beyond excited. Up to that point I'd only gotten them from the library, these would be my own to keep. I spent an hour searching for exactly the right ones (*Gone with the Wind* and *Robinson Crusoe*). While she was paying for them, the checker handed me a bookmark.

"What's this for?" I'd asked.

He'd leaned over the counter and talked to me very slowly, to make sure I would understand. "Well, honey, this is how you keep track of where you are in your book." He proceeded to demonstrate how to place it between the pages. He did it twice, probably thinking if I didn't know how a bookmark worked, how could I actually manage to read.

"Why wouldn't I just keep track of the pages in my head?"

He smiled. "It's very hard to do that, sweetie."

"No, it isn't. I'm on page two hundred and thirty-one in *The Hobbit*, one hundred and twenty-five in *Little Women*, three hundred and seventy-eight in—"

"Let's go, Jesse." My mom ushered me out of the store, but not before I saw the look of unease on his face.

I was very familiar by now with that look, and surprised to see it absent from Ander. He was smiling.

"Usually when people find out about it they get nervous around me."

"Truly? It seems like a great asset. It must really help with your job."

In the world of theoretical employment, that would probably be true.

"So…back to the man on the beach who attacked you. Did he say anything?"

I was about to answer when the bartender brought our wings and set them down, along with two shots of Orujo. "From your friends," she said, looking over at my quarters buddies.

They raised their glasses to us from across the room.

We picked up our shots and raised them back, clicked glasses, and drank.

"*Ugh.*" Ander grimaced. It was hard for me to imagine that it could be any worse than wine mixed with Coke. But maybe he just wasn't a shot drinker.

We dove into the wings. They were surprisingly good, and while not spicy enough for my taste, the first one had Ander red-faced and gulping his beer.

"Is all American food like this?" he said, little beads of sweat breaking out on his forehead.

"No, these are kind of unique." Good thing I hadn't ordered the jalapeno poppers.

The rest of the food followed shortly. While we ate he told me more about his family, and I told him about the Guggenheim and our engine tour. When I brought up my questions about the mechanical problems, and shared that the chief engineer seemed to be hiding something, he seemed less interested.

"It is probably nothing. Everything on this ship is backed up several times. They will not leave port unless everything is fine. I am sure the problem is very minor."

I wasn't sure how he could know that, but I was starting to have a hard time concentrating on anything other than his eyes. While we talked, he had inadvertently, or maybe advertently, moved his chair closer to mine. He smelled really good.

He was trying one of the sliders and seemed to like it. Since I would be eating all of the wings, I left the sliders to him.

"Did you do anything else in Gexto?" he said, now holding up one nacho chip and examining it.

"We did the trails on the top and saw some of the ruins, then we went to the Galea Fort."

After a thorough examination, he put the chip into his mouth, chewed for a moment, then reached for another. "Just you and Sam?"

"No, we took Tatiana, Svetlana's granddaughter."

He stopped eating and looked at me. "Tatiana?"

"Yes."

Up to now I'd held back about my investigation into Boris, but at this point shared with him their ongoing arguments, and Boris disappearing in Cadiz.

Ander seemed to be far more interested in this than the engine troubles. He leaned forward. "What do you think is going on? Is Tatiana dating Boris?"

"I'm not sure. It looks that way. That may be why her grandmother wants me to hang out with her. He's way too old for her. Not to mention kind of scary looking." I decided to spill everything. "There's one more

193

thing. I saw Boris meet with one of the crew members." I left out that I'd seen Ander meeting with Inigo, deciding to let him tell me in his own time. Mostly because I was having a good time and didn't want to spoil it by bringing up something he wouldn't want to talk about.

"When did you see that?"

"The first night. He gave him some kind of backpack. It could have been the one they found in the storage tank well."

"Did you see which crew member it was?"

"Someone named Gorka, one of the engine crew."

"Are you sure it was Gorka?"

I looked at him and raised my eyebrows. "The bartender has earrings in the shape of small ships that match her necklace. The man sitting at the bar on the far right is wearing mismatched socks, which means he is either color blind or single—"

"Oh, yes, right."

The bartender came over with two more beers, and I caught Ander glancing at her ship earrings. He continued to clean up on the nachos. I liked watching him eat.

Between mouthfuls he said, "You're running into Boris a lot."

"Well, I've kind of been following him."

A small frown crossed his face.

"What can I say? I'm the curious type."

His voice turned serious. "Jesse, maybe it is not a good idea to follow Boris."

"Do you think he could be dangerous?" I knew he was, but I wanted to hear Ander's take on it.

"Not necessarily. But if he is, don't you think you should leave it to the proper authorities?"

"You mean like Ballsy?"

"*Balasy*, yes."

"I tried. He wasn't appreciative of my efforts, and now he thinks I had something to do with it. He's been following me. Speaking of that, do you know what the security alert was about? We heard it was a bomb threat." Ander had known about the crew member going overboard, so maybe he would know about the Charlie code.

He didn't answer right away, taking a sip of beer and reaching in for a potato skin. "No…I assumed it had something to do with drugs."

"Really? They would lock us in our rooms for three hours while they looked for drugs?"

"Possibly. I do not know. As I told you, this is my first cruise."

I could tell he knew more about it than he was sharing. But he was even better looking when he smiled, and I didn't want to screw up our date by interrogating him. I let it go, and we moved on to other subjects.

He was enthusiastic about running his family's pig farm and told me more about that, along with more stories about his siblings, nieces, and nephews. I told him about the rest of our day in Gexto and the meal we'd had in the restaurant.

We went through most of our food and another round of beers. As before, our discussion ranged over a wide variety of subjects, and I found myself laughing frequently. I couldn't remember the last time I'd had this much fun on a date. At least, not one in which I hadn't put away my weight in alcohol.

Ander drained his glass and leaned close to me, our faces inches apart. His hand lightly brushed the hair away from my face. "Would you like to come back to my room? It is probably not as nice as yours, but I have a bottle of Jameson."

Nothing like the direct approach. I normally waited a little longer to hop into bed with someone unless I've had way too much to drink, which wasn't the case now. But I had Sam's voice in my head telling me there were only a few days left on the cruise, and it had been a very long time for me. And I was starting to really like this guy.

"Yes…give me a few minutes?" I said, wanting to freshen up.

Ander gave my hand a squeeze and told me his suite number. It was on deck seven. It made sense he would be on the lowest deck, the university that was sponsoring him didn't need to be set back six figures.

I tried not to run out of the bar. I took the stairs in the stairwell two at a time and burst into our suite, racing up to my room to brush my teeth and wash my face.

Sam was standing in front of the full-length living room mirror, putting some final touches on her makeup. "What's happening?"

"I'm getting lucky." I looked around. "Where are Alejandro and Valeria?"

"Waiting for me in the club." She gave her hair a quick run through with her fingers. "I'm heading out myself. Good luck." I ran up the stairs.

I made it in and out of the suite in five minutes flat, and ran back down the stairs to Ander's deck, narrowly avoiding knocking over a couple going the other direction. I was about to knock on his door when I heard voices coming from inside. I paused but knocked anyway. The voices stopped.

Ander opened the door but didn't invite me in. The warmth was gone from his eyes. "Jesse, I am sorry. We will have to meet another time."

I looked around him and saw Inigo and Gorka standing around the living room coffee table. There was a set of papers laying on top of it.

"Uh, sure, OK. No problem. See you around." *All engines full stop.* I turned and walked away as he closed the door behind me. *Merda.*

I wasn't excited at the prospect of going back to our empty suite, but didn't know what else to do, so I walked to the elevator. As I was waiting, one of the other suite doors in the hallway opened.

It was Boris. He looked up and down the hallway and our eyes locked. He glared at me. I wondered if he was going to think I was following him and come after me again, but he closed his door and turned away from me, walking to the stairwell.

The thing between Svetlana and Boris was making even more sense. Svetlana and Tatiana's suite was on deck thirteen, nearly as expensive as ours. Boris was on level seven with the Little Sisters of the Poor. So, in addition to being much older than Tatiana, he was also less wealthy. A weak match in every way.

Seeing Boris got me thinking less about being stood up, and more about what I'd seen in Ander's room. I knew there was something going on with Boris and Gorka, and between Ander and Inigo. Now three of the four of them were meeting in Ander's room, with Boris just down the hall. Another coincidence. They were piling up.

Ander hadn't bothered to share with me whatever was going on between him and Inigo. And when I'd told him about the meetings with Boris and Gorka, he'd asked if I was sure it was Gorka. Like that was somehow important. And he'd been hiding something when I'd asked him about the drugs they found.

Now that I thought about it, he had really kind of interrogated me about what I'd seen with the Russians, and about the bald guy who'd been following us. At the time I'd thought it was concern, but what if it was something else? He'd also dismissed my concerns about the ship's mechanical problems. How could he know they weren't serious if he wasn't involved somehow? He'd claimed he didn't know about the security alert, or what they'd found in the backpack, and that he assumed it was related to drugs. But I could tell he'd been holding something back.

Something was going on, something related to the ship, and it looked like Ander was in on it.

I needed to rethink things. Mattin and Ander had both said that the ETA violence was over. But what if it wasn't? He was Basque. The guy who had been following me was Basque, given that he'd swore at me in Euskara. Gorka and Inigo were Basque names. We were stranded in a port that was in the heart of Basque Country, and the ship had been tagged with ETA graffiti.

The Charlie code security alert that stuck us all in our suites made better sense if it were the result of a bomb threat, rather than drugs. And where better to place a bomb than next to fuel storage tanks?

It also explained why Ballsy had such a hard-on for me. Finding the backpack after he'd advised the captain to give the all clear put everyone in danger, and made him look incompetent. The captain had rightly chewed him out for it. This kind of fuck-up might affect his job security, for which he would blame me.

I thought about Ander's comment the first night in the pub. He'd said, "rightly or wrongly" the ETA was done. That sounded like he was at least ambivalent about the ETA. Unlike Mattin, who'd been very clear he wasn't in favor of the violence. And between the protests in Cadiz and at the Palacio, the explosion there and whatever had been going on at the quay in Barcelona, it didn't seem "done" to me.

Then there were the two "mechanical problems" on the ship. What were the chances that all of this happening at the same was an accident?

I wondered if I was getting ahead of myself. All of these pieces could be just that, unconnected pieces. When I boiled it all down, there had really only been a couple of minor engine problems, some small protests, which as far as I knew were a regular occurrence, some drug smuggling, not uncommon on cruises, apparently, and a couple of run-ins with a small-time thug with no agenda other than making some quick money. And I'd already determined that the arguments among the Russians had to do with the relationship between Boris and Tatiana.

That still left Ander meeting with Inigo and Gorka. What was so important that he would pass up sex with me to do that? Not that I was any great shakes, but he'd seemed very interested just a few minutes beforehand.

When I got back to our suite, I was disappointed but not surprised that it was empty. Putting a voice to my thoughts was helpful in recognizing patterns, and Sam was a great sounding board when I felt stuck. But she was out enjoying her date, and who knew how late she'd be out. I pulled a Guinness from the refrigerator and took it out to the balcony.

There was a text from Gideon. He'd found the guy whose picture

I'd forwarded, and sent me a report. I opened up his email and downloaded the document. It was short, only two pages. He'd added a light blue logo on the top of the first page. A baby riding a space shuttle. Very funny.

Gideon had run the goon's picture through their facial recognition database and got a hit. His name was Zuzan Zabala. Nice alliteration. He was from San Sebastian, and he had a record. Mostly small-time stuff, but some of his associates included known ETA members. The ETA had been labeled a terrorist organization, so anyone with ties to it was still in the database. There was a list of his criminal activity that looked like it started when he was a kid, possibly due to psychological damage suffered by being perpetually last in alphabetically-ordered lines. Burglary, assault, and he'd spent some time in jail for almost beating someone to death.

This guy was dangerous, but didn't sound like much of a mastermind. There was nothing in his background about bombs.

Gideon had also managed to get a hold of the crew list. I looked through and found the only Gorka on the ship. Gorka Viteri. There was nothing about Boris.

I looked at my watch. It was after midnight here but only five in Chicago. Maybe I could catch Gideon at work.

The phone rang a long time, and I was almost ready to hang up when he answered, sounding out of breath. "Spielberg."

"Hey, Gideon. Were you on your way out?"

"Hey! Yes. But I always have time for you. Did you get my report?"

"Yeah, thanks. Do—"

"Did you like the logo?"

"It's terrific. Do you have a minute?"

"Sure. Whaddya need?"

"Couple of things. First, did you find anything on Boris Alekseev?"

"I'm still looking. I've got the passenger manifest for your cruise and you were right, he's ex-military. Russian Commando forces. You've heard of Spetsnaz, right?"

"Russian special forces? Like the US Navy Seals?"

"Yeah, but even more specialized, like our Delta Forces. The top of the top. He was in a naval branch, but his files are sealed tight. I don't have anything more specific on him yet. Normally I don't have any trouble hacking into Russian records, but this one is super-snug. I'll keep on it though. I've got a couple more things to try."

"OK. Are you up for some real-time research on something else?"

Gideon was the fastest researcher I'd ever met. If you could articulate a question, he'd have the answer almost as soon as it came out of your mouth.

"Always. What's your pleasure?"

"You know we're in Bilbao. They're having some kind of convention here, Gastech. What can you tell me about it?"

I could hear him typing, then he said, "It's the largest energy conference in the world. It was a big coup for Bilbao to land it. And important for Spain, they're investing heavily in clean energy right now. They want to be a major player. You're very close to one of their flagship plants."

"You mean the one that's on the water in the bay? What can you tell me about it?"

"It's the Bahia de Bizkaia plant. You know what LNG is, right? Liquefied natural gas?"

"Yeah—well, a little. Our ship runs on it. That's about all I know."

"It's just what it sounds like. Typically, natural gas, methane, is extracted from the earth, then it's piped around to various places where it's burned as an energy source. But if it's super cooled, to -260 Fahrenheit, it becomes a liquid and takes up way less space. The amount of energy in liquid gas yields about six hundred times the energy in a similar volume of gas. As a liquid it can then be moved long distances much more cheaply and easily than in gas form. The plant in Bilbao is a regasification plant. So tankers—carriers—come in loaded with LNG and are hooked up to the piping system on the dock. The LNG flows from the ship to the storage facilities in the plant, and is later converted from liquid back into gas, and redistributed overland via pipelines."

I thought about what Paloma had said during our engine tour, about them closing the shipping lanes when the carriers came in. "There's one of those LNG carriers coming in to port right now." I waited a moment, hearing him type again.

"Yeah, it's the *Petris*. From Russia. It's carrying one hundred and fifty thousand cubic meters of LNG."

That seemed like a lot. "Are the carriers safe?"

"Hang on…" More keyboard sounds.

"There are some groups who are vocal about the dangers of shipping LNG. But it looks safe, especially compared to other forms of fuel. A good gauge is the insurance rates. They're twenty-five percent less for LNG container shipping than for crude oil shipping." More typing. "The carriers are pretty solid. It would take a lot of damage to cause any problems. They're double-hulled, and have all kinds of safety features."

"If they're so safe, why do they shut down the shipping lanes when they're coming into port?"

"I'm not sure. Maybe they're just being extra careful. It looks like the only real danger is if the LNG hits the air and gets ignited. But that's not likely to happen. When the carriers come into port, they're hooked up directly to pipelines, and the liquid is pumped into storage tanks before going through the regasification process."

I considered this for a moment. "OK…but what happens if there's a leak on the ship?"

"Not much. It usually just turns into gas and dissipates. Hang on… here's something. Two years ago there was a carrier that had a leak in the fuel storage system. The gas escaped and got ignited." I heard him suck in his breath. "Wow…a few people got pictures. I'll send them to you. It was a humongous fireball."

"That sounds dangerous."

"Not really. The tanker was out at sea and the gas is light, so it rose up above the ship. No one was hurt. Just a big fireball in the air. It went away within a few seconds."

I envisioned the two LNG storage tanks in the well behind the funnel turning into a huge fireball. "What are the dangers on a ship like ours that uses LNG?"

"I'm not seeing anything about problems with LNG on ships as fuel." More typing. "Can I get back to you tomorrow?"

I knew he'd spend his evening working on it, but still wanted to make sure he felt some urgency around it. "Bilbao was supposed to be a one-day stop. We're still here because we've had two engine problems in two days. I'm not sure they were accidents."

"Holy shit. You think someone is sabotaging your ship? Are you in danger?"

"I don't know. We've been told the mechanical problems were minor. If someone was sabotaging the ship, they did a lousy job of it. And I would think if there was any real risk, they'd get us off of it. But I know something is going on."

After over a decade together, Gideon trusted my Spidey Sense. "I'm on it."

"Hey, also, can you run some background on two more names for me. The guy whose last name you just found, Gorka Viteri," I paused, "and Ander Ibarra."

"OK. Are you looking for anything in particular?"

"Find out if they have any ties to the ETA."

"Roger Wilco."

We hung up. It was going to be hard to wait for more information. I didn't know if we were facing something violent, like bombs, or a drug smuggling operation, or both. And while the ship's mechanical problems seemed like a big fucking coincidence, there wasn't any hard evidence yet of sabotage. Getting some evidence of that would help tie things together.

I knew just where to start.

CHAPTER 26

I took the stairwell to deck four. It was late, and there were no people near the door to the lower decks we'd taken earlier on the engine tour. I walked over to the keypad and entered the four numbers I'd seen the doctor enter when I'd gone to get my stitches.

Nothing happened.

On a standard keypad there are ten thousand different combinations of a four-digit code. I was sure I'd seen him type in the numbers five, eight, and zero, but he'd shifted his hand while entering them, and the last number had been partially blocked from my view. I thought it was a six, but maybe it was a nine. I tried the combination again with a nine and heard a click as the lock opened. I opened the door and went into the stairwell.

I took the stairs softly down to the door leading to the crew's quarters on deck three and slowly opened it, peeking around. There were long corridors going in two different directions, each with a set of doors to the crew's rooms. The walls were white and shiny and blank, other than a large board with names and numbers near the door that looked like the duty roster. I moved closer to it and saw that next shift change was at five a.m.

I looked at my watch, it was 4:10. That meant the hallways would be filling up shortly. I needed to move fast.

I started to the right and walked quickly down the corridor, looking at the doors. Each door had a small sign on it with the crew members' names. There were two names on each door. There were about two hundred crew members on the ship, and with two to a room, that made one hundred rooms, minus the officers' quarters. That was a lot of rooms, and I didn't have a lot of time to find Gorka's room and search it before the corridors filled up again. I wasn't even sure all of the rooms were on this deck. But I figured I had about ten minutes to look, so got to it.

I continued down the corridor, running into a turn about every fifteen rooms. At each corner I stopped and listened for any sound of footsteps or doors opening before poking my head around. The floor was shiny like the walls, and my boots were making clicking sounds on it as I walked. I was moving slowly to limit the noise, but time was running out and I was getting impatient. I sped up, still trying to stay quiet. Without looking at my watch I knew I was cutting it close. I gave myself two more minutes to find his room and then get out of here.

Just before I got to another turn, I saw a door with G. Viteri/L. Salazar on the tag. Someone had crossed out L. Salazar and written *Mr. MOB* in pencil.

I knew Gorka was on shift right now. I didn't know about L. Salazar, who could be in the room sleeping or getting ready for his shift.

I waited, listening.

After a minute of hearing nothing, I tried the door handle. I wasn't surprised to find it locked, but it wouldn't be a problem. I was no stranger to breaking and entering.

As a kid I couldn't stand secrets, likely the result of growing up in a house with an alcoholic father and all of the deceit that entailed. In particular, locked doors drove me crazy. I'd downloaded the fifty-page *CIA Lock Picking Field Operative Training Manual*, that for some reason was publicly available, and taught myself how to pick locks. My parents thought it was cute when I opened locked doors in the house. They were less amused when I was returned home one night by the local PD who'd caught me breaking into a nearby restaurant. I was only eleven, and hadn't stolen anything, so they let me go with a warning. I was more careful from then on, getting caught only once more before I learned the three basic rules to avoid detection when I was trying to get into some place I wasn't supposed to be.

The first was to get really fast at picking locks. Lock picking is as much art as science, and developing the right feel for various locks comes with lots of repetition. I practiced over and over, on a variety of locked doors at home and at school until I could do it quickly, and in the dark.

The other two rules were standard B&E precautions, which were to act and dress as inconspicuously as possible, and be thorough with preparation. Thorough preparation meant, among other things, checking for any kind of surveillance. This was something I'd missed at the restaurant when the owners had seen me on a security camera. It also often included hours or sometimes days of surveillance to determine people's schedules and habits.

As an adult, I still viewed every locked door as a personal affront, and my compact Dangerfield lock pick set accompanied me everywhere I went. I pulled it out and picked Gorka's lock in under a minute.

I carefully opened the door, holding my breath. The room was empty and I exhaled, quickly closing the door behind me. It was small, just one set of bunkbeds, two sets of shelves built into the wall, a small shower, a toilet, and two tall standing lockers. One of the shelves held some pictures. I didn't recognize Gorka in any of them, so made the assumption that the other one was his. On top of the other shelf was a small wooden box. I opened it, finding a few pictures, one with Gorka and a couple of older people, probably his parents. I found a thin gold necklace with a small cross with an inscription on the back that was worn and faded.

I closed the box and moved to Gorka's dresser. Opening the drawers one by one, I quickly searched through the clothes. There was nothing there but a few sets of underwear and T-shirts. I put everything back into place and moved over to one of the lockers and opened it. Hanging inside was a set of white pants, a white crew shirt, and two empty hangers. On the floor was a set of white shoes. I got on my toes to reach the shelf above the hangers and swept my hand across it. Nothing.

I closed the locker door and opened the other one. Inside was a similar set of clothes and shoes. I swept my hand across the high shelf. There was something in the back. I couldn't see what it was so grabbed it and pulled it down.

It was a can of black spray paint. I couldn't be sure it was Gorka's, but I'd narrowed down the graffiti perpetrator to either him or his roommate Salazar.

There didn't seem to be anything else of interest, so after taking a picture of the can with my phone, I carefully placed it back where I'd found it and started to leave. I took one last look around the room and noticed a lump on one of the beds. They were tightly made, but one was bulging up in the middle. I lifted up the mattress to see a book underneath. As I was pulling it out from under the mattress, an envelope fell out. It wasn't sealed, and I looked into it.

It was full of money. I flipped through the bills and estimated it to be about five hundred euros. This must have been what I'd seen Boris hand to Gorka earlier. I took another picture, then put the bills back into the envelope and the envelope back into the book, and stuffed it under the mattress where I'd found it.

So Boris had paid Gorka. What for?

It occurred to me that what I *didn't* find was as revealing as what I did—there was no backpack in the room. This supported the theory that Boris's backpack was the one they'd found in the funnel. At least now I had something to work with. Boris had given Gorka money and the backpack that either had drugs or explosives in it. Now I needed to figure out what had been going on with the Charlie code. Going with the theory that Ander was lying, and that as Yanis had said, it was a bomb threat, who was behind it?

If there had been a bomb threat, the call would have come in just before the Charlie alert. Gideon would be able to track incoming calls to the ship during that time, and if he could link it to a call coming either from inside the ship or, ideally, to Boris, Gorka, or Salazar's cell phones, that would seal the deal. That, plus the can of paint, should be convincing enough evidence for Ballsy to identify who was responsible. Even with his epic level of incompetence he wouldn't be able to ignore all of this.

I looked at my watch—4:45. There was nothing else here and it was past time for me to leave. I needed to get out to call Gideon and get him to start looking into the ship's calls.

I opened the room door a tiny bit and peeked out. No one was in sight, so I stepped out of the room. I walked back around the hallways the way I'd come in, and eventually came to the one with the stairwell. I was near the door to the upper decks and started to relax.

"Hey!"

Damn. Missed it by *that* much. I looked behind me. One of the crew was standing at the other end of the hall. I turned and walked quickly to the stairwell door.

"*Hey!*"

If I could get to the stairs and up to deck five, I could get lost in the casino, which would be crowded at this hour. Maybe he hadn't gotten a good look at my face.

I made it to the door, threw it open, and rushed up the stairs, reaching the second step before running smack into another crew member. A very large one. He was apologetic, and started to move out of my way, when the one at the end of the corridor yelled at him in Spanish. I was almost past him when the big guy firmly grabbed my upper arm. I tried to get loose but he had no trouble keeping me in place while the other man caught up to us. Even if I'd been able to get out of his grip, he was blocking the whole stairwell. There was no way I could get by him.

"Hey, listen, this is a misunderstanding. I heard the trepidarium was down here. Can you guys point me in the right direction?"

They talked to each other in Spanish. Then the smaller one said,

"You please come with us."

They were polite, but the big one didn't relax his hold of my arm. They walked me down the corridor to a room with no names on it.

"You please wait here." They opened the door to the room and gently but firmly urged me in and closed the door, not before confiscating my phone.

I waited a few minutes until I couldn't hear them anymore and tried the door. It was locked.

I was in the brig.

CHAPTER 27

This wasn't the first jail I'd ever been in, but it was definitely the nicest. The brig was basically a remodeled crew's quarters room, the main difference that the lock was on the outside instead of on the inside. It wasn't exactly max security, but I guessed there probably wasn't a lot of serious criminal activity on a cruise ship, other than the occasional unruly drunk and elderly drug smugglers.

Comfortable or not, I didn't have time for this. I eyed the door. It wouldn't be any harder to pick the lock from the inside than it had been from the outside, but I could hear there was someone standing guard in the hallway. I lay back on the bed and waited, thinking about how this would have turned out differently if Ander had just done the right thing and had sex with me.

I must have fallen asleep, and woke to a sharp knock on the door. The knocker didn't wait for me to answer. The door opened and the first officer, Inigo, stepped inside. Another crew member stood behind him. It was Ballsy, who was making no attempt to hide his abject glee at my incarceration.

Inigo was very thin and tall compared to the other crew members. His face was clean shaven, pale, and gaunt, he'd completely nailed the cadaverous look. And *Love Boat* Ichabod Crane was not happy. "Dr. O'Hara, I am sorry we have to meet under these circumstances. Do you want to tell me what you were doing on the crew deck? I am sure you know that the lower four decks are off limits to passengers."

I'd seen Inigo talking alone to Ander on the deck the second day, and he'd been in his room earlier tonight with Ander and Gorka. Was he in on whatever was going on? That might explain why something as trivial as wandering around the crew's quarters would warrant what seemed like such a militant response. Or maybe Ballsy had told him I was a suspicious character, and they thought I was responsible for placing the backpack in the storage well.

Mr. Rodentia Face was almost giddy, and chimed in. "I would also like to know how you gained access to these floors. As I am sure you are aware the entrance requires a code."

While I was formulating a response, there was a throat clearing sound from the hallway. All three of us looked over.

It was the captain. Inigo and Ballsy immediately turned and walked out, closing the door behind them.

I moved closer, and could hear the captain and Inigo talking through the door. I didn't hear Ballsy. He wasn't part of the discussion, probably still in the captain's doghouse for missing the backpack during the search.

Inigo and the captain were actually having a conversation, which was a little strange, as in all the interactions I'd observed between the crew and captain, it had been a one-way exchange.

They were speaking Euskara, and while I couldn't understand a word of what they were saying, I imagined it was something like this:

"First Officer, we must let this lady go."

"But, sir, she is no lady, and she was caught on a restricted deck. We must interrogate her until she talks."

"Yes, but she is not only one of our passengers, she is a Neptune Suite guest. We must do everything we can to make her trip as wonderful as possible. Staying in this little room is not wonderful. And there is no designer furniture."

"But she might be doing something nefarious!"

"Everyone on this cruise is fabulously wealthy, so they have spent their lives doing something nefarious. Besides, isn't it enough that

she has to suffer by being trapped with many people for ten days, and endure the very high risk of catching norovirus?"

"Can we at least lock her in a room for a few hours with the tiny ugly dog?"

"No, that is a fate worse than death. And it is not a dog. It is a rat."

"Are you sure? I believe it is a dog. Why would the pretty lady bring a pet rat on board?"

"I do not know. The fabulously wealthy have strange habits. But if it is a dog, it is the ugliest dog in the universe."

The discussion ended, and I could hear someone walk away. The door to the room opened.

Inigo and Ballsy were both standing in the hallway, making no move to reenter the room. Inigo said stiffly, "Against my and the security officer's recommendation, the captain has decided that you will not face any consequences for accessing the restricted areas." Ballsy was red-faced and looked furious. I considered offering him some cheese.

I started to walk out, but Inigo blocked the doorway. "Before you leave, we must make sure you did not take anything. Please empty your pockets."

I privately breathed a sigh of relief that I hadn't taken the envelope with the money in it. I turned my pockets inside out and gave Inigo my jacket. He handed it to Ballsy, who went through it thoroughly, taking way more time than he needed to verify that I hadn't taken anything. Thankfully, he didn't attempt a body search, as I'd stuffed my lockpicks back into my boot. Still, it was creepy to have him touch my stuff. I'd have to wash and sterilize everything thoroughly.

When they finished going through my things, Inigo handed me back my phone, and stepped aside so I could leave the room. The two of them walked me out, one on each side, leading me down the corridor to the stairwell door and escorting me up the stairs to deck four.

When we got to the door Inigo opened it and faced me, his voice serious. "You are free to go. I do not know how you acquired the passcode for this entrance, but realize it will be changed by the security officer within the hour. Please do not do this again. If you do, you will spend the remainder of the cruise in the brig."

They turned around and went back down the stairs, closing the door securely behind them.

DAY 8

CHAPTER 28

When I got back to our room it was almost eight. The first thing to do was to call Gideon and get him working on tracing the bomb threat call. I caught him just before he was going to sleep, and he told me he'd get to it first thing in the morning.

It seemed pointless to go to bed. Sam wasn't up yet, but I needed some fresh air, so I walked up to the pool deck for coffee. At the railing I looked out over the water toward the mouth of the bay. The *Petris* LNG carrier was turning into the Bizkaia regasification plant terminal. It would dock soon, and we'd be on our way by the next morning.

Even from this far away I could see the ship was huge. I always had a hard time judging distance and size on the water, but the ship was at least a thousand feet long. There were four white domes, the LNG storage tanks, that took up most of the top of the ship. I could see why they'd restricted the shipping lanes while this thing was coming in. If anything caused those gigantic tanks to blow, it would be the mother of all explosions.

I leaned against the railing for an hour drinking coffee. I needed it. Other than the short nap in the brig, I hadn't slept in almost twenty-four hours. That, along with two bouts of head trauma, had me running on fumes. I looked longingly at the lounge chairs but resisted the urge to sit down. I could sleep later.

I looked at my watch. It was nine o'clock. Sam was usually a morning person, and I was a little surprised she wasn't on the pool deck yet. I headed back to our suite, telling myself I was getting a little worried about her, but was really just impatient to talk to her about what I'd seen in Gorka's room.

The door to her room was still closed, so I knocked. She answered in her robe, looking sleepy. She was alone, but her clothes were everywhere, along with two empty wine bottles, glasses, and a completely destroyed bed. At least one of us had gotten lucky last night.

"Alejandro or Valeria?" I asked her.

She raised an eyebrow.

"Both?"

She smiled.

"I hope you used protection, but if not, I can't wait to see your kids." I went in and leaned against the wall.

She walked to her small room kitchen and poured us both a cup of coffee. "How did you make out?"

"I didn't get lucky, but I did spend the night in another bed." I gave her a quick summary of my evening.

"Why do you think they let you go?" She was sitting on the bed, looking up at the ceiling. It was a little disconcerting that she wasn't more surprised I'd spent the night in the brig.

"I don't know. They probably don't want to lock up their luxury guests. Maybe it's a perk of the Neptune Suite, one get out of jail free card. How about you? What did you learn last night?"

"Well, for one thing, I'm way more flexible than I thought I was."

I looked up, confused. Then, "No, I mean what did you learn from Hugo? About the engine problems?"

"Oh. He confirmed that it was nothing serious. Somehow two of the electrical cables from one of the engines were broken."

I recalled from Paloma's engine tour that cabling can be a weak point in a ship's distribution system if it's not backed up. All of the major electrical cables on the ship were backed up. "Wait…*two* cables?"

"Yes. And normally it only takes a few hours to fix. But—"

"Yeah, I know. They have a no-fly rule when the LNG ships are coming in, and we missed our window. That's why we had to stay in port longer. Did he sound like it was something out of the ordinary?"

"Well, now that you mention it, he said he'd never seen it happen before, two cables from the same engine both broken at the same time."

"Kind of like it might have been done on purpose?"

"He didn't say that," she said quietly. She didn't like where this was going.

I didn't relish bringing her down from her post-awesome-sex-with beautiful-people high, but I needed her help. "He wouldn't. The last thing they need is the passengers thinking there's a saboteur on board."

"A saboteur? Is that what you think?"

"I'm getting there. Did you find out anything else from Hugo?"

"He told me who the man overboard was. As Ander told you, it was a member of the crew. Luix Salazar."

L. Salazar. Gorka's roommate. "Mr. MOB."

"Yes." She gave me a funny look. "How do you know that term, Mr. MOB?"

"Someone wrote it over his name plate on his room door. What does it mean?"

"It's gallows humor. Cruise ship crews often refer to the man overboard as Mr. MOB. Not very funny in this case, given that he's dead."

Out of two hundred crew members, Gorka's roommate goes overboard? No way this was a coincidence. Someone was willing to kill people to do whatever it was they were going to do. Shit was getting very real, very fast.

"Do they know what happened to him?" I asked.

"I don't know. And there's one more thing. They found black paint on his hands. They think he was responsible for the graffiti."

No huge shock there. I'd found the can of paint in his room. And it made sense that if Gorka was involved, his roommate would be too. But they'd pulled Salazar out of the water *before* the mechanical problems. There was more to this whole thing than Luix Salazar.

"Did Hugo tell you anything else?"

"No. I imagine the ship's officers aren't too eager to share all of the details with the crew, and especially not with the passengers. I doubt most of them would care anyway."

I walked to the bed and handed my cup to her. "I know someone who cares."

It was time to see the captain.

CHAPTER 29

I called Ben. When he arrived I asked if he could arrange a private meeting with the captain. An hour later he came back to our room and said the captain would be able to speak with me for a few minutes before lunch.

Ben came to our suite at the appointed time and escorted me to the captain's cabin. He politely knocked at the door. The captain opened it and gestured me in. Ben left, and the captain closed the door softly behind him.

The captain's quarters were spacious, including a full bath and a large kitchen, an office, a bedroom, a living room area, and a dining room with a table that looked big enough to hold at least ten people. There were two doors leading out, one to the hallway with the elevator from which we had just come, and the other that I presumed went directly to the bridge. This made sense, as if he was sleeping and there was a problem, he could be on the bridge within seconds.

The captain took a seat on the couch in his living area. He tried to smile at me and failed. I'd already cost him a trip to the brig, and I recognized the "you're the one that's going to be the biggest pain in my ass" look on his face. Something between a frown and a grimace. I'd seen it many times before, often on the faces of my employers.

"Yes, Dr. O'Hara, how can I help you?"

I took a seat across from him in one of the chairs. "I think we're all in danger. Someone is sabotaging the ship. I think the ETA is behind it."

He looked surprised, then his face relaxed into a small smile and he leaned back into the couch. "The ETA? The ETA is over. They have not been a threat for years. I know Americans are very worried about terrorism, but there is nothing going on with the ETA anymore. Every now and then there are some minor protests, but they are small and completely nonviolent."

"Yes, I know. But there was the graffiti, and the engine problems—"

He cut me off. "Those were minor problems that caused very little damage. They were easily fixed. I am not happy that someone defaced our ship, but a little graffiti is nothing to be afraid of."

I didn't like being cut off. "What about the bomb threat? And the backpack with the explosives?" I went with my hunch that it was explosives and not drugs they'd found in the backpack. If I was wrong, I'd be able to tell by his reaction.

He looked shocked. "How do you know about that?"

Bingo. Bomb threat and explosives in the backpack confirmed. I tried not to look too satisfied.

"Dr. O'Hara, this is very serious. You are fortunate that we have already determined who was responsible, otherwise you would be a suspect."

"You did? Who was it?" Knowing who was in charge of security, I was dubious that they'd managed to figure that out, although it would be a huge relief if true.

He looked at me stonily. "That is not for me to share. In any case, the matter is closed. We know who was behind it and he is no longer a threat."

What? "Wait…you're not talking about Luix Salazar, are you?"

His shocked look confirmed again that I was right. This time he didn't bother asking me how I knew about it. He just stared at me.

I tried not to sound frustrated, and failed miserably. "He wasn't even *alive* when the mechanical problems happened. I saw—"

He cut me off again. "As I told you before, the mechanical problems were very minor. Please, Dr. O'Hara, leave the ship security to us."

He was being condescending, and I was getting irritated. "You mean Ballsy?"

"*Balasy*, yes."

"Good luck with that. Your security officer has the IQ of a rhesus monkey. He's a brain stem in a uniform. So far, we've had a bomb threat, two probably sabotage events, drug smuggling, and a man overboard. And he's been following *me*, for fuck's sake. So whoever is behind all of this, the likelihood that Ballsy's going to be the one who figures it out is about the same as the likelihood that you and I are going to hook up and produce a love child."

We both cringed at that visual. I didn't know where it came from, sometimes it felt like my mouth was completely unconnected to my brain. I struggled to get the horrifying image out of my mind. *Puppies and bunnies...puppies and bunnies...the one hundredth decimal place of Pi...Ander in the shower...*

I took a big breath. OK now.

The captain had to be aware that in comparison to Ballsy, Barney Fife would be a candidate for the American Mensa Committee. I pressed on. "Look, *sir*, members of your crew are meeting with passengers under what look like suspicious circumstances. Most of them are from the Basque region, and I've seen—"

He cut me off again. I was very quickly moving from irritated to angry.

"Dr. O'Hara. You will please *not* speak to me about my crew. It is bad enough you have been caught sneaking around where you are not supposed to be. You are a passenger and our guest, but I will not tolerate any talk about the conduct of this crew. There was one bad apple, and he is gone. Given what has transpired, I suggest you pay more attention to your own behavior."

I couldn't believe he was dismissing me like that. I ramped things up. "You have to admit it's kind of an unbelievable coincidence, *don't you*, that we've had not one but *two* engine problems? And that one of your crew went over the side and is now dead? You think he was acting alone? That's not even taking into account the protests at *every single port* we've been to. I can't *believe* you can't see—"

"That is enough!" His face had become dark red. It was very striking against the bright white of his uniform. Like the Swiss flag. "We are done here." I noted a slight increase in volume, and his tone was deeper. He was using his Captain Voice.

"*Done?*" The Captain Voice had no power over me. I was just getting started. And while I realized at this point it was probably a lost cause, I couldn't give it up. I got louder to match him. "You must be kidding. Are you *blind?* Your ship is being sabotaged and some of your crew are involved. There is a—"

"Please leave." He pointed to the door.

I really, really hate being cut off. Especially when I'm right. This wasn't a new situation for me, and I knew exactly what to do.

"Listen, Ahab, the captain of the *Titanic* called. He wants his inevitable disaster back."

Sarcasm. That's the ticket. "You should rename this thing the *Minnow*. I'll bet there's a huge market for three-hour tours."

He got up from the couch and moved toward his desk, reaching under it.

"This will be awesome for you the next time you run into Captain Phillips. You two will have lots to talk about."

He stayed behind his desk, looking toward the door.

I heard it open but didn't turn around. "Let me guess. Competition for this year's Hazelwood Award is fierce."

I was running out of famous maritime disaster captains, but was saved by the entrance of two very large crew members. They were both over six feet tall and built like body builders. Impossibly large biceps bulged out from their short-sleeved uniforms. I looked in vain for their necks.

The captain nodded to them, and as they walked toward me, he said, "As a result of the delays the ship has experienced, we will be missing two of the last three ports of call. You will all be receiving refunds and vouchers for that, but I hope the extra time in Bilbao has been to your liking." Now that he had things under control, he calmed down. and was no longer using the Captain Voice, although his face retained its bright red hue. "Enjoy the rest of your cruise and let us worry about keeping everyone safe. And please stay out of my brig." He nodded again to the Twin Terminators who took up positions on both sides of me. Clearly my work there was done.

I expected them to just escort me out of his cabin, but they walked me all the way to my suite and stood waiting until I opened the door. As I walked in I gave them a salute. "Thanks, guys. It's been real. Take it easy on the steroids. It's hard on the boys, if you know what I mean." I was pretty sure that gelding had left the barn. I closed the door, wondering if they'd be out there the next time I left the suite.

Sam was sitting on the couch, holding a sleeping Chaz on her lap. She looked at my face. Tilting her head to the side, she said, "I'm going to go out on a limb and guess the captain didn't appreciate your concerns." She looked up at the Amelie clock on the wall. "Hmmm… let's see if I can recreate what happened. You spent two minutes telling him what was going on, and when he didn't immediately catch on and agree with you, you spent the rest of the time insulting him." She knew my standard approach with people in authority.

"Yeah, in retrospect, maybe it would have been better for you to talk to him." This wasn't the first time I'd gotten frustrated and sabotaged my own communication efforts.

"You don't make it easy for people. Not everyone picks things up as quickly as you do." This was Sam's positive spin on the cesspool of traits that made up my personality.

"I did get confirmation that there was a bomb threat, and that it was explosives they found in the backpack. And whether the captain sees it or not doesn't change the fact that someone is doing something to this ship. And it's not over. He thinks it was all Luix Salazar, the man who went overboard. But I know Boris and Gorka are still up to something." I didn't want to mention Ander out loud.

I pulled out my phone. Nothing yet from Gideon, so I called him.

He answered after ten rings, sounding sleepy. "I know you can do math. It's four a.m. here."

"Things are heating up. Do you have anything for me?"

"I'm still looking into a few things."

"Can you send what you have now?"

"Sure. Night." He hung up.

I sat down on the Eichholtz and waited, checking my email every few seconds. A few minutes later the one from Gideon arrived with an attachment. It was big and took a while to download.

Sam had gotten up from the couch, setting Chaz gently back down on one of my shirts that I'd left there. I thought it was her way of getting me to pick up my things, given that we both knew he would chew it to pieces as soon as he woke up. She picked up her bag and headed to the door. "Do you mind if I leave you to this? Tatiana and I are going to meet at the gallery and then have lunch together. It would be great if you could join us for lunch, we'll be at the Basque restaurant on deck seven."

"I'll see how it goes." I was already reading the report and didn't look up when she left the suite.

CHAPTER 30

As usual, Gideon had been fast and thorough. Included in his report, topped off with what I feared would be a permanent baby and space shuttle logo, was a summary of LNG, the Bilbao regasification plant, the history of LNG carriers and LNG-fueled ships, and a treatise on the risks associated with LNG.

He'd also looked into the calls to the ship around the time of the security alert. A call had come in during that window of time. The origin was a pre-paid burn phone, and while he couldn't tell whose it was, he could tell it had originated from our ship. I wasn't surprised. The captain had essentially confirmed for me we'd had a bomb threat. But it was useful to know it had come from somewhere on the ship.

I skimmed through the rest of the report quickly. At the end were a few pages about the crew and passengers. He'd looked into any possible ETA connection, and found nothing on Inigo. Gorka was a little more interesting. Similar to Zuzan, the bat-swinging thug, he had some ETA associates. But nothing linking him personally to any action, or any criminal history. I'd need to ask Gideon to also check on Luix Salazar.

There was nothing about Boris. That must have been the part Gideon was still working on. I was surprised and a little relieved to see nothing about Ander. I wasn't sure I wanted confirmation about him being a bad guy just yet.

I went back to the beginning of the report and read through again more deliberately. In terms of LNG safety, it looked like opinions varied depending on who you talked to. The LNG industry touted itself as one of the cleanest and safest forms of energy available. That looked to be true, although there were a small group of dedicated opponents who believed it posed enormous risk. These groups pointed to a few accidents that had resulted in numerous casualties.

Digging in, I realized there was really only one notable LNG disaster, and it had happened in the forties. A plant in Cleveland had blown up, causing explosions that leveled a square mile of the city. Hundreds of people died and many more suffered burns. It was a terrible tragedy, but it had happened seventy years ago. The safety systems had been massively upgraded since then. I moved on.

The carriers themselves didn't appear to be that vulnerable. Every LNG carrier was required to develop and implement a threat-scalable security plan that established things like access control measures, security measures for cargo handling and delivery of fuel, surveillance and monitoring, security incident procedures, and training requirements. The plan also had to identify a Ship Security Officer responsible for ensuring compliance with the ship's security plan. This seemed extensive, but I made a note to myself to have Gideon look into the *Petris*'s security officer.

He'd included information about the Gastech conference. As Mattin had told us earlier, it was the leading exhibition and conference for oil and gas industries. Anybody who played any role in the global energy value chain attended this conference, including major NOCs (national oil companies), IOCs (international oil companies), integrated energy companies, global utilities, contractors, shipbuilders, pipeline companies, manufacturers, technology providers, and service companies. About forty thousand people attended every year.

This was all helpful background, and explained the crowded restaurants in Bilbao, but it resulted in more questions for me than answers. If the ETA was engaged in some kind of action, what were they doing? It didn't look like our ship was in danger, and it was hard to see how a largely defunct terrorist organization could pull off any significant action against a tightly secured energy plant. The captain had been right about that. Gideon's report included an entire section on plant and carrier security, including identifying potential terrorist actions and the steps taken to mitigate that risk. The industry had recognized the possibility that plants could make good targets for terrorists, and there was a lot of proactive planning that addressed a variety of contingencies. Again, all very interesting, but nothing that shed any light on what might be going on with our ship.

I thought back to what I'd seen in Ander's room. They'd been looking at some papers together. I wanted a look at those papers.

I checked the time and put my phone away. I left the suite quietly, heading for the stairwell, hoping that Chaz could continue to sleep through my absence, and I might avoid losing another T-shirt.

I knew all of the suite doors opened with electronic key cards, but it was midday, when the cleaning crews were working the suites. I would get one of the maids to let me in to Ander's room. I didn't expect it would be too hard.

I walked down the stairwell to the seventh floor and opened the door. The floor housed twenty suites in two hallways that made an L shape. The concierge station was at the juncture of those two hallways. As I expected, there was a maid crew cleaning the suites. And while I didn't have a master key card, I was confident in my ability to talk one of the maids into letting me into Ander's suite.

Unfortunately, I hadn't counted on the custom security measures on this cruise. As Sam had noted, there were few cameras in the passenger suite halls, done to accommodate the camera-shy nature of the ship's uber-wealthy passengers. This was helpful to me in that I wouldn't be caught on camera sneaking around. But in an effort to offset the lack of cameras, they'd restricted access to the suites. As they finished cleaning each suite, I saw the maids close the door and signal to the concierge, who opened up the next one. None of the maids themselves had key cards. Not only that, but the concierge would have no trouble seeing me go into Ander's room. From his station he only had to slightly turn his head to see every single room on the floor.

Dammit. Even if I could figure a way to distract the concierge, I would still need a way to break open a magnetic key card lock.

One problem at a time. I looked at my watch. It was almost one, which meant six a.m. in Chicago. Gideon was probably up by now.

I went back up the stairwell to our suite and called him.

"You're lucky I'm a morning person." Gideon sounded way better than he had at four in the morning. "But I don't have any information on Boris yet. I've been, you know, sleeping for the last two hours."

"I know. I'm sorry. I owe you." I gave him a quick overview about the man overboard, the explosion at the Palacio, and what I'd seen in Ander's room. "I need to get in there. Do you know anything about hacking hotel keys?"

"You mean the key cards?"

"Yeah, the suite doors all have those card reader things where you put in the card with the magnetic strip."

"Hacking hotel keycards is actually fairly easy. You just need a few components…" he paused, "…that you probably don't have." He went silent for a moment.

I was impatient, but had learned over time that it was best to wait him out when he needed to think.

"Does your room have any motion detection lights? Or anything activated by motion?"

"I don't think so. It's all designer-this and designer-that, and everything's got a switch."

"Hmmm…"

I waited.

"Is there anything that requires your fingerprints to be scanned? Or any kind of robotics?"

"No and no. There's a safe with a lock, and the keycard for the door entry. Everything else looks pretty low-tech."

He paused again, longer this time. Then, "Is there a makerspace on board?"

"What's a makerspace?"

"It's a collaborative workspace. They often have them in schools and libraries for kids to explore technology. Depending on the venue, they'll have some really high-tech tools like 3D printers and soldering irons. Lots of hotels and resorts are starting to offer them. Some cities even have mobile ones, vans that drive around to different neighborhoods. They bring it to kids who normally wouldn't have the opportunity to play with technology."

That sounded like a pedophile's dream, but I assumed Gideon would know about that if it were a problem. "Hold on." Like a hotel, the ship had a binder that described all of its amenities. I pulled it out of the coffee table drawer and quickly scanned through the pages.

"Yeah, here it is. Deck six." Of course this ship had a makerspace. It had everything.

"Look through the description of what's in it, and see if the word 'Arduino' is listed."

I flipped to the makerspace page and skimmed it. "Yeah, it's here. 'Full suite of Arduino kits and components.'"

"OK. All you need to create a hotel master key card is an Arduino microcontroller, a battery, a switch, and a DC connector. If the makerspace has Arduino kits, they'll have those components. Once you have them, we'll just pop some code into the controller and you'll be good to go."

"How will I know what they look like?" I didn't know how to identify a DC connector, and was sure I'd never seen an Arduino before.

"I can send you images of each piece. After you get them, call me back and I'll tell you how to put them together."

I couldn't believe that was all there was to it, but Gideon had never steered me wrong.

"Are you going to tell me what you're up to?"

"Later. Bye." I hung up and headed down to deck six.

***

There were only a few kids on board and no activity right now in the makerspace. Gideon's pictures were helpful, and I had no trouble identifying the components. He was right, they were all there, along with a bewildering array of other things, most of which I didn't recognize. I was a whiz with math but had little interest in developing my technical skills. I had Gideon for that.

I pocketed the components and headed back to our suite and called him back. He walked me through the assembly, and we spent another half hour inputting the code into the microcontroller. It was a little scary how easy it was. I made a mental note to never again leave anything of value in a hotel room unless it was in a locked safe. Not too difficult for me, as I had few things of value, or at least of value to other people.

I was a little skeptical that it would actually work. "It's hard to believe it's this easy,"

"Believe it, although there's probably only a short window of time where this is going to work anywhere. This hack was discovered just last year by a guy who put it on the internet. Made the keycard companies really mad. They'd installed millions of these things all over the planet, and it will take a while for them to be retrofitted. The hacker took a lot of flak for not talking to the companies first before sharing it online with the world."

"Yeah, that seems like kind of a dick move."

"I can kind of see his point though. If a company knew about it, they probably would have done everything in their power to keep him from publicizing it. This way, at least people checking into hotel rooms can know to keep their things safe until the room locks are retrofitted. Even so, I'm a little surprised they didn't retrofit your ship right away. Isn't it supposed to be the best of the best?"

I wasn't surprised at all. "Rich people are used to keeping their valuables in safes when they stay in hotels. And it's unlikely this clientele includes many thieves. At least not the kind that break into rooms. Should I test it first?"

"Yeah, they don't work on all keycard systems."

"What? Now you tell me." But I plugged the connector into our own door and heard a satisfying *click* almost immediately. "It worked! Thanks, Gideon."

"Great! It's actually a pretty cool little hack. It basically takes the code from the existing systems, and reads it back to itself. Very—"

"Gotta go. I'll let you know how things shake out." I didn't have time to learn how the fucking thing actually worked. I packed up my little system and headed back down to deck seven.

CHAPTER 31

The deck seven concierge was still at his station. As before, he would see me as soon as I stepped out of the stairwell. I'd come up with a solution to that while we were putting together the Arduino thing.

I walked out into the hallway and waved at the concierge. He watched me warily but waved back. I went straight to suite 702 and knocked.

The door opened. "*Jesse!*"

"Hey, Trish. How are you?"

"I'm *great*!" She ushered me into the room.

My ears were already ringing. It hadn't been hard to find their suite. I knew they were on this floor and all I had to do was follow the shouting.

"Can I get you something to drink?" She was bursting with enthusiasm, her smile impossibly wide.

"Sure, thanks."

She bustled into the kitchen, and I sat down on the couch and looked around. Trish was by herself; John must have stepped out, likely to some place quiet. Their suite was similar to ours but considerably smaller, and took up only one floor. There was a large living area filled with designer furniture, a bedroom and master bathroom, a bar, and a kitchen. The balcony was a quarter the size of ours. Like ours and every other suite, it had the Ming steward call units placed conveniently in each room to summon their floor's concierge. I'd been counting on that.

Trish came back out from the kitchen carrying a tray, on which was a bottle of wine and an opener, a glass of what looked like whiskey, and a bottle of Guinness, along with a bowl of salty snacks.

"Jameson and Guinness, right?" she yelled at me, setting the tray on the coffee table.

"Uh...yeah, thanks," I said, picking up the beer. I wondered how she knew.

She opened the wine. After pouring herself a glass, she raised it to me, and we toasted.

"I'm so happy to see you! How is your cruise going?"

"It's been great. How about you?"

"It's wonderful! I love Spain!"

I realized if I wanted to save my hearing, I'd need to do more of the talking. "Yeah, me too. We saw the Guggenheim. It was fantastic. And the food has been terrific." I shared the details of our meals.

She hung on my every word, refilling my whiskey and going to the kitchen for more beer when I finished the first one.

She was polite about my descriptions of Bilbao, but very eager to know more about my business. Leaning forward, she asked, "What's your next case going to be?"

"I'm, uh, not sure. I didn't help myself too much with the last one."

"Why not? You're terrific on the stand!"

"Well, the prosecutors pay me to be unemotional, and I kind of blew it with the baby and space shuttle comment. I haven't had much business since that trial." Actually, no business, but I didn't want to tell her that.

"Oh." She looked disappointed, but it only lasted a moment, then she brightened. "That's OK! You'll find something else! Whatever it is, I hope they put you on TV!"

I was starting to feel bad that I'd disappointed her by losing my business, even though she appeared to get over it in a few seconds. She seemed to be a terminally positive person. I wondered what that would be like. It made my head hurt even trying to imagine it.

"What do you do when you're not cruising?" I asked, momentarily forgetting that I wanted to keep her yelling to a minimum.

"We own a real estate business, but John does most of that! I spend most of my time doing volunteer work!"

I hadn't seen that coming. Trish had a little more going on than I'd realized. "With who?"

"SOS Children's Villages and GirlForward!"

Two solid Chicago nonprofits focused on foster kid support and refugee girls empowerment. *Huh.* "That's great, Trish." I was starting to like her. But my ears were ringing, and I needed to get out of there and into Ander's room. I looked around. "Can we go out to the balcony?"

"Of course!"

We grabbed our drinks and walked out. "It's so beautiful!" Trish was leaning against the railing, looking out over the bay. "I love to come out here and look at the water. I do it every day!" She was still shouting but it was less of an issue outside, and I decided to let her talk for a few minutes, although if the word "cerulean" came out of her mouth, I'd have to push her overboard.

While she continued to talk about the view, I finished both of my drinks and waited for her to notice, which she did almost immediately.

"Can I get you another?" she offered.

"Sure, thanks."

She left the balcony and headed for the kitchen. When she turned her back, I took the Ming call unit I'd pocketed from her living room table and heaved it as far as I could out into the water. If there'd been a first basemen eighty-four feet out I would have hit the center of the mitt.

Within thirty seconds there was a knock at the door to the suite. Trish left the kitchen to open it. As I'd hoped, it was the seventh-floor concierge.

"Hi, Vicente!"

"Hello, Mrs. Henderson. I am sorry to bother you, but my station console indicates that there might be a problem with one of your call units. Do you mind if I look at it?"

All of the concierge stations were equipped with consoles paired with the Ming call units in the suites. When a unit button was pushed, the light associated with the corresponding suite number would light up on the console. It would also notify the concierge if the unit malfunctioned or, for whatever reason, stopped sending signals. Like if it was out of range. Or under sixty feet of water.

She looked over at me. "That's no problem, Trish. I need to get going anyway. Thanks for the drinks." I put my glass on the table.

"No, thank you! Let's do this again sometime!" She made a "call me" sign with her hand.

As I walked out, I took one last look into the room. Trish was following Vicente as he looked for the living room call unit. His back was turned, but she looked back and gave me a conspiratorial wink.

Well then. She knew I'd done something to bring in the concierge, and was playing along. She was loud but no dummy. I winked back at her and left the room, closing the door.

I fast-walked four doors down to Ander's suite and stopped in front of his door, listening. I waited one minute and, not hearing anything, plugged in the Arduino controller and heard the door click open. *Wow. Very cool.*

I'd already decided what I would say to Ander if he was in the room. That I'd wanted to see him, and when I'd knocked on his door it had accidentally opened, having been not shut completely by him or the maid the last time they'd used it.

But the room was empty. I was relieved. I don't enjoy lying, and I hate liars, probably because I grew up with one.

I closed the door softly. The papers I'd seen the other night on the low table were gone. I'd need to look around.

I started with the bedroom. On the floor next to the bed was a briefcase. It was unlocked. I found some blank paper, pens, and a number of journal articles about law enforcement. They looked fairly technical. I sighed. Ander wasn't just another pretty face.

Not finding anything interesting, I went to the closet. It wasn't a walk-in like ours, but it was large, with two oversized sliding doors. There were several suit jackets and pants hanging up. I leaned in to flip through them. They smelled like Ander. Earthy and clean, with a slight hint of the sea. I looked wistfully back at the bed, wondering what it would have been like to spend the night here with him. Probably really great.

I forced myself to stop thinking about him and get back to it. I had no idea where he was or when he'd return, and I didn't want to get caught going through his stuff.

I was looking at his shoes and starting to close the door when I saw something leaning against the back of the closet. It was a tube of papers with a rubber band around them.

I pulled out the tube and took off the rubber band, unrolling the papers on the bed. It was a set of blueprints. The top page was the ship's main control room, with a hand-drawn circle in red pen around one of the components. It was the fuel gauge; I assumed the same one that had needed repair. Flipping through the pages, I found another one with markings. The schematics on this page were of one of the engine rooms, the crude marks were near the wall on lines that went from one room to the next. Likely the cabling that had been broken.

This was pretty convincing indication of sabotage, and Ander had clearly played a role in it. I pulled out my phone and took pictures of the two pages, and then quickly flipped through the rest of them to see if there were any other marks signaling future or as-yet undiscovered engine problems. There was one other near the funnel on deck twelve, next to where the backpack with the bomb had been placed. I took a picture of it.

Not seeing any other marked pages, I rolled the papers back up and put the rubber band around them.

I debated taking the blueprints with me and showing them to the captain. Even if he would agree to see me, which was doubtful, how convincing would they be? He could think I'd put them together myself. And while they'd blamed the whole thing on Luix Salazar, Ballsy was still itching to link shit to me.

Or worse, what if the captain was in on it? There was a good chance all of this was related to the ETA, and he was Basque too. Maybe he'd dismissed my concerns not because I was a pain in his ass, but because he was in on it.

Whatever I was going to do, I needed to get out of Ander's suite right away. I had proof that he was definitely involved in something, and he wouldn't take kindly to finding me there. He didn't seem like the dangerous type, but one guy was already dead, and I didn't want to find out about Ander's dark side up close and personal in a private space.

I put the blueprints back into the closet, taking care to put them exactly as I'd found them, and closed the closet doors. I walked out, giving one last look around the room before opening the door to the hallway. I peeked around to make sure the concierge was still busy in the Henderson's suite. The hallway was clear, and I could still hear him talking to Trish. Well, I could hear her talking to him. I said a silent prayer for the loss of his hearing and walked quickly back to the stairwell. Once I was inside, I leaned up against the door and let out a long breath I hadn't realized I'd been holding.

I was blinking back tears. *What the fuck.*

Lack of sleep and multiple head traumas all caught up with me at once. I slumped down to the floor and wiped my eyes with my shirt. I hadn't realized how much I'd started to like Ander. He was warm, thoughtful, smart, and really grounded. In many ways the opposite of me. And he had the one other essential quality—he seemed to like me back. But I'd found definitive proof that he was mixed up in something dangerous and criminal, which meant that he was not only not Mr. Right, or even Mr. Right Now, but instead, Mr. Never, and possibly, Mr. Terrorist Who is Doing Something that Might be Putting Everyone in Danger for Reasons I Don't Know Yet.

I felt like I'd been punched in the stomach. Not just that a potential relationship was no longer on the table, but also because now I was questioning my own judgment. I prided myself on reading people and noticing things. *How had I missed this?*

I mentally reviewed our interactions to-date. My recollection of our conversations was uncharacteristically incomplete, although I realized I could recall in vivid detail exactly how he filled out that tight, long-sleeved T-shirt. Well, no great mystery there. I wasn't immune to distraction from a pretty face. Or other parts. I sighed. Like a lot of things, I'd found out he was too good to be true.

A bigger issue was that now that Ander was in the bad guy category, there were few people left on this boat who I could rely on. I couldn't trust the captain or the first officer, and Ballsy the Bungler wasn't going to be any help. But something was going on, something potentially very bad, and I needed to get myself together.

I stood up and walked up the stairs to deck eight to join Sam and Tatiana for lunch. I wasn't sure what my next move should be, but talking things over with Sam never failed to give me a boost.

CHAPTER 32

I found Sam and Tatiana at Cafe Rufo on deck seven, enjoying traditional Basque cuisine. They were finished eating, but Sam was working on a cup of coffee and Tatiana on a large glass of whatever wine they'd been drinking.

"Hey, sorry I'm late," I said when I got to their table.

Sam reached over to pull a chair out for me. "No problem. I'm glad you could join us." I could see her looking questioningly at my red eyes, but she said only, "Are you hungry?"

"Ravenous. Is the food good?" Kind of a stupid question. All of the food on this ship had been fabulous.

They both nodded. It was a little shocking to see Tatiana communicate something positive. Sam had definitely made progress with her. I was surprised they'd bonded so quickly, though it was kind of par for the course for Sam.

Sam waved down a waiter who brought over a menu and an extra wine glass. I glanced at the menu and ordered. He poured me some of the white that was on the table and left.

"How was the gallery?" I took a large sip of wine, wishing it were something stronger.

"Very nice. Tatiana has quite the eye for art."

"All Russians have eye for art. It is the essence of our culture. Unlike Americans." All of a sudden her reticence to talk had disappeared. She gave me a look of what I interpreted as a mix of superiority and utter disdain.

Holy shit. She'd barely said anything to me since we'd boarded, and was opening up now to extoll Russian cultural superiority? *I'll give you fucking cultural superiority.* Something about her brought out my competitive side in a big way.

I leaned forward. "You think? OK, hot shot, let's talk writers. You have Tolstoy and Solzhenitsyn. Both great, but we have—"

"And Dostoevsky, Chekhov, Pushkin, Golgol, Gorky, Vasiliy Grossman, Nabokov—"

"Yeah, *Lolita.* Not sure I'd be really proud of a pedophile journal." I wondered if her propensity for dating older men came from reading Nabokov at an early age. But other than that, it was an admittedly solid list. I'd have to come back strong. "We have Mark Twain, Edgar Allen Poe, Harper Lee, Stephen King, Henry David Thoreau, Faulkner, Hemingway, Flannery O' Connor, Kurt Vonnegut, Harlan Coben—"

"Who?" Sam and Tatiana asked in unison.

"Harlan Coben." Whatever. It wasn't my fault neither of them read suspense novels. And Myron Bolitar was one of my all-time favorite literary characters. "I think we can call authors at least a draw."

Tatiana gave her snort of contempt, which I interpreted as tacit agreement. "Russia has Chagall and Kadinsky."

Visual artists. *Fine.* "Warhol, Pollack, and Leibovitz," I countered. *Hmmm...probably point to Russia.*

She knew it and smirked. "Tchaikovsky and Stravinsky."

I didn't bother bringing up Gershwin and Lloyd Weber. Russia wins composers. *Damn.*

She went on. "Baryshnikov, Anna Pavlova, Rudolf Nureyev, Alexander Godunov."

Fuck. Ballet dancers. We might have some, but it wasn't my strong suit. I couldn't name one American dancer, ballet or otherwise, other than the gopher in *Caddyshack.* Would fictional dancers even count? I did see *Flashdance...*

America was getting creamed. It was true, Russia really had

produced an inordinate number of gifted artists in multiple forms.

I hated losing. I searched my brain for accomplished American artists.

"*Hah!* Actors and singers. Kate Hepburn and Elvis alone crush Russia." This was true, as I couldn't name a single Russian actor or singer, and no bands other than Pussy Riot, who admittedly was worth several points. Thankfully Justin Bieber was Canadian.

She snorted. "Acting and singing not true art forms."

"At least our most famous actor isn't a ballet dancer. And we also destroy you in movies." This was undoubtedly true. We had the *Stars*, both *Wars* and *Trek*, along with *The Thin Man* series, all of which were enough by themselves to defeat the entirety of Russian cinema.

Our cultural competition was interrupted by the waiter with my food. I still wanted to share what I'd found in Ander's room with Sam, but didn't want to do it in front of Tatiana, so I focused on eating.

I'd ordered cassoulet, which is essentially a slow-cooked white bean casserole that includes duck confit, some kind of sausage, and an additional meat, often pork. Cassoulet originated in France, but they were serving the Basque version. It was made from similar ingredients, but in one bite I could tell that it bore little resemblance to the French form. The casserole itself was much thicker than the French variety, which was often soupy and came served one-bean thick on a large plate. This one was baked in a ramekin, producing a very crunchy and delicious crust on the top. It was also spicier; I could taste tomatoes and the distinctive Basque pimenton.

I was in the process of scouring my dish for the last bits of it when Tatiana looked over to the entrance and gave a small sound. She put her glass down and got up. She seemed eager, in odd contrast to her customarily bored affect.

I watched her walk over to Boris, who was standing by the opening to the restaurant. He leaned down and whispered something, and they stepped out into the atrium. We could see them talking through the full-length window.

Now was my chance. "I found something in Ander's room."

"Hmmm?" Sam was looking out the window at Boris and Tatiana.

"*Sam.*" I nudged her arm. "This is important. He's got blueprints of the ship in his room and they're marked with the locations of the two engine problems and where they found the bomb. I think he's involved in sabotaging the ship."

I had her complete attention now. "His room? Did you actually break into his room? How did you get in?"

"Yes, never mind about that. I found blueprints. The locations of the engine problems and the bomb were marked. This is proof that the mechanical problems we've had were definitely sabotage, and that he's involved in the bomb threat."

"What are you going to do? Are you going to go back to the captain?"

"I don't know. He's not going to let me near him at this point." That was the understatement of the century.

"I could try to talk to him," she offered. "*I* haven't been thrown in the brig yet."

That could work. Or it could be dangerous. "What if he's in on it? He completely dismissed me when I tried to talk to him about it."

Sam, to her credit, didn't bring up the fact that he may have done that because of my suboptimal communication approach. "Sabotaging his own ship? Why would he do that?"

"I don't know. I don't know who we can trust at this point," I said. "But I'm more convinced than ever that all of this has something to do with the ETA. They practically signed their work with the graffiti. And we've seen three different Basque protests since we've been here: one when we boarded, one at the port in Cadiz, and another at the Palacio. That one might have included a bomb. Gorka, Inigo, Ander, and the captain are all Basque. Luix Salazar was Basque, and he's dead. And Zuzan, that guy who's been following us and who tried to kill me on the beach? He's Basque, and he has ties to the ETA *and* a criminal record. So if the captain is in on it, we could put ourselves in danger by talking to him."

I looked over at Boris and Tatiana on the other side of the window. "And we still don't know what's going on with Boris. He met with Gorka a couple of times, and we know he gave him some money and the backpack with the bomb. Not to mention him threatening me in the stairwell." I sighed and slumped into my chair. We really had nowhere to turn.

Sam took another sip of coffee. "What do we really know about Boris? Other than he's paranoid about being followed, and he's carrying on with a woman who's half his age?"

She was right. Boris was the outlier.

"Gideon is digging into Boris's background and will call me when he finds anything out."

"OK. Why don't you go back to the room and lay down for a while until he calls? You look exhausted."

A nap sounded really good. I nodded and got up to leave.

Looking back out the window at Boris and Tatiana, Sam said, "I'll see you up there. I'm going to wait for her." She turned back to me, her brow furrowed. "I hope whatever he's doing he's not involving her. Do you think she's in danger?"

"I think we all are."

CHAPTER 33

I'd just laid down on the couch when Gideon called.

"How did the break-in go? Did it work?" He was always excited to hear about how his hacks worked for me.

"Yes. And I found something in his room. I'll give you the details later, but it definitely points to sabotage. Did you find anything on Boris?"

"Yeah! Man, were his records sealed up tight. But no match for me. All I had to do was—"

"*Gideon...*" I was beyond tired, and didn't have time to listen to him wax eloquent about his technical prowess.

"Right. Anyway, he's got quite the resume. I told you he's former Russian Spetsnaz. He was actually a black beret in the PDSS, the Counteraction Underwater Diversionary Forces and Facilities. It's a special group on the naval side. He's been out of the service for a while. It looks like he's on his own, working private jobs. Guess what his specialty is?"

"Gideon, please, I haven't slept in a while..."

"Underwater demolition. He's a commando frogman and an explosives expert."

There it was. Explosives expert. We'd had the one bomb on the ship that didn't go off, likely from Boris's backpack that he'd given to Gorka to plant. There was also the small one at the Palacio. I'd seen Zuzan running from where it went off, but Boris could have made it and given it to Zuzan to plant.

"Did you find any links between Boris and the ETA?" I asked, hope creeping in to my voice.

"No, none."

"Damn." I guess that that would have been too easy.

"Why isn't that a good thing?"

"Because we still don't know what Boris was up to, and why." It wasn't outside the realm of possibility that he was just a mercenary. But I was certain he'd given Gorka the envelope full of money. So if the ETA was behind everything, and using Boris to supply explosives, wouldn't they be giving *him* money rather than the other way around?

"And something else is bugging me. Boris is an explosives expert. Given his experience in the Russian elite forces, he's among the *crème de la crème* of bomb makers, right?" I didn't wait for Gideon to answer. "What are the chances he'd build a bomb that didn't work? Or make one that resulted in only a tiny explosion like the one at the Palacio?"

"Slim to none." I could hear the enthusiasm going out of Gideon's voice.

It was eight days into our trip, and it made sense that if Boris really intended to blow our ship up, it would have happened by now. That meant that the objective wasn't our ship.

There were plenty of other potential targets in the area, like the LNG carrier. But from what Gideon had found, even if the LNG on the carrier was ignited, it wouldn't be that big of a deal. Any fireball it produced would rise harmlessly into the air.

There was another other high-value target in the port area though. I broke our collective silence. "Gideon, what if someone blew up the LNG plant?"

He gave a low whistle. "Christ, I don't know. The Cleveland plant that I told you about, the one that blew up in the forties? The Bilbao plant has one hundred times the amount of LNG that the Cleveland plant had. An explosion at the Bilbao plant would flatten everything around it, maybe for miles.

"But it's a moot point. Those plants are guarded like nobody's business. No one gets in without going through a metal detector. Everyone is vetted. The perimeter is completely fenced."

He was right. We were missing something. Boris's demolition background was another piece to the puzzle, but I couldn't see what he was going for, and I still didn't know how Ander, Gorka, Salazar, Inigo, and the ETA were tied in. I didn't have anything to take back to the captain, even if I could be sure he wasn't involved. Without something more substantial I wouldn't get within fifty feet of him without the Incredible Hulk brothers intervening.

As far as I could see, I had one option. We'd be leaving port tomorrow. Whatever was going to happen would happen in the next twenty-four hours. Boris was the explosives expert, and if something dangerous was going down, he would be playing a key role.

The only thing left to do was tail him and find out what he was up to, hopefully before it happened. But I would need to be careful. I wasn't sure what he'd do if he caught me following him again, but it wouldn't be good.

The first thing to do was to check to see if Boris was still in his room. I said good bye to Gideon and took the stairs to deck seven, which was starting to feel very familiar. I opened the door to the hallway slowly, peeking around to make sure no one was there. It was empty except for the concierge. I walked over to Boris's door and pretended to knock.

I heard movement. He was in there. Good.

Trying to look disappointed, I walked back to the stairwell and waved again to the concierge. I would wait until Boris left his suite and then follow him. I didn't think I'd be waiting long.

I waited a short while, peeking out of the small window on the stairwell door, when I saw one of the doors open. Out came an elderly couple looking like they were heading for the pool. A few minutes later I heard the elevator, and then loud voices. It was the Hendersons returning to their room. Even after they closed their door I could still hear them.

God, I hope they don't start having sex. I imagined miked-up feral cats in heat going at it. *I really don't want to hear that.*

I waited a half hour before Boris opened his door. He walked toward the elevator, dressed to go outside and carrying a large black bag that looked heavy. It wasn't a shopping bag, and he wasn't going to the pool to work on his tan. He got on the elevator, and when it closed I went into the hallway to see what floor he went to. I wasn't surprised to see the elevator stop at the deck with the gangway leading off the ship.

I went back to the stairwell and ran down the stairs, making it to the gangway just in time to see him open the driver's side door to the black sedan he'd driven the first day we'd been in Bilbao.

I called Mattin and asked him to meet me at the car pickup right away. He pulled in and barely came to a stop when I opened the back door and hopped in. By now Mattin was used to our strange requests, and was unperturbed at my direction to follow the car. We left the terminal area and drove out to the main road.

There was little traffic around the port, and I could see Boris's sedan getting on the highway to Bilbao. But instead of heading into the city, he went the other direction, toward Gexto and the east side of the bay. It was the same way Mattin had gone when he'd driven us to the Point de Galea for our hike.

The sedan turned up the coast, following signs for the Real Society of Golf de Neguri. I wasn't shocked when we turned before reaching the golf club. Boris didn't strike me as the links type. He turned off the road and parked in the large lot above the Galea Fort we'd walked through the day before. He turned his car off and sat there. We sat too.

An hour later, Boris still hadn't gotten out of his car.

I didn't know how long this was going to take, and it didn't seem fair to make Mattin wait when he could be doing something else. I told him I'd call him when I needed him and got out of the car. He gave a mild protest but left, making me promise to call him when I was ready to go.

I walked behind a small tree on the edge of the parking lot, out of

Boris's line of site but where I could still see the sedan, and settled in on the ground to wait.

Almost two hours passed before Boris got out of his car. It was dusk, and all of the tourists had gone for the day. The only car left in the parking lot was his. He got out and opened the trunk, pulled out his black bag along with a metal suitcase, and started walking toward the fort. I would lose sight of him soon in the vegetation around the parking lot, so I got up from my spot and followed him at a distance.

He walked past the fort and through the low stone wall that I'd gone through when I'd chased Zuzan. At the edge of the grassy area with the cement retaining walls, he climbed over and disappeared. I gave it a minute, then headed over and looked down. He'd made it down the slope to the beach. The bag and the suitcase were on the ground, and he was pulling things out of them.

I couldn't get a good look at what he was doing and needed to relocate. A few yards away on the cliff was a partially hidden outcropping directly above him. The footing was precarious, and I had to be careful not to slip on the loose rocks. But he couldn't see me from there, and I had a good view.

He pulled a wetsuit out of the bag. Boris was going for an evening swim.

It was getting dark, but I pulled out my phone and took a few pictures. I wasn't sure they'd come out but it was worth a shot. After he got the wetsuit on, he pulled out a tank, a mask, and a regulator. From the metal suitcase he pulled out two mesh bags full of what looked like green dishes. He put on his tank and regulator, and with the mask set above his eyes, he slung the mesh bags over his shoulder and waded into the water. Once the water was up to his chest, he adjusted the mask over his nose and put the regulator in his mouth, then disappeared under the water.

The sun had set by now, and even if he resurfaced I wouldn't be able to see him. It was time to call Mattin and get back to the ship. With this new information I might be able to get the captain's attention. I would just have to hope he wasn't part of it.

I looked at my phone. No bars. I took a few steps to see if I could improve the signal. I stepped closer to the ledge and felt the ground give way under my foot, loose dirt and rocks sprinkling down to the beach. I tried to pull myself back but it was too late, and I tumbled over the cliff.

CHAPTER 34

It was still dark when I came to. There was a golf ball-sized lump on my head. The fall had only been ten feet or so, but I'd landed on one of the large rocks that littered the shore. My skull was really taking a beating on this trip.

I didn't know how long I'd been out. I felt around on the ground next to me and was relieved to find my phone. I held it up to my face. Still no bars. *Great.*

I got up and dusted myself off, and walked unsteadily to where Boris had gone down earlier to get to the beach. I climbed up the steep slope on all fours. Once I got to the top, I walked toward the road until I got a better signal and called Mattin. He would be here in a few minutes. I sat down on the side of the road to wait.

Twenty minutes later I saw headlights coming up the road. The car slowed as it approached me and I stood up. The driver was rolling down the window. I realized too late it wasn't Mattin's Mercedes.

"Jesse…"

It was Ander. *Shit.* I turned and started running up the road to the parking lot. Maybe I could find someone and get help. I looked behind to see him following me in the car.

I made it to the lot with him close behind me. I reached the end of the pavement and ran up the grassy hill that led to the homes I'd seen on our hike a few days before. Ander stopped his car and got out, and was now chasing after me on foot. "Jesse, wait!"

I was in good shape and could run for days, but I wasn't fast, and I was still feeling the effects of the fall on the beach. He caught up to me and grabbed my arm. I pulled away and turned to face him, getting into a defensive position. "Get away from me!" I yelled, frantically looking for anyone who might be around to help.

I was dizzy and felt like I was spinning. I almost fell back down, and had to resist the urge to throw up. I reached for my boot knife and pulled it out, showing it to him as I backed up.

Ander put his hands out in a calming gesture.

"What the hell is going on?" I yelled at him. "Who are you?" All of my pent-up disappointment at how things had turned out with him was coming out now. I felt betrayed. As a kid betrayal had left me depressed; as an adult it made me angry. "How could you do this? You fucking motherfucker!" I was hyperventilating.

He sighed. "Please, Jesse, let's go to the car."

"I'm not going anywhere with you, you fucking asshole!" I said, rubbing the bump on my head.

"Jesse, look, I am not a teacher—"

"No shit! You're a fucking terrorist. And to think I almost slept with you." Actually, sleeping with a terrorist might have been kind of cool, in a "who's the most interesting person you've ever slept with" kind of way. That is, without the actual terrorism part of it.

"Let me explain—"

"I give zero fucks about your explanation. You can shove it up your ETA terrorist ass!" I was feeling a little better and turned to storm off. Toward nowhere really, as at this point I had no idea which direction to go. I kept my knife up as I walked away, in case he was thinking about getting close to me again.

"Jesse, I'm a detective."

I stopped and turned around.

He reached into his jacket and pulled out a badge.

"I'm with the GEL, the Grupo Especial de Operaciones."

"Sure you are," I said sarcastically.

"We work with CITCO, the Centro de Inteligencia contra el Terrorismo y el Crimen Organizado, Spain's counter terrorism organization. We received a credible alert of a terrorist action associated with your cruise ship. I have been leading the investigation, working undercover."

"Sure you are," I said again.

I was getting less sure. I played back in my head everything that had occurred in the last few days: Ander's meetings with Inigo, the blueprints in his room, his interest in the Russians, the job teaching about law enforcement, the articles in his briefcase. Him being with law enforcement made as much sense as him being a terrorist. Actually, it made more sense. I was starting to feel a little silly and lowered my tiny knife.

"Please, will you come back to the car?"

I waited a moment, mostly to save face, but I knew he was telling the truth. We walked back down the slope to his car and got in. I looked around at the completely empty parking lot as we drove away and remembered why I was here in the first place.

"Boris's car is gone. We've got to get back to the ship right now."

"Why?"

"I'll tell you on the way."

Ander pulled out of the parking lot and drove carefully down the dark road.

"You might want to hurry. He's going to blow something up, probably very soon."

He looked at me, frowning, but I felt the car speed up.

"I saw Boris here earlier tonight. He was wearing scuba gear, and swimming toward the west side of the bay. He's ex-Russian military and an underwater demolition expert. He had two bags with him."

"Bags?"

"Yeah, bags. Full of mines."

Ander nodded. "Ah…that explains it."

"Explains what?"

"Boris left the ship in Cadiz. We had a team follow him. He drove to Bilbao from Cadiz and made some stops along the way. Perhaps he was picking up his gear and the explosives. He would need to do that, as he could not easily bring them aboard the ship." He was still thinking, then shook his head. "No…"

"No, what?"

"The terminals have very tight security, and ships in port are regularly swept for mines. They would be discovered immediately if he put them anywhere on or near any ship."

"Metal mines would. I'm guessing the ones he's using are made of plastic or ceramic, and not detectable with their normal minesweeping procedures." I'd recognized the green color of the "dishes" in his bag as similar to what I'd seen in old Cold War movies. Back in the day, the Soviets had been big on plastic antipersonnel mines. They were the same green color as what I'd seen in Boris's bag.

"Even if you are right, and they are plastic mines, what would he be blowing up?" Ander was right, we'd figured out the how, but still didn't know the what.

I thought about what Gideon had said about the amount of gas at the regasification plant, and what would happen if something caused it to explode. "What about the LNG plant?"

Ander shook his head. "The Bahía de Bizkaia Gas plant? It has extremely tight security. No one could get in. The perimeter is under heavy guard twenty-four hours a day. And the tanks themselves are reinforced to withstand severe impacts, even from cars crashing into them."

"If it isn't the plant, we're back to ships. Our cruise ship has already been sabotaged, likely twice, but not badly enough to do any real damage. And I doubt he'd blow up our ship with Tatiana on it," I mused aloud. "You knew about the sabotage, right?"

"Yes. Wait…" He frowned. "How do *you* know that?" The sabotage had understandably been kept quiet among passengers, and most of the crew.

Uh-oh. "I…uh…kind of searched your room. I found the blueprints. That's part of the reason I thought you were in on it."

He leaned into his seat and tilted his head back, exhaling slowly. Through clenched teeth, he said, "You were in my room? How did you get in?"

I looked out the window.

"We will talk about that later." I could tell he was vacillating between wanting to give me a hard time about breaking into his room and focusing on the immediate danger. Immediate danger won. He said, "Yes. Inigo picked Gorka up that night while you and I were at dinner. We wanted to interrogate him right away."

I guess that was a good enough excuse for turning down sex with me. "What about the bomb threat? And the backpack with the bomb in it?"

Ander rolled his eyes. "How do you know about *that?*" He waited, and when I didn't answer, said, "I do not think there are more bombs. The ship underwent a full inspection with a bomb-sniffing dog in Cadiz and was declared clear. It is now undergoing another one with both drug and bomb sniffing dogs."

"Did Gorka tell you Boris paid him to do it?"

"No." He looked at me sharply. He'd speeded the car up while we were talking, and I wished he'd pay more attention to the road. "How do you know *this?*"

I told him about the exchanges I'd observed in the hallway between Boris and Gorka, and the money I'd found in Gorka's room.

Ander considered this new information before answering. "Gorka admits to sabotaging the ship, but not to making the bomb threat. And while he knew about the bomb, he swears there was never any danger of the bomb going off. Our technical team has confirmed that this is true. The bomb was inoperable. And he has not talked about Boris."

"Let me guess. He blamed it on Luix Salazar."

He nodded. By this point he'd given up trying to figure out where I got my information.

I'd noticed all of this without really even looking for anything, at least at first, and wondered how the entire security staff could have missed it. "What the hell has Ballsy been doing this whole time? Isn't he the one who's supposed to be keeping tabs on this kind of thing?" His incompetence was at a uniquely superior level, but it seemed unlikely that the whole security team could be that worthless.

Ander looked like he knew something but hesitated to talk, so I stared at him until he said, "Balasy and his team have been busy dealing with the drug smuggling operation."

"It seems like explosives should be a bigger priority than drugs. Because, you know, blowing shit up and stuff."

Like me, Ander was doing some of his thinking out loud. "The Marchands could not have done it alone. The chances are that crew members and maybe other passengers are involved as well. The drugs found in their room were not packed in such a way that they would have gotten by the drug dogs that went through everyone's luggage during boarding. They would have had to get them from someone else on the ship, probably a crew member. Balasy is still looking into that. And it is curious…"

"What?"

"The amount that they were paid. It was over one hundred thousand euros. That is a lot for the quantity of cocaine found in their room. This is the other reason he thinks there are more people involved."

Sam had noticed that too. The amount of money they were paid was high by about ten times.

I looked at him and raised my eyebrows. "I assume you've been working with Ballsy. Did you know he suspected *me* of all of this shit?"

"*Balasy*. And, yes, he told me you were under suspicion. I convinced him you were not involved. He is not a bad man, and is dedicated to his job, but understandably feels that the ship's security is his business. He is not happy about having federal investigators on board, and has been difficult to work with. But at this point he is overwhelmed. There is just too much going on for him and his team to handle."

This was true, it was a total clusterfuck. Sabotage, a bomb threat, a man overboard, and drug smuggling…even if Ballsy wasn't the second coming of Frank Drebin, this was an almost unbelievable amount of stuff to handle.

"What else do you know?" he said tightly.

"Not enough." We were missing something. "Why would Boris pay Gorka to *slightly* sabotage our ship? And go to the trouble of planting an inoperable bomb? It makes no sense. The only result was a few extra days in port. And even that wouldn't have happened if we hadn't changed our itinerary and gotten here early because of the storm."

A few extra days in port.

That was it.

I turned to Ander, my pulse quickening. "He's going to blow the plant."

"What? No, we already ruled that out. The security is too tight."

"Ander, do you know what happens when the gas on an LNG carrier escapes and gets ignited?"

"Yes, it creates a fireball. But the gas is light, and the fireball rises. The carrier loses cargo, but it is not much of a danger of explosion."

"If it's at sea."

"Yes, at sea."

I waited for the light bulb to go on for him. Three, two, one…

"Oh." Then, "OH!" He hit the gas, speeding the car forward.

Gideon had said that an LNG carrier catching fire wasn't catastrophic when the gas ignited because it would create a fireball that was lighter than air that would rise harmlessly above the ship. That is, if it were at sea. It wasn't at sea now. The LNG carrier was connected to the regasification plant. A plant with a half million cubic meters of gas in storage. Boris was putting mines on the LNG carrier, planning to blow up the plant while they were connected.

"Excuse me." Ander pulled out his phone and punched in a number, then spoke rapidly in Euskara and hung up. "So the sabotage was not about damaging *our* ship. The ship arrived in Bilbao early because of the storms, and Boris needed us to stay in port long enough for the carrier to arrive, to give him time to set the mines on it."

"Yeah, the fuel gauge that Gorka damaged was fixed too quickly. They had to do something else to keep us there longer. That's why he cut the cables."

Ander was now driving very fast.

I was still bugged by the fact that we didn't know anything about Boris's motivation. "Do you think Boris is working with the ETA?"

"Why do you think that?" said Ander. He sounded evasive.

"Well, for one thing, there was the graffiti. Isn't *Euskal Herria* an ETA thing?"

He stared straight ahead, his hands tightening on the steering wheel.

"C'mon, Ander. I've given you a lot. We need to trust each other at this point."

"I am sorry. I am not in the habit of sharing information about my investigations with civilians."

"Well, maybe you should start. Do you think he's working with the ETA?"

He sighed. "I do not know. Maybe. We are looking into that. At least two members of the crew with ETA connections were working with him, maybe more. Gorka admitted that he caused the engine problems, and he blamed Salazar for the bomb threat. But he did not say anything about why, other than the money. Maybe he did not know. And we have not been able to find much out about Boris."

I wasn't surprised they hadn't found anything about Boris. Even with his superior hacking skills, and access to the most sophisticated databases in the world, Gideon had struggled to get into Boris's background. It seemed curious, though, that a mercenary for hire would have that much security around his information. But I left that mystery for later.

He continued. "Our initial intel was from chatter among people with known ETA connections. All lower-level operatives, but this is when we first heard Boris's name, and suspected he might be working with them. It is why we followed him in Cadiz when he left the ship. But as far as we can tell, Boris has no history with the ETA. If he is working with them, it is a new relationship."

"What about Luix Salazar? Do you have any information about why he ended up dead in the water?"

Ander's face turned grim. "We do not know that either. Gorka swears he does not know anything about what happened to Salazar. I find that hard to believe."

"Is the captain in on it? He's Basque."

"No." He chuckled grimly. "But we did not know at first. When we finally cleared him and told him what was going on, he was angry at being kept in the dark. But we could not say anything until we were sure. The only executive officers I knew I could trust at first were Inigo, Paloma, and Balasy."

I wasn't sure I would trust Ballsy with anything, but I let that go, and said, "The guy I told you about, who was following me the last two times I went ashore? His name is Zuzan Zabala. He has some ties to the ETA and was involved in the protest when we disembarked in Barcelona."

"How do you know it was him? Are you sure?"

I rolled my eyes.

"Oh, yes, right."

"So, does this change your thinking at all, as to whether or not what's happening is about the ETA?"

He stared straight ahead. He clearly didn't want to go there, despite all of the evidence that was piling up. I couldn't really blame him, given the implications of a resurgence of ETA violence in his homeland. The last decade had seen a cultural renaissance of sorts in the Basque Country. The Guggenheim by itself was bringing hundreds of thousands of new people to Bilbao every year. That, along with the growing energy industry, had lifted the economy of the whole region. The implications of an ETA attack could be devastating and long lasting. Not to mention the loss of life, which, given the amount of gas at the plant, would be unimaginable.

It wouldn't help either of us to dwell on that, so I changed the subject. "I saw you go to the lower decks with Inigo. I thought you guys might be together. And then I thought you were both in on it."

He allowed himself a small smile. "No, and no."

"Did you know Inigo and Ballsy wanted to keep me in the brig?"

"Yes. At the time they thought you might be involved. After all, you were caught sneaking around on the lower decks. Because of the intel we had, and then the bomb threat, the ship was in a security alert. I told the captain you were not involved, but it *was* suspicious that it was you who found the backpack with the bomb in it." He looked over at me. "You are very nosy."

No newsflash there. One more thing was bugging me. "Ander… how did you know to look for me on the hill back there?"

"Mattin." He looked at my puzzled expression. "Mattin does work on the side for us from time to time. I asked him to keep me informed about your whereabouts. When he told me you'd been out at the beach for several hours, I was worried something had happened."

We were turning into the terminal. He stopped the car and I opened the door to jump out, but Ander put his hand on my arm and leaned close. "Jesse, you have been a great help. But this is a law enforcement matter, and Boris and the people he is working with are dangerous. I have alerted the security officer on the *Petris* about what we think is going on, and am heading over there now. Please go straight back to your room and leave this to me. *Please.*"

I nodded and got out of the car. I ran up the gangway and took the stairs to our suite.

Sam was on the couch with Chaz, but jumped up and threw her arms around me when she saw me. "I was out of my mind with worry. Where have you been?"

She'd left about fifty texts for me since the night before, none of which I'd answered. She wasn't usually the worrying type, even with my penchant for getting into trouble. But I'd always been good about staying in touch.

"Taking in the local scenic views. Listen, have you seen Boris?"

Day 9

CHAPTER 35

I was stacking up concussions and going on two days with no sleep, but there was no way I was going to leave it to Ander and whoever he was working with to stop Boris. We believed something was going to blow up very soon, and the more people working on it the better. Boris might be at the plant, but he could still be on our ship. Since Ander was at the plant, and it sounded like Ballsy was busy looking for drugs, I would look for Boris on the ship myself.

I gave Sam the quick rundown of the situation and then ran to deck seven, to Boris's suite. I listened at his door for a minute, ignoring the concierge's scrutiny. No sounds. I assumed he was either asleep or roaming around the ship. If he was asleep he wasn't any danger at the moment, so I moved on.

With no idea where he would go, I decided to start on deck four and work my way up. I ran down the stairwell, grateful that most of the passengers used the elevators.

Deck four was more crowded than usual, but there was no sign of Boris. I looked up into the expansive atrium. This would take forever, and I had a strong sense there wasn't much time. But I didn't know what else to do, so I started moving quickly up the central staircase to the next level.

"*He-ey!*" Trish Henderson yelled down from three decks above me, waving.

For once I was glad she had a foghorn of a voice. I yelled back, "Trish, have you seen Boris?"

"*Who?*"

"The Russian man," I yelled. He was the only Russian man on the ship, and the only one with a suite on the same level as the Hendersons.

"I saw him leaving his suite! He had a coat on!"

If he'd left the ship, there was nothing for me to do. But he could be out on one of the outside decks. It was worth checking out.

I cupped my hands around my mouth and shouted, "Do you know which deck?" It was either the main pool deck on twelve or the sports deck on ten.

"No!"

"Thanks!"

She made the "call me" sign as I turned to run to the stairwell. I sprinted up the stairs, heading to the larger pool deck first. It was 7:30 in the morning and there weren't many people out yet other than a few crew members setting up for the day. I ran all the way around the deck next to the railing. No sign of Boris.

I went back inside and down the stairs to the sports deck. It took longer to search this one, the climbing wall and various other activity equipment making the sight lines shorter. I fast walked around the climbing wall and each of the walkways on the deck, and then along the railing. No Boris.

It occurred to me that Svetlana might know where he was. She'd been trying to keep tabs on her granddaughter, which likely meant also keeping tabs on him. She'd not been extremely talkative so far, but I was sure if I explained to her what was going on she'd be eager to help. There weren't many better ways of keeping Boris away from Tatiana than getting him arrested.

I ran back up the stairs to deck thirteen and knocked on her door.

She opened it, not looking at all surprised to see me. "Hello, Dr. O'Hara."

"Hi, Svetlana. Have you seen Boris?"

"No, why?"

"It's very important that I find him."

"Please come in." She stepped aside. "May I get you a drink?"

That was surprisingly gracious. And for fuck's sake, 7:30 a.m. is a little early, even for me. "No, thank you. Can you tell me where you think he might be?"

"His suite is on deck seven. Have you checked there?"

"Yes." I turned around to leave.

"Dr. O'Hara, since you are here, can you help with something? I have not heard from Tatiana since yesterday morning. Have you seen her?"

"Not recently." I thought Tatiana could take care of herself. But she'd been with Boris yesterday at the restaurant. "Do you think she's with him now?" Sam had wondered if Tatiana was in danger. I didn't think so, but who knows what Boris was doing, or what he was capable of.

"I don't know, but I am concerned. She is not usually gone this long, and she does not answer her phone."

Was it possible Tatiana was involved in what Boris was doing? I didn't think so, but how could I be sure? In any case I didn't have time for this. Whether or not Tatiana was involved, it was Boris I needed to find. And if she was in danger from him, I'd help her by finding him.

"Look, Svetlana, I will look for her, but first I need to find Boris."

"But—"

"I'm sorry," I said as I ran out the door.

I hated cutting her off. I didn't like being rude to someone's grandmother. But depending on what Boris was up to, there were a lot worse things that could happen than not hearing from her granddaughter for a few hours.

I went up the stairs to our suite. Sam hadn't moved from the couch, and was sitting with Chaz, who was unfortunately now a permanent fixture there.

"I can't find him. Any ideas?"

"Maybe he's left the ship?"

"Yeah, maybe. Trish said he was dressed to go outside. I checked both decks but found no sign of him." I was pulling out my phone to give Ander a call.

"Aren't there three outside decks?" said Sam.

"No, two. The pool deck and the sports deck."

"What about the foredeck?"

"That's off limits to passengers." I realized as the words were coming out of my mouth how stupid I sounded. If Boris was involved in blowing something up, he wasn't going to be too concerned about a minor breach of ship security protocol.

I went out to our balcony and looked down. From up here I could see down to the large H of the helipad on the foredeck. And one lone figure standing next to the railing.

I rushed back into the living room. "You're a genius."

"Be careful."

"Always." Actually, almost never. I didn't bother turning around to see Sam's reaction to that.

I hurried out the door and took the stairwell to deck eight. As I was running down the stairs my phone rang. I didn't recognize the number.

"Yeah?"

"Jesse, this is Ander. I am at the gas plant. You were right, they found mines on the tanker. But we are not able to remove them safely. We need time to get everyone off of the ship and disconnect it from the plant piping system before the mines are detonated. Boris is not here—"

"He's here. I'm going to him now."

"Can you buy us some time?"

"I'll try." I put the phone away and continued down to deck eight. The landing on this level had three doors: one to the atrium, one to the hallway with the passenger suites, and a third to the foredeck. The foredeck door required a keypad code. Hopefully they were using the same code throughout the ship, and hadn't changed it since my break-in to the crew's quarters.

I entered in the code I'd used before and heard a click. Inigo had said the security staff would be changing the code right away, but I wasn't all that surprised to find another thing Ballsy had screwed up. In this case, the consistency of his ineptitude was helpful. I let myself outside.

Boris was standing next to the railing, holding a small black box in one hand and looking at his watch on the other. Occasionally he looked toward the mouth of the bay, in the direction of the LNG plant. As I moved closer to him, I saw the box had a large red button on the front of it, covered with a clear square plastic casing. There was a wire leading from the box and running over the railing.

I'd never seen a real-life detonator before, but assumed that's what this was. Probably an acoustic one, given that the mines were underwater.

"Hey, Boris."

He looked up but didn't say anything, then looked back at his watch.

I needed to stall him. I took a step closer. "The ETA is over. There's no point to this."

He ignored me, flipping up the plastic safety cover.

I expected he was waiting for the optimal time to blow the ship, which I knew would be when the plant's piping system was hooked to the carrier's LNG tanks for the unloading procedure. Ander said the tanker was hooked in and the liquid gas was currently flowing from the tanker into the facility's piping system. An explosion occurring while the gas was entering the facility would carry into the plant, and there would be no breeze to carry a fireball safely above the facility. Instead, it would spread through the piping in the plant and into the storage tanks. If there was even a small amount of air in the system, it would cause a half million cubic meters of gas to explode, destroying the ship and leveling the plant and everything around it. Hundreds, possibly thousands, of people in the area would be blown up or burned alive.

Ander said they were in the process of disconnecting the tanker. I didn't know how long that would take, but I knew we didn't have much time.

Boris was about twenty feet away from me. If I tried to rush him I wouldn't be able to get to him before he hit the button. Not knowing what else to do, I took a tentative step toward him.

He looked up briefly, reaching down to pull a long knife from a sheath on the outside of his leg. The blade must have been at least seven inches long. It wasn't shiny. Like his bombs, it was made out of ceramic to get past ship security. It would still do the job though.

He held the blade toward me and turned back to his watch. "Stand back. I do not want to hurt you." That seemed like a strange sentiment, coming from someone who was getting ready to blow up an industrial plant full of people.

"Why are you doing this? Why do you care about the ETA?"

He looked at me, scowling, then back at his watch.

I wasn't sure exactly what he was waiting for to push the button, but given the frequency with which he was checking his watch, he was getting close to doing it. I was frozen in place, not wanting to provoke him and risk him activating the detonator.

All of a sudden it hit me. "You're waiting for the tour to start."

Gideon's report on the Gastech Conference had included the agenda. There was a VIP tour of the plant scheduled for eight a.m. The leaders of virtually every major player in the industry would be at the plant this morning.

"You're going to take out the heads of the energy companies along with the plant."

He looked again at his watch.

"Boris, don't do this. Tatiana loves you." I didn't know what else to say. Maybe the prospect of never seeing her again would help him come to his senses.

At the mention of her name he looked up. "There is no choice." I was a little surprised to see what looked like real pain in his eyes.

He looked back down at his watch, his finger hovering over the button.

I couldn't stall him anymore and was out of ideas, so I decided to rush him, even though he'd be able to hit the button before I got there. But it might distract him, and give Ander a little more time. Looking at the knife in his hand, I realized he'd probably kill me, but it would take some time, maybe enough for Ander to disconnect the tanker and get it away from the plant.

As I was taking my first step, I heard a loud *pop*, a ping of metal against metal, and then another *pop*.

Boris grunted and grabbed his shoulder. He staggered away from the railing and dropped the detonator. His knife clattered to the deck.

I looked around. No one else was here.

Boris's arm was dripping blood and hanging limp. The detonator was hanging by the wire over the railing.

I ran over to grab the detonator and stood there looking at it, snapping the safety casing back down over the button. I looked over the railing, my eyes following the attached wire. It went all the way down and into the water. As I was looking down I heard footsteps, and turned around to see Boris coming at me, his shirt darkening with blood.

He hit me low, like a linebacker making a tackle. The blow lifted me off my feet and drove me back.

I felt the railing make contact with the lower part of my back as I flew over the side. The next thing I knew I was in the air, falling toward the water.

The foredeck was a long way above the water. And while I'd seen divers go off cliffs at least this high, I knew that belly flopping from this distance would not end well. I tried to orient myself vertically, to hit the water with as much of an edge as I could get with my feet. I crossed my arms and held them tight against my chest.

I heard a splash just before I entered the water. When I hit I wasn't perfectly vertical, and the force of the entry snapped my head back. My breath was knocked out with a whoosh, and I could feel the bones in my right foot give way. Pain radiated up my leg. *Damn it.*

I was disoriented as I struggled for the surface, kicking with one leg. When I finally broke through, I took a huge breath and lay back, looking at the sky, trying to get my bearings. It was then that Boris grabbed me.

We struggled, him trying to take the detonator from me with his one good hand, and me trying to move away with my one good leg. We were thrashing around and sank together below the surface. I was glad he'd dropped his knife, although it would probably be just as easy for him to kill me with his bare hands.

Eventually, he gave up trying to pry my fingers from around the box, and instead wrapped his hand around mine and forced it into the button. Even with only one working arm he had no trouble crushing my hand around the box. The hard plexiglas edges of the safety shield cut into my skin. I cried out, letting in a mouthful of salty water. But I continued to hold onto the detonator.

He let me go, and started to punch me in the head. Being underwater made his punches slower than they would have been, but he was powerful, and my head rocked with each blow. I tried to block him but was using one hand to hold the detonator, and the other to help me tread water, already made difficult with only one usable leg.

He continued to bang away at my undefended head. How much time had passed? I didn't know, but I was now having more immediate problems. I was running out of air, and though my eyes were open, everything was getting fuzzy. My good leg was no longer working very well, and I was sinking further beneath the water.

Boris stopped punching me and grabbed my arm. Lack of air and what was likely my third concussion in as many days was taking its toll, and he easily took the detonator from my hand that no longer had any strength. Once he had it, he kicked powerfully to the surface.

I was still sinking and focused on trying to make my good leg move.

It was weak but I was able to get it to flutter, and it took me slowly to the surface. I broke through next to Boris, gasping huge mouthfuls of air. Even if he was interested in killing me, at this point I didn't have the strength to do anything other than keep my head above water. But he looked completely focused on the detonator. I watched him flip open the plastic safety shield and push the button. I heard it click.

We were next to each other, treading water, looking in the direction of the LNG plant.

There was a dull rumble, then three more. I looked to the sky. There were bright flashes in quick succession, I counted four of them. We both waited for the cascading series of much larger explosions and fireballs. I braced for a shock wave.

A minute went by, then another. It was quiet.

Boris looked down at the box and pushed the button again, then over and over. He was banging on it, cursing in Russian.

Something had happened, but it wasn't anywhere close to what should have happened with an exploding LNG tanker hooked up to a pipeline and a plant full of millions of cubic meters of gas.

Boris let go of the box and lay back, the water around him growing red as he stared up at the sky.

CHAPTER 36

I looked back toward shore and saw that a group of cars had pulled up on the roadway near the terminal. People were getting out and walking to the shore, and I could hear police sirens in the distance. I started a painful swim toward land. Once I got to knee-deep water among the rocks I tried to stand, but my broken foot gave out, and I sat back down heavily on the ground. A couple of men waded in and helped me to the side of the road.

Boris still floated in the water. It was over, but it looked like he had no intention of making it easy on anyone. Police officers gathered on the edge of the water, and eventually someone brought over a small inflatable boat. Two uniformed men got in and paddled out to him. I heard them yell and one pulled his gun. Boris refused to acknowledge them, so the one without the gun jumped in the water and led his unresisting form over to the boat. With one hand on the boat and the other on Boris, they towed him to shore, where he was handcuffed and led to a car.

"Jesse, are you OK?" I was beyond relieved to hear Ander's voice. He'd walked down the beach next to me. He put his hand on my shoulder and squeezed it.

"Yeah, but I think my foot is broken." And my hand was bleeding, but it didn't seem like a priority at the moment.

"I need to take care of some things, but Raphael will take you to the doctor." He gestured at a deputy nearby.

They spoke rapidly in Euskara, and then Raphael leaned down to take my hand and helped me to his car.

***

There were four broken bones in my foot. The doctor put on a cast and gave me a pair of crutches, along with a bottle of painkillers. He also wrapped a bandage around my bleeding hand. It hurt but didn't require stitches. Raphael waited for me, and when we were done he took me back to the ship. He left me at the door to our suite.

I walked in to see Sam sitting on the couch with Chaz, who for the first time in his life didn't growl at me. Ander was standing next to them. Sam didn't say anything, just walked over and gave me a careful hug. I put the crutches down and limped over to sit on the couch.

I looked at Ander. "What happened? Was anyone hurt?"

Ander explained that while we'd been in his car, he'd called his friend on the *Petris*, the security specialist. He'd told him what we suspected, and they'd sent in divers who found a series of mines laid along the keel of the ship. The mines were expertly placed in such a way that they would blow up the ship, double-hulled or not.

"There was no time to remove or disarm the mines, so they disconnected the tanker from the pipeline, got everyone off the ship, and backed it out into the bay before the mines blew. And while the ship was destroyed, it did not result in any loss of life, and the plant was undamaged. If it weren't for your information about the mines and delaying the detonation, we would not have had time to clear the tanker. We barely had enough time as it was. You saved a lot of people, Jesse."

He paused to clear his throat. "When we took Boris into custody, we noticed he had a gunshot wound."

I nodded. "He was shot while we were on the deck. Do you know who did it?"

"No." He looked pointedly at Sam. "Of course, anyone who fired a gun would have to be taken in for questioning, and probably be required to spend time in jail."

Sam looked to the side and down at the floor.

Ander went on, still looking directly at Sam. "But as of right now, we do not have any suspects, and have bigger issues to deal with at the moment."

Sam made an attempt to not obviously exhale but failed.

Ander ignored it. "We are in the process of rounding up Boris's accomplices. He is not talking yet, but he will. We think there are a few of them on the ship in addition to Gorka, and others elsewhere. And we still do not know why he did it. We are just starting to gather some background on him, but so far we are not seeing any connection to the ETA."

Boris's motivation was still a mystery. Whatever, it wasn't my problem any longer. "Where is he now?"

"We are keeping him in the brig while we sort out jurisdiction."

"That's not exactly high security," I said, recalling my time there.

"He is handcuffed, and there are two police officers from the local agency posted at the door. And I do not get the sense that he is going to try anything else. He seems…done."

Defeated was the word I would have used, thinking about how the fight seemed to go out of him after the too-small explosions.

Ander got up to leave. "I wanted to make sure you were OK. I am going now to talk to Boris." He looked at me and smiled. "Good work."

Sam and I stayed on the couch and watched the door close behind him. I waited until I heard the elevator door open and close. "Impressive shot, from the balcony no less," I said.

"Thank you. I was disappointed that it took two."

"Well, we *are* on a ship."

"I suppose."

"How did you get the gun past the ship's metal detector?"

"It was in Chaz's little pack, the one he was wearing when we boarded. They don't generally search small dogs."

Especially if they look like rats. Even if they thought he was bringing a nuclear warhead on board, they probably would have decided it just wasn't worth getting that close to him.

"Wow," I said, leaning back on the couch.

Four years of graduate school and that was all I could come up with. I was beyond tired. My foot ached and my head was throbbing from multiple concussions. Not bad for one vacation.

I was in the process of closing my eyes when I heard a familiar noise, one that sounded like a cross between a hack and a cough.

Chaz was throwing up on the Surya rug. I could see pieces of black fabric coming out of his mouth. One of the larger pieces had part of a band logo I recognized as from of one of my favorite T-shirts.

"He hacks up like a cat! He has no hair! Are you sure he's a dog?" I said irritably. Sam denied it, but I was sure there was a 666 birthmark on him somewhere. I stood up unsteadily to get some paper towels to clean up the mess.

"Don't get up, I'll do it," said Sam.

"No, I'm *fine*." I could manage well enough on one foot and wanted a reason to continue to sulk.

As I was hopping on one foot to the kitchen my cell phone rang. The "Rhinestone Cowboy" ringtone was Gideon's.

"Hey, Gideon. I'm kinda busy…" I was looking around for paper towels, and not finding any, searching for any suitable substitute for cleaning up dog barf.

"You're going to want to hear this." He sounded serious.

"What?"

"Does the name Victor Ivashchenkov mean anything to you?"

"No. Should it?" I found some designer towels in one of the cabinets. Probably $250 a pop. I grabbed a handful.

"He's the former CEO of Rusgaprom. It's the largest energy company in Russia. They're into all forms of energy, but most of their assets are tied up in natural gas. Their infrastructure wasn't built to handle LNG technology, and with LNG starting to replace non-liquefied gas, they're losing market share. Spain, on the other hand, has been investing heavily in LNG. They already have the most regasification capacity of anyone in the EU, over two billion cubic feet. Spain is not only Russia's biggest competitor, their investments will dramatically increase their capacity in the next three years, much of it coming at the expense of Rusgaprom."

I was focused on cleaning up dog barf and wasn't sure why Gideon was sharing all of this.

"Ivashchenkov died a year ago in a car accident." I heard him take a deep breath. "His wife's name is Svetlana."

I stopped cleaning and stood up.

"Her maiden name is Peshkova."

I felt the air go out of my lungs. "You're telling me that Svetlana Peshkova was Ivashchenkov's wife?"

"Yes, and she's currently the CEO of Rusgaprom."

"Shit…"

"Jesse, you need to be really, really careful. This woman is no joke. Her husband had ties to the FSB, and there's evidence that she's involved with them as well, including some we know are really bad actors. She's linked to a number of assassinations. She's way too wealthy to be arrested for anything, but her fingerprints are all over them." He paused again. "One more thing…"

"What?"

When Gideon gave me his last piece of information, I resisted the urge to smack myself on the head. "OK. Thanks. Bye." I hung up. *Son of a fuck.*

Sam had been listening and saw the look on my face. "What's the matter?"

"Sometimes I think I'm the dumbest smart person I know. In Russian, Boris means 'fighter.'" I grabbed my crutches and headed for the door. "But I missed the important part."

"What?" she called out after me.

"Alekseev means 'defender.'"

CHAPTER 37

I took the elevator down to deck four. It turned out that Ballsy still hadn't gotten around to changing the passcode to the lower decks, and I caught up to Ander on deck three outside of the ship's brig. He'd been talking to the guards and was just about ready to go into the room. I fast-crutched my way to him.

"Ander, wait."

He turned around. "Jesse. I am busy right now. Can we talk later?"

"It's not the ETA. It's Svetlana."

"What?"

"She's not Shelly Winters. She's Ruth DeWitt Bukater."

He gave me a blank expression.

"You know, Kate Winslet's mom on the *Titanic*."

He looked even more confused.

"*Really*? You go on a cruise and that doesn't warrant watching the two most famous cruise ship disaster movies *ever*?" There was no time to take him through everything. "Please, Ander, trust me. Let me talk to Boris."

I could tell he wasn't thrilled with the idea, but whatever discomfort I was causing him was overridden by his dedication to getting things right. I'd found out more in nine days than his whole team had in a month, and at this point he trusted my investigative skills, if not my methods.

He opened the door to the brig. Boris was laying on his side on the small bed, staring blankly at the wall, his hands still cuffed behind him.

"Boris," Ander said.

Boris ignored him, his face impassive.

I stepped around Ander and moved directly in front of Boris's face. "We know about Svetlana."

At the mention of Svetlana, Boris looked up at me.

"Let me see if I have this right. Spain is not only Russia's biggest competitor in the LNG market, but they're in the process of investing billions to become the dominant player. Rusgaprom is taking a big hit, and they don't have the money or the technology to compete. What better way to damage your biggest competitor than by creating an explosion at its flagship plant? And the timing is perfect. Not only is the Gastech conference happening right now in Bilbao, but the leaders of the LNG technologies are all taking a tour of the plant today. Even if the damage to the plant could be fixed, Spain's reputation as a reliable source would take a long time to repair. At the very least, an apparent ongoing terrorist threat from the ETA would require LNG customers to find backup suppliers. Like Rusgaprom.

"That's what you were waiting for, wasn't it? You wanted the muckety-mucks from Gastech to start their tour of the facility that was scheduled for this morning. Then you could assassinate the whole group at one time. What a spectacular way to announce to the world that Spain's LNG capacity is unreliable. Blowing up a plant would be one thing, but killing all of the energy leaders? It would guarantee the industry would turn elsewhere for LNG capacity."

Svetlana was really an evil fucking bitch. A very smart, evil fucking bitch. I leaned closer. "You're not aligned with the ETA, are you?"

He looked at me, his face a stony mask.

"I've been trying to figure out what would cause you to try to kill so many people for a cause you don't care about. And it's not about money for you."

He turned his head away from me, and I saw him in profile. Now that I was looking for it, the resemblance was obvious. "Tatiana is your daughter."

At the mention of her name, he looked sharply at me and broke his silence. "Svetlana was going to kill her if I didn't do it."

I turned to Ander, who'd been struggling to keep up. "Ander, we need to find Svetlana. Right now."

He didn't move.

"*Ander!* Svetlana is behind all of this. We have to find her."

His brow furrowed and he gave a small nod. "I will get her. Please go back to your room. If she is involved, she is extremely dangerous."

I nodded and tried to give him a thumbs-up, which almost made me fall over on my crutches.

"I mean it, Jesse. Promise me you will go straight back to your room."

"I promise." This time I meant it. Now that all the excitement was over and the adrenaline had worn off, I was almost asleep on my feet.

I followed Ander out of the room. He spoke briefly to one of the guards, who followed him to the stairwell. I took the elevator back to our suite. Even if I hadn't been on crutches, ten flights of stairs right now seemed like an impossible task. I hit the button to our floor and leaned back against the wall, closing my eyes.

CHAPTER 38

When I got back to the suite, Sam was still on the couch with Chaz. I was surprised to see Tatiana there as well.

"Sam, you're never going to believe this." I looked at Tatiana. "She's Boris's *daughter*. And Svetlana is behind the whole thing." I put the crutches down and limped toward the couch. "It's OK now. Ander is on it."

Sam looked at me strangely, then turned her head toward the other side of the room.

"Hello, Dr. O'Hara," Svetlana said from the entrance to our kitchen. She had a gun in her hand. It looked like Sam's Beretta.

Fuck me.

"Sit down."

I didn't want to take orders from her, but I was tottering on one foot, so I sat down next to Sam. "What's the point, Svetlana? The plant is fine, and no one got hurt. Your plan failed."

I could feel Sam nudge me. Maybe now was not the most opportune time to gloat.

"There are other plans. But maybe I kill you for ruining this one."

She looked very comfortable holding the gun, which didn't surprise me a whole lot.

I realized then that I'd seen her the second night on the pool deck. She'd been the woman next to the "drunk" man near the railing. "Like you killed Luix Salazar? You set him up as the fall guy, didn't you?" She hadn't been holding him up, she'd been helping him over the side. She'd likely paid him to put the graffiti on the funnel, and then made sure there was paint on his hands to take the suspicion away from Boris and Gorka.

She nodded. She didn't need to admit anything to me since she was the one holding the gun, but I could tell she was proud of herself.

I wondered how she got Salazar over the railing. She was sturdy, but no match for a young man. On the other hand, she and her husband were tied into Russia's FSB, formerly known as the KGB, who had a long history of political assassinations via poison and radioactive toxins. She'd probably not brought anything that toxic on board, but some kind of fast-acting paralytic or sleeping drug would have done the trick. It probably wasn't hard to get him up on the deck to help her with some imaginary problem. All she'd need to do then was get close enough to inject him with something that would make him appear drunk, and render him easy to get over the side.

Looking at her expensive clothes and perfectly styled hair, I wondered if she really would be interested in, or even capable of, murdering someone by heaving him over the side of a ship. But the gun was sitting comfortably in her hand, and I thought back to the pub that first night, when she'd smacked Boris in the face with calm alacrity.

No, this was a woman who liked to get her hands dirty.

She confirmed it by laughing. Or, at least, trying to laugh. It came out like more of a hack. I got the feeling it wasn't something she did very often. "He was problem. Like you."

I was running through the events on the ship in my head. "And the bomb threat, and the Marchands...you set up the drug smuggling, didn't you? It was all a misdirect. You wanted to keep the security officers busy, so Boris could focus on what you really wanted to do. And then you packaged everything up to make it look like the ETA was behind it." Holy shit that was a lot of stuff.

She looked at me and cocked her head. "They were stupid."

I couldn't disagree with her there.

"You are not so stupid. You are smart, for American."

"For *American*?" Were all Russians this arrogant? "I figured *your* shit out without too much trouble."

Sam nudged me again, harder.

Svetlana looked down and fiddled with her enormous diamond ring. "I need smart people to help with company. You are unemployed now, yes?"

"Yes." Wait...*what? Is she actually offering me a job?* "By 'help with company' I assume you mean help blowing shit up and killing people? No thanks."

"I make you millionaire."

"Not everything is about money."

She couldn't comprehend what I was saying and looked at me blankly. Part of me felt sorry for her. An infinitesimally tiny part.

"Besides, you're done, Svetlana. You'll never get off the ship."

Sam was punching me now, trying to get me to shut up.

"I think I do get off ship." She said this matter-of-factly, as if it were a foregone conclusion. She looked up at the Amelie clock on the wall.

"No way. It's surrounded by police at this point." I hoped that was true.

"I think you are wrong. Police are gone. Anyway, they can do nothing." She glanced again at the clock.

I couldn't believe I had ever thought of her as a loving grandmother. She was as suited for that as I was to hospice nursing.

"Just in case, I take hostage," she said.

Please let it be Chaz. Please let it be Chaz.

Svetlana gestured to Sam with the gun. "You come."

Sam gently moved Chaz from her lap and put him on the couch. She stood up and I stood up with her. The exhaustion I was feeling disappeared instantly. I looked straight at Svetlana, my eyes boring into hers. I no longer felt sorry for her. For the first time in my life I had the urge to kill someone.

I said flatly, "If anything happens to her, I will do everything in my power to see you die the most horrible death I can think of."

The first thing that came to mind was being slowly gnawed to death by Chaz. But I was sure given enough time I could come up with something more horrible. Maybe.

"No one follows. If you follow, I shoot her. I have men on ship watching."

"Your 'ETA' thugs?"

"ETA is good to blame for things." She grimaced, her version of a smile.

Even though the end result wasn't what she'd wanted, she was apparently pleased with how cleverly she'd framed the ETA for the mayhem she'd caused. I wondered if the money was secondary, and the primary motivation for her boiled down to power and the ability to manipulate others.

"So you were behind the protestors in Barcelona at the quay," I said, thinking out loud. "And the guy who followed us..."

"You are nosy person. I have good idea to have you watch 'granddaughter', yes? Kill two birds with one stone, as you say." She hacked again.

She'd used me to keep an eye on Tatiana and make it easier for her thugs to follow both of us. *Jesus.*

"And the Palacio?" I was incredulous, but I guess I shouldn't have been surprised. If she could throw one hundred thousand euros at the Marchands to persuade them to smuggle coke, she could throw enough money around to get a hundred people to show up in front of a museum.

She grimaced again.

"You're pretty proud of a plan that failed."

"As they say, there is always next year."

Something was bugging me. I turned sharply to Tatiana. "Why didn't you say anything?" We'd been alone several times, and she'd had ample opportunity to talk to us on shore. "Or just leave?"

She looked down, her hand moving up to the locket around her neck. "She says she will kill my father if I talk to you. I believe her. She is devil." She was caressing the locket. I thought back to our earlier conversation, an awful realization dawning on me.

"She killed your mother, didn't she?"

Tatiana's head was still down but she nodded slowly.

I turned back to Svetlana. "You're a monster."

She looked up at the clock again. "Your phone, please," she said impatiently. She held her hand out.

I pulled my phone out of my pocket and tossed it onto the floor in front of her. She glared at me, then stepped on it sharply with her heel, breaking the screen and grinding it into several pieces. Then she gestured with the gun to the door.

Sam walked through the door, turning her head to look back at me. Our eyes locked. It reminded me of the first time we'd seen each other, in the bathroom in Kresge Hall. But this time Sam didn't look terrified. She actually looked calm, all things considered. She knew I would do whatever it would take to get her back. Sam was not just my best friend, she was my link to humanity. Without her, the world would be an even more dark and awful place. *I'm not letting her spend the rest of her life in a Russian beet cellar.* I would work with Gideon and find her. I'd go to Russia if necessary. I was sure her family would finance whatever efforts it took to get her back.

As Svetlana followed Sam out, I caught a blur of movement out of the corner of my eye. Chaz had jumped off the couch and was running toward the door. He took a few steps and went airborne, and before Svetlana could react, he locked his teeth around the wrist of the hand that was holding the gun.

She cursed in Russian and stopped in front of the door. She used her other hand to try to pry Chaz's mouth off of her. She was grabbing and pulling at his muzzle, but he held on. I was a little surprised that his Austin Powers teeth could actually grip like that. Blood was starting to drip from his mouth.

Still cursing, she was now trying to dislodge him by shaking her arm back and forth, first slowly, then more violently. His little body was swinging around, but it did nothing to separate her wrist from his teeth, which were firmly sunk into the skin. She stepped back inside the suite and started to smack her arm against the wall near the door.

"No!" yelled Sam, as Svetlana smashed her hand and Chaz against the wall. Two, three, four times…I couldn't believe he was still attached, she was really banging him hard. But he couldn't keep it up forever. On the fourth try he finally fell off, crumpling to the ground. But not without leaving her wrist and hand a bloody mess.

Beating her arm against the wall did more than get Chaz off of her. With the last whack the gun fell from Svetlana's mangled hand and bounced away.

"Chaz!" Sam pushed Svetlana aside and ran back inside the suite. While she knelt next to his unmoving body, I took a couple of limping steps toward the gun and picked it up.

Svetlana didn't waste any time and ran out the door. I started after her, but Sam's shoulders were shaking in quiet sobs. I sighed and turned from the door, moving over to her.

Leaning down I put an arm around Sam's shoulder, and my hand gently on Chaz's small head. As much as he got on my nerves, he was really not a bad little dog. And pretty fucking loyal. As I was brushing his tiny tuft of head hair over to one side, I felt a small vibration. His thin lips quivered, and as I leaned closer, I could hear a soft growl.

"Oh, *for fuck's sake*," I said, shaking my head. I pulled my hand away and he opened his eyes, baring his teeth at me. Sam hugged him in relief.

"Now you know truth. My father is not terrorist." I'd forgotten about Tatiana, who was still sitting on the couch. But I really didn't give a shit about her father right now. We needed to contact Ander so he could go after Svetlana.

I reached for my phone and remembered it was in pieces. I was looking around for the Ming unit to call Ben when I heard a deep *thump, thump, thump* coming from outside.

We all looked out the window to see a black helicopter emerging from the smattering of clouds above the ship. As it got closer, I could see large white letters on the side of it: Русгапром. Rusgaprom.

I hobbled out the door as fast as I could and took the elevator to the foredeck. I opened the door just in time to see Svetlana being helped into the helicopter, lightly perched in the center of the large white H on the deck. When she got in she turned around and gave me a small wave. Two long dark rifle barrels peeked out of the door on either side of her.

I stood there while it took off, watching it shrink into a small black speck, and eventually disappear.

CHAPTER 39

"So that's it then? She just gets away, and Boris goes to jail for the rest of his life?" I was slumped on the couch, staring at Ander. Now that we were safe, I was free to be outraged at the notion that Svetlana could get away with almost killing masses of people, including me. Next to me were Sam and Chaz. He hadn't left her lap since his attack on Svetlana's arm. There was still a little of her blood on his muzzle.

"I will work with my contacts at CITCO to see what kind of case we can bring against her. Once everyone involved starts talking to make deals, we should have more information."

I sat up, encouraged. "Yeah, after everyone hears about the plot to blow the plant, the Russians will want to give her up. They won't want the scandal."

Ander looked down at the floor. "I am not sure it will be that easy."

"What are you talking about?" I was almost yelling, my pent-up relief making me a little more emotional than usual. "She tried to blow up a fucking gas plant!"

He sighed. "There is no real evidence yet that Svetlana was behind the bombing. Even if Boris talks, it is just his word and that of a few known criminals. And she has a lot of money. A *lot* of money. And she controls one of Russia's largest companies. Her government is very careful with people like that." He looked at my face and stopped. "But we will try.

"What will happen to my father?" Tatiana asked quietly. She

was leaning against the door and had said little since I'd returned to the suite. We'd gotten a hold of Ander and told him about Svetlana's helicopter escape, but at this point there was little left to do. She was gone, and by now far away from Spanish airspace.

"Boris, for his own safety, will be staying in Spain. He is being taken to the Centro Penitenciario in San Sebastián. In exchange for a lighter sentence, he is going to tell us everything he knows about Svetlana's plan, her network, and the group of criminals she conspired with to blow up the plant. That should help us make a case against her."

"And Tatiana?" Sam asked quietly.

"I do not know. Spain may allow her to stay. It is not safe for her in Russia right now."

CHAPTER 40

Sam, Tatiana, and I stood at the bottom of the gangway. Sam was holding Chaz, who had recently completed a session with the dog groomer. The pathetic tuft of hair on his head looked like it had been oiled, and was combed flat and lay jauntily over to one side. I could tell he thought he was extremely cool, but he looked more ridiculous than usual, if that were even possible. He was still walking a little stiffly from Svetlana smashing him against the wall, but other than that he seemed fine.

Boris was being led away in handcuffs to the waiting police car. Ander was standing next to it, holding the door open.

Sam leaned down to Tatiana and said something.

Tatiana looked at her for a long moment, and then walked over to her dad.

The police blocked her way, but Ander put his hand up and they let her through. She went up to Boris and threw her arms around him. As they pulled apart, she whispered something in his ear. He looked over at Sam, then back at Tatiana and nodded.

"What was that all about?" I asked Sam.

"She's going to come home with us. She'll live with me until her father's sentence is over. It's the safest option. Svetlana is still out there, and it's too dangerous for her to go back to Russia."

I shook my head in disbelief. "Are you *nuts*?" I couldn't imagine Tatiana and her "Russians are the best at everything" fitting into Sam's community, of which I was a prominent part. And I was pretty sure that spending an extended amount of time with her would lead me to drink. More.

Sam said simply, "She doesn't have any other family."

***

Ander and I said goodbye in Bilbao. He left me with a non-brotherly kiss and hug, and an open invitation to visit him at the earliest opportunity. I was pretty sure I would take him up on that. Sam and I decided to finish the cruise, and stayed aboard as it headed to the terminus in Southampton.

The next two days were uneventful. We spent them eating, drinking, and talking with Tatiana, who had finally opened up. Sam was right, beneath the grumpy Russian exterior was a likeable and talented young woman. That is, if you could get around the unrelenting snorts of contempt and apparently limitless arrogance about Russian cultural superiority. She was devastated at losing her father, but he was at least alive and relatively safe outside of Russia.

It was surprisingly fun to be out with her now that she had grown to trust us. And she was an excellent drinking companion, the two of us managing to hold our own with the Aussies on the last night at Joe's Place. We actually had a lot in common. We'd lost our moms at about the same age, and our fathers were both in jail, albeit for very different reasons. And we were both highly competitive, which kept things interesting.

On the eleventh day of the cruise the ship pulled into Southampton port. As she did on all of her cruises, Sam made the rounds to the restaurants and clubs, personally thanking each of the crewmembers who had taken care of us on the trip. This took a couple of hours. When we were done, we took our time packing, then sat together on the couch, sharing one last drink.

Sam looked at me apologetically. "I'm really sorry about all of this. I just wanted you to have a nice vacation."

I was incredulous. "Are you kidding? I couldn't be happier with this trip." It was true. "I mean, it was a little bit of a goatscrew. But drug smuggling, a chase on the beach, international intrigue, and we helped foil a terrorist plot? Completely awesome. I could have done without the multiple concussions, but this was *way* better than I thought it was going to be. I thought I'd be bored out of my mind. Other than not actually hooking up with Ander, this trip has been perfect. And I didn't get legionella."

There was a knock at the door, and I opened it to see Ben.

"Dr. O'Hara, this came for you. It was delivered to the terminal today." He handed me a brown paper-wrapped package.

"Thanks, Ben, and thanks for everything."

"You are very welcome. You have been my most...*interesting* guests." He gave his little bow and left.

"What is it?" Sam asked.

I shook it gently. It was heavy. "I don't know. Maybe a gift from a grateful nation?"

There was no return address. I tore open the brown paper to see an expensive looking box, with one side open to view. Inside was a bottle of vodka shaped like a skull.

Acknowledgements

This is my debut novel, and before I wrote it I would look at the list of names in other book acknowledgements and think, "Who the hell are all of those people?"

Now I know better. There is no way I could have produced this without the help of many humans. For starters, Molly Friedrich and Lucy Carson from the Friedrich Agency, and Jason Pinter and his team at Polis Books - thanks for taking a chance on Jesse O'Hara.

My beta readers…wow…every single one of you made this book better. Mark Patterson, Kathryn Meuwly, Chris McComb, Sue Hunt, Pam Kassner, Dawn Rodney, Jennifer Schultz, Lesley Carmichael, Lynne Smith, Anna Hurwitz, and Daniel Doolittle, thanks for taking the time to read this and for your thoughtful thoughts. Monica Depiesse you have an amazing artistic eye.

Special thanks to the Happy Hour Ladies - Suz, Lesley, Dawn, Monica, Teresa, Laurie, Dona, Melissa and Anna - for your heartfelt support and unwaveringly positive energy.

Debra Hartman at the Pro Book Editor (theprobookeditor. com) did the editing on the early draft of this work. Debra somehow managed to be critical and supportive at the same time, and hung in there during our epic battles over my use of commas. Many thanks.

I really need to appreciate Jane Friedman, who I've never met, but whose website (janefriedman.com) I consulted at every stage of this project. I started writing at the beginning of the Covid lockdown, and made liberal use of the internet to learn how to construct and publish a book. Jane's site provided the most consistently and apparently useful advice on the whole process.

Jennifer I'm not sure I would have even attempted this if not for you. Thank you for that, and for your insight and warmth.

Mom you supported my love of reading to the nth degree, taking me to the local library on a regular basis when I was a kid, and patiently waiting while I carefully selected the maximum thirty books per visit. I don't know where you found the time.

At its core this is a novel about loyalty and friendship. Kristen you're my model for these things. I'm so lucky you're in my life.

Last and definitely not least, I'm grateful Anna for your emotional support, your inputs on the many drafts, and in particular for moving your home office to the basement to give me space to write.

About the Author

Wendy Church has been a bartender, tennis instructor, semi-conductor engineer, group facilitator, nonprofit CEO, teacher, PhD researcher, and dive bar cleaner. Her first suspense novel, Murder on the Spanish Seas, is set on a luxury cruise in the Iberian peninsula and introduces smart-mouthed amateur sleuth Jesse O'Hara, whose adventures are partly informed by Wendy's expertise and international travels.

Follow her on Twitter at @DrWendyChuch and visit her online at www.WendySChurch.com.